THERE AND BACK

ERIC BEETNER

ROUGH
EDGES
PRESS

Rough Edges Press
An Imprint of Wolfpack Publishing
5130 S. Fort Apache Rd. 215-380
Las Vegas, NV 89148

roughedgespress.com

Paperback ISBN 978-1-68549-158-1
eBook ISBN 978-1-68549-157-4
LCCN 2022944095

THERE AND BACK

OUT THERE

THE ROCK SLID from the hand and turned twice in the air, the edge serrated in a peak like a mountain range, blood filling the cracks and fissures. Droplets of blood spun off as the rock fell to the forest floor. A soft pillow of pine needles and rotted leaves cushioned the fall. The rock bounced slightly, landed on an edge and then rolled to a stop, as still and lifeless as the body beside it.

All eyes were on the rock. On the blood, the bits of hair and skin stuck to the jagged edge. Lichen covered by remnants of murder.

No one dared look at the face. Even after all they'd been through, it was too gruesome. It meant maybe they'd reached the bottom, or worse, the descent still had far to go.

The forest sounds continued, not caring about the dead body. Slowly, in shuffling steps, they moved away and left the body there, the rock beside it dripping blood.

BACK HOME
DAY 1

THE FIVE SURVIVORS step from a white Sheriff's Department van. A fireworks show of flashbulbs assault them. Shouted questions merge and roil through the air into a flat noise like the rushing of a flooded river.

They raise hands to block the light. The men haven't shaved yet, the one woman hasn't showered or done her hair. It's been less than a day—twenty hours —since the rescue and they've slept nearly the whole time, a ranger station high in the hills acting as a makeshift triage and bunkhouse for the five battered survivors.

Uniformed police officers form a pathway with their bodies holding back the hungry reporters. Suit-jacketed higher-ups lead the five through the crowd, waving their hands to part the masses, a guiding hand on an elbow where it is needed.

Sean wants to turn back for the van. Only twenty-eight, he looks a decade older than he had nearly a month ago when he left for the wilderness. He scans the crowd for his wife, but the flashes and wall of reporters make it impossible to see. He doubts she is there anyway.

He wants more water, more food. They'd given them enough to regain their strength after the rescue, but it isn't enough. They seemed only interested in making them strong enough to answer questions. What happened out there? How did it happen? Where are the others?

Ten went into the woods. Only five returned.

———

Maia hears her name among the cacophony of shouts. They are interested in her—the only woman to survive. She is a story to them, an angle. Part victim, part heroine. She can't see who asked the question. She doesn't know if she has any more answers in her, the police had asked so many.

And they all gave the same responses. All five. Rehearsed and agreed upon.

———

Grady tugs his elbow free from the grip of the detective beside him. He doesn't need help. He doesn't want to seem weak in any of the photos they are snapping at three frames a second. He is a survivor. He made it. The others made it because of him, mostly. Yes, that's what he did—he survived. And now these animals are trying to attack. Vicious, rabid, more feral than anything they encountered in the forest. He purses his lips together and spits at the crowd. Cameras hidden behind lights meant to fake for the sun, to lie about the dark. Well, he'd seen true darkness and he wouldn't be fooled anymore.

———————

The wall of police holding back the reporters funnels to a point ending at the entrance to the office building. The Wallis building, number Nine Fifty Seven Royal Street. A glass parallelogram with black steel beams. Industrial and modern. The opposite of where they've been.

Sean moves forward toward the point like a steer moving up the slaughter chute.

"Out of the way. You'll get your chance," the cop in the lead says to the reporters.

The sound muffles as Sean is the first to pass through the revolving doors and into the lobby he knows so well. Three years at this job, in this office. Late nights, weekends. The Wallis building had never seemed like a sanctuary, but there had never been a mob after him before.

Sean steps aside as the others push through into the lobby. Maia, smoothing her hair and letting out a breath. Grady, scanning the space for an exit already. Wes, unsteady on his feet and distant in his eyes like he hasn't fully returned from the forest yet. And Nathan, taking a deep breath as if he'd been underwater.

The five survivors. And here came Allison Gates, head of this office and the one who sent them on their adventure for "team building," as she called it. Sent eight. Got back only five.

Allison's hand is out, her smile is wide and almost

sincere. Sean spots the glisten of a tear in her eye, ready to fall at the opportune moment.

"My God," she says. Allison retracts her hand and spreads both arms wide. This occasion is worthy of more than a handshake. "My God," she says again and offers her open self to Sean. He stands still and lets her envelope him.

Inside are a trio of photographers from the company. Much more discreet. Much more quiet. Behind Allison are a dozen junior executives, company publicists, office coworkers. One of them starts to applaud and quickly the others follow suit. Sean isn't sure if they are clapping for the returning employees or for Allison's generous hug.

She releases Sean and spreads her arms open to Maia.

Ten minutes later and all the hugs have been given out, the photos posed and taken. Allison is stepping to a podium and a microphone. Speakers and a video screen are on the outside of the building to satiate the throng of reporters while keeping the lobby to company personnel only.

The five survivors stand shoulder to shoulder. Shell shocked, weaving on weak knees and lacking focus, they look as if they've lined up for a firing squad.

Sean nudges Wes beside him. "From zero to a hundred, right?"

"Huh?" His right pinky finger is fixed into a metal splint wrapped in white medical tape, frayed at the edges from where he's been nervously picking at it.

"I just mean from the quiet and alone of the woods...now to this..."

Wes stares out over the lobby crowd but Sean can tell he isn't really seeing. Sean is still thirsty.

To his left is Maia. He looks at her and raises an eyebrow.

She rolls her eyes. "I know, right?"

"This building isn't exactly the first place I wanted to come to."

"Seriously. I want to be at home in my bed."

Sean lets his eyes drift over the assembled crowd, looking for Kerri but knowing he won't see his wife here.

Allison taps the microphone with a polished fingernail.

"Ladies and gentlemen, we here at Synergen Dynamics can't express to you how happy we are to have the safe return of a part of our family."

The applause starts up again. The group of five all take a moment to realize it is for them. Weak smiles and a short wave from Nathan and Sean to the assembled mass of Synergen workers, some they recognize and many they don't.

Allison checks a small notecard in her palm. Sean knows that card was prepared by Kelsey, her assistant. Everything Allison does and says is prepared by Kelsey. Does Allison even know what she's saying, these heartfelt feelings?

"Of course, in many ways, the joy in our hearts is eclipsed by the tragic loss of three of our own."

A more muted round of applause accompanies the bowed heads in the room. There is a moment of silence, the pause measured like the moment before a drummer counts off the start of the next song. When the rhythm is right, Allison starts again.

"When all had given up hope, we here and at the corporate office never doubted these bright faces and members of the Synergen team would walk through these doors again. David Hellinger, our CEO, even lent his personal helicopter to the search and rescue efforts."

Allison tilts her head down to the survivors and gives them a thin smile that says: *didn't know that, did you?* A vigorous round of applause circulates the lobby even though David is a thousand miles away in his lake house.

Grady sneers at the clapping suits. He almost spits again.

"As proof of our never-ending confidence in your return," Allison waves a hand over the five like a model on a game show displaying the prizes. Sean wonders if that gesture is marked on her card. "Your jobs have been kept open for you, and when you are ready, the Synergen Dynamics family is ready to welcome you back home."

More applause. And then the speech is over. They've been promised as much time as they need to recover from the harrowing experience.

"Yeah, that's so we won't sue," Maia says.

"How long before they bring us the paperwork to sign that says they aren't to blame?" Grady asks.

"They sent us out there," Nathan says. "But nobody could have expected..."

"Yeah," Wes says. "But we wouldn't have been out there if they didn't have this stupid tradition."

Grady smiles. "Anyone wanna bet this is the last year they do this?"

The group fakes a laugh then let themselves be led away by the police again.

As Sean moves back out of the lobby he thinks how odd it is to be talking like normal coworkers again with these people. What they've been through. What they've done. The things they said to each other out there—all gone now like the morning after a Thanksgiving blowout with family. But would it last?

Detective Greg Kettner gathers them together in a back room for one final briefing before they can return to their lives.

"If anyone remembers anything else that could be relevant, please give me a call."

"You've already been asking us questions since yesterday," Grady says. "We all want to go home."

The others mumble in agreement.

"I know. But this is an unusual situation. I've got five people dead and no bodies. This is a big story, like it or not, so there is a lot of scrutiny and that will continue for a few weeks or until the next news cycle plays out."

Maia holds up a hand like a child in grade school. "Was everyone talking about us like we were dead?"

"Some were. Some had counters for how many days you were missing."

Wes scoffs. "They should have been out looking for us instead of making counters."

"Everyone was very concerned and I'm sure you'll all like to get home to your loved ones. I'm sure we'll follow up in the next few days, but for now you're free to get home. Thank you for your patience."

Sean smiles at him. "Thank you, detective."

They are led through a side door to the parking garage where their cars have been since they left. A woman squeals and runs into Grady's arms. She is all blonde bouncy hair and a short skirt. She clamps onto him and he pries her off. Undeterred she covers his face in kisses.

Nathan is met by his parents in a tearful reunion they try to make as private as possible by stepping away from the others.

Wes is escorted by a company representative, who explains tomorrow's schedule and his accommodations for the night. Nobody is there to meet him from home.

Maia walks alone to her car and gets in; the people in her life were already in the building. Her work is her social life. She hasn't fully realized it until now. Tomorrow she'll call some friends she hasn't seen in too long. Then she thinks twice. All they'll want to talk about is...out there. She'll have to retell and retell the story.

She'll take a few days to herself.

Sean sees Kerri waiting her turn. She doesn't rush to him, she doesn't cry. She stands by his car and waits for him to walk to her.

"Not rid of me that easy," he jokes. He tries to follow it up with a smile but she is stone faced and his smile dies a quick death.

"Are you okay?" she asks.

"As well as could be, I guess."

"Sean." She stares at him like he's a ghost. "I really thought..."

"Yeah. I thought it, too."

Kerri rests a hand on his arm. "I'm glad you're home."

"Are you?"

"Yes." She leans in and kisses his cheek. It's almost warm.

BACK THEN

IT HAD BEEN six weeks since they'd been told about the trip, but they didn't know who all was going. When Sean found out earlier in the week that Grady had also been selected, he contemplated not going.

Their last project together hadn't gone well. Grady tried to assume all control and take all credit. Sean felt like he was back in high school working on a science project. Grady spoke first in meetings, dominated conference calls, called clients by their first names. The guy was a jerk, but he got results.

Didn't mean anyone liked working on a team with him, which seemed to be how Grady liked it. He was setting himself up to be the maverick. The one man team. The go-getter.

Sean often wondered if he should be more like Grady, but it wasn't in his nature. And here they were, with Grady four years younger than Sean, climbing on the same next rung of the company ladder.

It must have been obvious they hadn't made a good team since they hadn't been partnered again, but Sean always feared Grady had gone behind his back and requested not to work with him. A week in the woods, though—they'd have to face each other then.

But for now, Sean let Grady walk ten paces ahead of him down the hall, determined to be the first in the door like it meant a damn thing at all.

They met in the conference room. Allison was there at the head of the table to welcome them, three strangers seated beside her.

"Come in, come in," Allison beckoned.

Maia stepped in behind Sean and Lara followed Maia, as usual. Always stepping on her shadow. Nathan came in last and eyeballed the three newcomers.

"I'd like you to meet your three counterparts from the northern office." Allison pointed at them one by one. "This is Ken, Ron and Wes."

The three men nodded and lifted hands in short waves. They got a stone-faced greeting from the locals as they found seats around the conference table. Sean noticed the three from up north wore suits and ties. He and his colleagues were more casual. Sean in a v-neck sweater and hiking boots that had never seen a trail. He was short in stature, a lifelong burden from his mother's Korean heritage, though he'd long ago given up on fighting it.

Maia kept even her casual wear form fitting and crisp. Her hair stopped sharply at her shoulders, her makeup was always understated and natural looking—learned from hours in front of YouTube video tutorials on how to achieve a 'no makeup' makeup look. The idea of using her looks in an office setting repulsed her when she saw other women do it. She was on the executive track, and she was going to get there with her work skills only. Having Allison as her boss helped. It was no office secret she was Allison's favorite.

Grady seemed to wear his shirts a half size too small to emphasize his wide chest and thick arms. Working in tech, he was allowed to keep his sleeves rolled up and expose the tattoos running below the elbow on his right arm. A twining rose bush with blood dotted thorns. He'd perfected the three-day growth of stubble that never seemed to materialize into a full beard.

Lara, with her red hair from a drug store box, studied the three men from up north, seeing if any of them were worth going after on this little trip. Camping wasn't her thing, but if she could share a sleeping bag with one of these guys, maybe she could warm to it. Ken looked good. She'd never been with a black guy. If she squinted he could pass for a cousin of Idris Elba and that wasn't bad at all.

Wes was average in nearly every way, and his hair line had already betrayed what was to come for him. His youthful face was pudgy in the cheeks and made him look even younger.

Ron was nothing much to look at either. Generically soft with dark features and a shadow of whiskers lurking under the surface no matter how recently he'd shaved. Lara knew he was the kind of guy who had hairy shoulders. All she had to do was look at his knuckles. Yep. No way.

Ken it was.

Nathan shot his cuffs and made sure his Rolex could be seen by all. He turned to Allison, practicing all the moves he'd learned in his business seminar. Maintain eye contact. Lean forward. Keep your hands visible at all times. Hidden hands beneath a conference room table were a sign of mistrust.

He wore his six-foot-four frame well. Trim and fit, only his hairline gave him away as being any older than the others in the room. Mid-thirties may have been old for the tech industry, but his experience and maturity would make him a prime candidate for one of the promotions coming up. A better choice than the others in the room—his competition.

"I'm jealous, you know that?" Allison stayed standing, arms leaning over a high-backed chair at the head of the table. "I remember very well when I went on this retreat. I won't say how long ago it was." She smiled and waited for the others to smile along with her, and maybe give a chuckle which Nathan and Maia did. "But it was a really formative time in my career. If you're like me, you might not know exactly what five days in the woods has to do with coordinating business solutions in a digitized world..." She'd quoted directly from the company banner in the lobby of Synergen Dynamics. "But trust me, you will come back here as a better team, better leaders, better employees, and for four of you, better jobs."

Nobody around the table really tried to hide the evaluating looks and sizing up stares that crisscrossed the table. Promotions were coming down, and this Roman Gladiator mode of weeding out the weaker ones was how Synergen Dynamics worked. They had all heard about this trip in their first interviews. Employees who had been with the company for at least two years and who were on track to move up when positions became available all went on the trip. It was a little bit rite of passage, a little bit reward, a little bit job interview.

To those around the table it was a week off work and the trip of a lifetime to hear any of the higher ups tell it. They spoke of it the way college kids talked of a semester abroad.

"You know I wish I had positions to offer all of you, but I've only been authorized to move four of you into new positions. For now. Even if this round of evaluations doesn't go your way I don't want you to get discouraged. In fact, I'll let you in on a secret. When I got back from my retreat, I didn't get promoted right away. I also didn't let it get me down. I got back to work, did my best, and here I am now. I can't say the same for anyone but one other person who went with me on that trip. And she and I still see each other and have formed a great bond. You won't believe it can happen in just five days, but it can and it will."

Grady lifted his hand but didn't wait to be called on before speaking.

"So is our time out there like a final test? Will you have company representatives out there evaluating us?"

"I don't want you to think of this as a test. This is mostly for you to come together as a team and to learn valuable leadership skills. The only people with you will be the wilderness guides. Most of the evaluations will happen here while you're gone. But while you're out there you'll be assigned various leadership tasks and we will hear back from the guides how well each of you perform when it's your turn to be team leader. Everyone gets a chance, don't worry. You'll have plenty of opportunity to prove yourself. But we put much more emphasis on the work you've already done in the office."

"I can't believe I have to shit in the woods." Maia loved to say things she felt the others couldn't get away with around Allison.

Allison smiled. "It's all part of the experience."

Wes from the Northern office cleared his throat. "I just want to say how pleased we are to join you on this adventure. We really look forward to getting to know all of you."

The northerners nodded in unison. The five locals nodded back, minus the fake smiles.

"Us, too," Sean said.

"Oh, I wish I could go again." Allison gripped the chair back and closed her eyes with the memory. "You'll come back changed. I guarantee it."

As they exited the conference room Maia felt a hand on her arm. She turned to see Allison holding her back from the crowd. When the others had gone she stayed close to Maia, speaking in a conspiratorial tone.

"I'm rooting for you, you know."

Maia tried hard to suppress a satisfied grin.

"I want you to know all your hard work isn't going unnoticed," Allison said. "I'm sure a lot of it is how much you remind me of myself at your age and in your position. Not that it was that long ago."

She smiled and Maia joined her.

"Thank you," Maia said. "It really means a lot to hear that I have someone on my side. Someone who sees my work for what it is."

"You mean not just the skirt?"

Maia looked away. Was it that obvious she had such

a blatant feminist agenda? Oh screw it, she never tried to hide it. And why should she?

Allison dropped her voice even lower and put a hand on Maia's. "We have to stick together you know. The glass ceiling won't break unless someone is there to bang on it."

She squeezed Maia's hand and motioned her out the door.

"The retreat is a good thing. You have nothing to worry about. See you next week."

"Okay. Thanks."

————

That night Sean set his backpack of newly acquired clothes by the door. The car would be there at five a.m. to pick him up and take him to the chartered bus. He'd been given a list of clothes to bring, equipment to buy, and been told that everything else he would need on his week in the woods would be provided for him.

He knew he should get to bed early, but he wasn't tired.

Kerri always seemed tired these days.

"You got everything?" she asked from the top of the stairs.

"I think so."

She folded her arms across her chest. Loose t-shirt, flannel pajama pants, hair in a ponytail. Sean tried to see her but she stood mostly in shadows. That was how he felt about her a lot lately. No, how he'd felt for a long time.

"You think you're gonna get it?"

"I don't know, Kerri. There are eight of us and only four spots."

"Fifty-fifty."

"Yeah."

"And if you don't get it?"

"Then I don't. I keep going."

"Same job? Same salary?"

"There will be other chances."

Kerri shook her head at him. He knew the look on her face even with her standing shrouded in darkness on the top step. She thought he was a fool. She thought he was a sucker. He should be making twice as much by now. He should have stock options, a 401K. He'd joined on with a tech company, for God's sake. They were all swimming in cash and handing it out left and right.

"Maybe..." she started. "Maybe I shouldn't be here when you get back."

"Maybe you shouldn't? Why not?"

She unfolded her arms, flung them up and then brought them down to slap at the sides of her thighs. She'd gone from zero to full argument again in no time flat.

"Because, Sean."

He waited. Asking "Because why?" would only make her angrier.

"Because if you come back and you don't get it and then I leave it's like I'm leaving because of that."

"Aren't you?"

"You really don't get it." She refolded her arms. "It's like you haven't been paying attention for the past two years."

But he had. He'd seen it coming. He wasn't surprised. Money issues led to other issues. He'd agreed to buy too much house because he thought it would make her happy. All it did was make them poor. He kept his mouth shut when she shopped too much until it came out in angry bursts that did them no good.

He had been paying attention.

He shook his head and turned to walk away and try to get a few hours sleep on the couch. This time tomorrow, he figured he'd been aching for a soft couch to sleep on.

BACK HOME

THE FIRST THING Sean does is shave. His beard has grown in patchy and itchy as hell. A few of the whiskers came in gray and it bothers him.

Clean shaven again he stares at himself in the bathroom mirror. His face is thinner, his eyes deeper set. He knows his cheeks will fill out again, maybe he'll even over compensate and get a little fat. But his eyes will never be the same. Not after what they've seen. They won't be able to hide the visions that plague him.

He tells himself this is his chance. To reinvent. To start over. He doesn't want to say the old Sean is gone, but he knows a part of him really is.

The room is quiet. The indoors—so void of sound. The sounds he came to know in the woods confirmed life all around him. Now the indoors sounds dead. He turns on the faucet for the sound of moving water. It used to be white noise to him, but now it dredges up flash memories. He shuts off the tap. He knows it isn't the river, but it is too close. Too soon.

The river, where it all started.

Kerri stayed downstairs. She knew he'd have so many questions. She knew he'd notice the changes she made to the house. The myriad ways she removed him from his home.

"I thought you were dead," she explained before they came inside. "We all did."

Walking in was like being brought through the house by one of Scrooge's ghosts, showing him a life in which he never existed. No photos. His books gone. The framed painting of the pier they'd bought on their honeymoon—absent from the wall with nothing there to cover the thin outline of discoloration where it once hung.

Kerri had threatened to leave and Sean couldn't help thinking how happy she'd been when she learned she wouldn't have to. Did she quietly thank him in his death for making her decision for her?

He knows the discussion will be coming soon. Should he sleep on the couch? Would she welcome him into their bed? Did his near death have a reconciling effect on Kerri?

For the moment he continues to stare at his new face. At the ranger station he glanced in a mirror but didn't recognize the face looking back. He was too tired, then, to think about it. Now he can study the new lines and creases and chart the damage done. Now his face reads like a diary of the madness out there.

Beyond the door, in the bedroom they once shared that Kerri now claims as her own, he can hear the door shut and her moving in the room.

"I made up the couch," she says to the door.

Sean says nothing.

"I bet it will feel good to sleep on something soft, huh?"

He looks into his own eyes, beyond the mouth of the caves surrounding them, and begins to cry. Not for her, but for everything. He cries for something soft, for the memories he knows will never leave him, for the woman who had already forgotten him.

He forces himself to stop. Wills his eyes dry again. A new start. A chance to say the things he wouldn't have said before.

Sean opens the bathroom door. Kerri is there, decision made for him about where he would sleep.

"You didn't seem happy to see me," he says.

"What?"

"You didn't seem happy. You wanted me to stay gone, didn't you?"

Kerri stands speechless for a moment. She isn't used to Sean speaking exactly what's on his mind. At first it was a quality she liked—his aversion to conflict and his willingness to give in to her at every turn to avoid it—but after too long it became a liability. A weakness.

Now it comes so unexpected she doesn't know what to say.

"You didn't ask if I wanted to sleep on the couch," he says.

"I figured...after our talk before you left..."

"Do you know how many nights I dreamed of my own bed?"

"I guess I could stay on the couch."

"No. I want us to stay together." He watches her curl her arms around herself, unthinking, guarding herself from him. Or maybe from her own feelings. He reads it on her face—she's made peace with it, with him being gone.

"Kerri." He takes a step forward. "I need to make something whole again. I need to be a part of something good. I need to fix...I need to set things right."

"Sean, I thought you were dead. I *knew* you were dead."

"I know it's not easy for you, but this could be a new start. I need a new start. More than you know."

She reaches out a hand, palm down, not quite halfway between them. He moves closer, takes the hand. He leads her in and closes the bedroom door with both of them inside.

———

Grady does not shave. He does not look at himself. He sits and drinks a beer brought to him by his girlfriend, Natalie.

She hasn't noticed that he has barely spoken since she brought him home. She hasn't noticed what is broken inside. He hasn't noticed, either. To him, it is as if something has been repaired.

"Oh my God, baby, I thought I lost you."

He sips. The beer is good, but he takes his time. He's waited for this moment, wanted it, but didn't obsess over it. He didn't let himself become preoccupied by what lay at home for him when he was trying to survive. Now he knows that life here—in this apartment, in this city, at this job—is not that different. It's still survival. You have more tools, more basic needs taken care of, but the goal is the same. The instincts remain. Survive.

"So this is weird, but, um...they let your rent go for

an extra week. Well, nine days actually, since nobody knew what was going on. But Mr. McKinney said he needs it by the weekend now that you're back."

Natalie has her own place with two roommates, but she stays with Grady a lot. Too much. Not enough to feel like paying rent, though.

"It sucked," she goes on. "As soon as they announced it on the news, like an hour later. Less. He calls me up and is all like, 'He's gonna pay me the rent now, right?' and I'm like, back off, dude."

"He'll get it," Grady says.

"That's so awesome they kept your job for you. I mean, we all knew you would come home, but still."

"You knew it?"

"Yeah. Totally."

She smiles, sits on the edge of the couch. Space between them. Something keeps her from moving closer.

Grady thinks of his time out there. The debates and arguments about what to do to make it out. To survive. Grady thought a lot about dead weight. About who was holding them back.

He looks at Natalie now. She is not essential to his survival. She is holding him back. And now he is home, in his shelter. All he needs to survive is contained within. And he is tired.

"I think you should go now."

"What? Are you sure?"

Natalie gives him a smile with a hint behind it. Surely after so long without a woman...

"Yes. Go home."

Grady finishes his beer and sets the bottle on the table.

"Oh, come on, I'm sure you've had enough time being alone."

"I wasn't alone. I had all those people with me. All day, every day. Too many damn people. Now I want you to leave."

"But I missed you." She slides closer to him. Sets a hand on his cheek. "And I think I'm digging the beard."

His face is stone. She feels a coldness coming from him. *You are not essential. You are not needed.*

"Go home," he says again.

"Okay." Natalie begins to stand. She wears a pout and lets the strap of her tank top slide off one shoulder. "If you're sure."

"I'm sure."

"I just thought..."

Grady stands and takes her arm in his wide hand. In his ears is the sound of the river rushing, masking all other sound. He lifts her, the strap falling lower on her arm.

"Ow, Grady."

His grip tightens. He moves her toward the door like she is an intruder in his home. His domain.

"Jesus, Grady, you're hurting my arm."

Natalie twists away from him. She slips the strap back onto her shoulder. The pout is gone, replaced by a stern warning look.

Grady stands with his legs shoulder width apart. The sound fills his ears, but she can't hear it. She doesn't understand the sound, she wouldn't even if she could hear. Dragging him down. Slowing him. Maybe drowning him. Maybe getting in the way of his survival.

Grady reaches for her, takes her hair in his fist, and pulls. With a yelp she bends with him, protecting her hair from being pulled out at the root. Grady continues his march for the door, dragging her along behind him on scrambling feet. She grunts in pain but can't form words. Her feet give out and he is dragging her on her heels, both her hands around his wrist to keep her body weight from being solely supported by her hair.

He opens the door to the apartment and shoves her out. He lets go of her hair, long brown strands cling between his fingers.

"Go home," he says between heavy breaths.

Natalie is crying. He can't hear her over the sound of the river.

"You're an asshole," she says.

No, I'm not, Grady thinks. *I'm a survivor.*

Maia's key to her condo was in the personal effects the police turned over to her. Everyone was grateful to get back their cell phones, car keys, credit cards. All the things stripped from them before they left.

She stands at her door reading the note left for her by a neighbor, Elizabeth, a sweet older lesbian woman who thought for the first year Maia lived there that she, too, was a lesbian. Not that she ever hit on Maia, but she noticed that Maia never brought anyone home. No men around. The suits she wore more often were pants rather than skirts.

"I thought…"

Assumed, you mean, Maia thought. *I can't get a fucking break. If the men don't assume one thing my goddamn lesbian neighbor thinks something else. This is an uphill battle on a mountain that only goes up. No downslope to the fight for equality or to be taken as a person and not a gender.*

Elizabeth's door opens. Maia has finished the note. She looks at Elizabeth, questioning.

"You read it?" Maia doesn't move. "I fed her for those first few days, like I said I would. I emptied her litter box. But then when it went on for so long...it became cruel to leave her in there locked up all day with only me popping in twice a day for three minutes at a time."

Maia folds the note. It said as much only in a calmer voice. Elizabeth is on the verge of tears.

"We didn't think you were coming back."

"Did they find her another home?"

Elizabeth nods.

"When I heard you were alive...that you were going home, I called them. But..."

Maia nods.

"She was such a sweetie," Elizabeth says. "I'm sure she went to a good family."

"I'm sure."

Elizabeth steps forward as if maybe to hug Maia, but she stops. Something there between them, hanging in the air like a fog, makes her stop. Maia doesn't want her affection. Doesn't want any affection. Elizabeth doubts if she ever would have wanted it from the cat. She seems void of all capacity for it.

Instead she says, "We're all so glad you're home."

"Me, too."

Maia goes inside.

The company has put Wes up in a hotel. The hour is late and the three-and-a-half-hour drive back north is too much to ask. Plus, there is a meeting scheduled for tomorrow with all the survivors and the company HR department. They plan to discuss the "events" and get everyone's "feelings" about those events. It's group therapy, although nobody is coming out and calling it that. Wes knows. He's been to plenty of meetings from his years in AA. Six years sober now, since senior year in college when he was on the verge of getting expelled or dropping out from embarrassment at his slumping grades.

Since then he's been the poster boy for turning around your life. And nobody at Synergen Dynamics knows of his history. Not even Allison.

Here in the hotel room, alone, he is grateful for his habit of calling the front desk before check-in to have them empty the mini bar. Still, he is here hundreds of miles from his sponsor. Not that Gordon had done him much good the past year. The old man kept blowing him off and claiming to be "dealing with some issues," which Wes assumed meant falling off his own wagon.

Other than Gordon, nobody was waiting for him back north. His parents were both dead—the start of his drinking—and work kept him from finding a girlfriend. Not going out to bars didn't help any. He'd spent three years with Synergen avoiding outside social events. A long while back they stopped asking him.

So here he is, waiting for tomorrow to come. Grateful to be alive, but raw and unsure of what comes next. He hasn't shaved. It seems too daunting a choice right now. Like to make any decision means life is moving again. He needs it to stand still for a moment. He needs to pause and just be alive.

The room is stifling. It is a weird thing—for days upon days to want nothing more than to be inside a real building. To have room service on call. Linen sheets. A TV. But now it all seems to be closing him in.

Wes throws on a jacket with the Synergen logo over the breast and leaves the room. Fresh air. He'd grown used to it.

The city sounds are so different. He puzzles the tiny changes. Rushing cars going past versus rushing water. The chirp of cell phone calls versus trill of birds. The murmur of people passing versus the constant drone of insects in the trees. Maybe not so different.

He hears a sound unlike any in the woods. Familiar and welcoming. Distinctly human. Laughter mixed with music mixed with glass chiming. A bar. It stops him. He waits on the sidewalk outside, his eyes half shut, ears tuned to the sound. He knows it so well. Here, back home, in college, in any city in America. It stirs a deep nostalgia in him, like hearing the song that played during your first kiss. A slow pull of sadness in his gut for lost time, for memories of better times. He didn't want to be welcomed back into the world of hotel rooms and room service. He wanted to come back to this. This was home.

He dials Gordon. Voicemail. The tone sounds and Wes draws a breath to speak, but he can't think of how to explain it. He knows he doesn't need to. He only needs to say, *I want a drink and I need your help*. But he wants Gordon to know this isn't ordinary weakness. This is a powerful combination of factors beating at him in an already weakened state. He wants to explain it to someone so he might understand it himself. He hangs up the phone.

Three men about his age—mid-twenties—walk past and toward the door. One of them stops.

"Hey man."

Wes stops listening to the bar sounds. The city noises all around him turn up in volume.

"Are you...?" The guy looks at him, studies his face. "Yeah, shit, from the news."

He slaps his buddies on the shoulder, gesturing to Wes, pointing to the splint on his finger as evidence.

"This is one of the guys lost in the woods."

His two buddies perk up. Wes is frozen.

"Holy shit, dude. You're him, right? Yeah, you are."

"Oh, my God," a buddy says. "You were out there for like a month. That's badass, man. That wasn't like a game show or anything, that was real."

Wes nods slowly. "Yeah. It was..." Something. It was something, but he doesn't know what yet. He can't describe it. He doesn't even know if he's completely felt it yet.

"Dude, we are buying you a drink."

The one who recognized him puts an arm around his shoulder like Wes is now one of the buddies. They push for the bar like the three friends are walking in with a prize they won, the trophy that will give them all the attention.

Wes is swept along like he is back in the water, being pushed by the river. There is too much might, too much behind the push. No resistance. No point.

"Check it out," the buddies say. "It's one of the guys who almost died out there lost in the woods."

The crowd cheers. It doesn't sound like the woods anymore. It sounds like home.

———————

Nathan finally convinced his parents to let him get some sleep. They went back to their hotel room. His mom never stopped crying. Now Nathan sits alone in his apartment looking at a dead plant.

He'd thought about a dog last year, but quickly gave up the idea. He wasn't home enough. He preferred running at the gym to being on the street. He didn't like the idea of paying thirty or forty bucks for a bag of dog food like some people he knew. Living alone suits him better.

There'd been three girls. Real relationships. Nothing under a year. A serial monogamist, a friend had called him. All three women treated him like crap. They hadn't started out that way, but all fell into the same pattern.

"I don't like who I became when I was with you," Donna had told him after the breakup. "It's like you invited me to abuse you. You've got to get a spine, Nathan."

Not the first speech with those headlines. He doesn't know why. Before they left for the retreat, he knew he wasn't going to get the promotion. It doesn't even make him sad. He's used to it.

Maybe it's the dead plant, but he feels terrifyingly alone. He starts to shallow breathe, to feel his heartbeat. He has to get out.

Down on the street he starts to calm. A man in the bodega on the corner. Two couples hailing a cab. People in cars going places he can't imagine. He's not alone. He is among them and he is alive. And he doesn't have to fear death. Not the way he did a day ago.

He realizes the fear had consumed him. Had calcified his bones. It was all that filled his thoughts the entire time they were out there. From that first day he waited for it around every tree trunk. How did he let it go now when it clung to him like a tattoo?

Since Donna there had been no one. He knows a place. Somewhere he can go. Somewhere he's gone before.

The walk is long but it settles his nerves. He comes to the shop offering Thai massages. Nathan knows the code words to say. He knows the person to ask. He goes inside.

They give legitimate massages here. They also do more. Nathan says the right words and he is led to the end of the hall and through a door marked NO ADMITTANCE.

He recognizes a girl who walks by. He's not a regular, and he is sure she doesn't know his face, but he remembers. A different girl comes out to meet him. She is white, not Thai. Nathan figures some men would send her back, wanting what is advertised out front. He does not. He stands and shakes her hand. She wears a thin kimono that stops mid-thigh.

"How are you doing tonight?" she asks him. She doesn't ask his name or give hers.

"Okay. I could use some company."

"That's what I'm here for." She smiles and it reads as genuine. Nathan is glad she is a good actress. It helps.

His cheeks are still red from the shave. They blush a deeper hue. He is grateful for the half hour long shower he took. He stayed under the hot water until his mother knocked on the bathroom door and asked if he was okay.

The room she leads him to is small and functional. The decoration is a tangle of tapestries and potted bamboo. There is a small water fountain that he almost asks her to turn off, but the sound of the pump motor is louder than the sound of the water so he lets it go.

The girl unties the sash at the waist of her kimono but Nathan stops her.

"Can we...can we just sit for a while?"

"Whatever you want. We have an hour."

He paid up front when he gave the code word. His time is ticking now.

"I don't really need...I mean, I could use some company."

"Yeah, you said that."

She sits on the red blanket covering the bed and pats the open space next to her. She's surely seen every type of foreplay there is. Nathan sits.

"Can I...I mean, can you just hold me?"

She pauses as he can see her wheels turning to see if this has ever happened to her before. Her mind is reviewing the catalog of freaks and trying to match this particular fetish. But this isn't one. Nathan settles against her, and when she wraps her arms around him he begins to weep. He is quiet about it, the tears fall as soundlessly as the fountain behind him. The girl is tense at first, but she relaxes. She strokes his hair. She might feel sorry for him. She might be grateful that this will be the easiest trick she has all night.

Nathan holds her and continues to cry.

OUT THERE

DAY 1

THE BUS DROVE them six and a half hours into the wilderness. Sean watched the landscape change outside the window and couldn't decide if they were going towards somewhere or away from somewhere.

The bus was short, lined with seats along the interior and had a run of string lights along the ceiling. Ken joked that they were like seniors on their way to Vegas. Lara said it felt like a bachelorette party she went to once.

Everyone had been given a list of things they could take and what to leave behind. They all had their cell phones but they knew they would be losing them soon. Most of the supplies would be provided by the tour company. They didn't expect everyone to have their own tents, their own sleeping bags rated to forty below. Everyone on the bus except Grady wore new hiking boots purchased for the trip.

"Did you break them in?" he asked Sean.

"Kind of. Not really, I guess."

"They're gonna hurt your feet. You should have

worn them wet and let them dry on your feet. It fits them to the shape of your foot." He shrugged. "Too late now. They'll probably start to break in about the day we leave."

Sean grinned like Grady was making a joke but he knew he wasn't. Grady was always pulling tiny power trips like that. He seemed to operate in a mode where he couldn't make any forward progress without pushing you back. Every achievement of his came at the expense of others. He seemed primed and ready to continue the streak out in the forest.

Wes and Ron napped for a while. Maia nodded off, but mostly so Lara would stop talking to her. She seemed nervous and clung to the only other woman on the trip with white knuckles.

They traded stories of one or two camping trips when they were younger. Some made regular hiking trips in the hills overlooking the city. Easy trails frequented by dog walkers and boy scout troops.

Already they started talking about food they would miss.

"Man, I wish there was booze on this bus," Ken said.

Wes laughed a bit too hard.

Nobody said a word about the promotion waiting for half of them when they got back.

They started to ascend. Sean's ears popped and he could see some others working their jaws and tugging on their earlobes to get theirs to shift to the changing pressure and thinning air.

No one had bothered to research the area they would be living in for the next five days. They trusted the company, and knowing that all executives before them had gone through the ritual, each figured this was *glamping*, as it was called. Camping for non-campers. Plenty of food, comfortable accommodations, probably even beer at the end of a long day.

A week off from work is what it came down to. Everyone there was looking forward to it.

Their two wilderness guides met the bus. They had pulled over at a seemingly random bend in the road. There were no buildings, no welcome center. No bathroom facilities.

Rick and Karina, the guides, were all smiles as the newest team of junior executives exited the bus. Rick wore a scraggy beard, well-worn hiking boots, a cluster of carabiners on a clip at his waist. A sun bleached bandana looped around his neck and a tattoo of one of the figures from the Nazca lines ran along his forearm.

Karina had long hair that clumped into dreadlocks at the ends. Her eyes were a bright blue and her face freckled with markings of a life in the sun. When she smiled she closed her eyes for a moment as if the brightness of the good in the world was too much for her.

"Welcome, welcome Synergen Dynamics," Rick said. "I'm Rick and I'll do my best to remember your names, but don't quiz me on it too soon."

He shook hands and repeated everyone's name as they introduced themselves.

"Hi, I'm Karina," she said to each person stepping off the bus. "And you are?"

"Sean, hi."

"Sean. Great. Welcome, Sean."

Her name memorization techniques were the same ones they taught in business school.

After everyone was off and standing in the dirt, nervous eyes scanning the dense thicket of trees in every direction, Rick held up a woven bag.

"It's time," he said.

"This is everyone's least favorite part," Karina said. "Cell phones in the bag."

With a reluctance that was familiar to Rick and Karina, each person handed over their phones.

"Thought it was gonna be easier than that, huh?" Rick said to Nathan.

"Yeah. Jeez, we're really out there, huh?"

Karina smiled at Maia. "This is when it gets real."

Maia smiled back, then dumped her phone in the bag. Lara stood next to Maia and handed in her phone.

"I guess we're really doing this."

"We are," Karina said. She stopped and put a hand on Lara's busy hand to calm her. "It's gonna be great."

One by one Rick and Karina went through the supplies everyone had brought, then pointed to their backpacks that had be pre-prepared for them.

Grady pulled a short folding knife from his pocket.

"I brought this." He flipped the blade open with his thumb. The sharp serrated blade looked mean.

"Spyderco, cool," Rick said, calling out the brand name. "You'll definitely use that."

Grady clipped it back inside his front pocket with a smile. He'd come more prepared than the others. The winning had already started.

Ken clapped his hands together. "Whoo. Already cooler up here than it was in the city."

"Oh, yeah," Karina said. "But don't worry. You'll

warm up a lot on our first hike. We've got to get to our campsite and it's a two mile trek."

"Two miles?" Lara said.

"More like two and a half, really. A lot of it is down-hill," Karina said, calming her with a warm grin. "Down into the valley. A little warmer, less exposed. Close to the river."

"Karina," Rick mock scolded. "Are you spoiling our surprise about the river?"

"No way," she answered with a rehearsed-sounding stiffness.

The bus had started out at five a.m. and it was nearly noon. Rick gave a speech about the importance of hydration and made everyone take a drink from the water bottles provided to them. He explained this was the last bottled water they would be drinking. From here on out it would be the freshest mountain snow runoff they'd ever had.

He showed everyone a protein bar they've been given in their packs and made everyone eat it for some energy before the hike.

He checked the sky as if it were his watch and he could tell the time down to the minute.

"We gotta move out if we want to make camp on time. The rest of our supplies are waiting there. Let's roll out, what do you say?"

The group gave a less-than-enthusiastic yay. Lara, Ron and Wes all grunted when they hoisted their back-packs over their shoulders.

"Cinch it up real tight," Rick explained. "Let your core carry it, not your lower back. It should feel like a part of you, not something you're carrying."

A quick pass down the line to make sure everyone

was properly outfitted and the bus pulled away. Once the engine faded they were left with only the sounds of the forest and then the crunch of ten pairs of feet on the ground as they moved away from the open road and into the trees.

———

For the first few hundred yards the trail was wide enough for them to walk two and three abreast. The ground sloped gently downward making the walking swift and easy going. Sean looked around him at the trees trying to find the birds making calls, but he couldn't see any of them even though they sounded right over his head. His pack felt heavy, but not unmanageable, and his shoes snug and comfortable.

Ahead the tress closed and seemed to form a wall. The trail narrowed to a single lane. Rick led the way.

"Doin' great, guys."

Grady angled ahead of Sean, bumping him with his backpack as he stepped in front like someone merging in traffic with no turn signal. Sean stopped and took a half step back, not sure if he wanted to say anything or let it go. While he paused on the trail, Maia passed him in a hurry to keep up with Grady. Sean fell in behind her. He knew the type. Make everything a race, a competition. Well, this was, in a way. But Allison had said the decision was being made back in the office without them around. Whatever they did out here didn't weigh too heavily for the outcome. Try telling Grady that. Or maybe he was that kind of asshole all the time.

Maia had her own thing to prove, and he let her go

ahead with no hard feelings. He knew she had one of the spots sewn up. Really, this was a fight for three spots. If they didn't give it to Maia, they were idiots. Nobody worked harder or had less of a life outside the office.

Lara couldn't keep up with Maia and watched her duck in front of Sean. Not that she wanted to stare at Maia's backpack all afternoon. What she really wanted to look at was Rick. As soon as she saw him her thoughts of Ken faded. A genuine mountain man. He was lithe and a little bit dirty around the edges. But hell, she was out in the woods for a week. What better type of guy to have a roll in the tent with? Plus, no awkward run-ins back at the office. One in the pro column for Rick, and one in the con column for Ken. Besides, with Ken she had time. Rick she'd never see again beyond these five days. The perfect relationship.

The canopy of trees closed over them, throwing the bright mid-morning into dusk. The path continued to slope down. A river of pine needles that had turned rust colored made a snake through the dense trees and a cushioned path for the hikers.

Sean noticed the deeper they went into the valley the taller the trees got, all reaching higher as the ground sank lower. They muscled into each other like they were rubbing shoulders and throwing elbows to grab the sunlight. He didn't think thin pine needles could block out that much light but the density wove together to make a solid sheet of green. Thicker trunked trees with wide leaves grouped together to fend off the pine trees dominance.

Sean didn't know the name of a single tree. He didn't know if any of the bright berries on the bushes down lower were edible, didn't know if the fungus clinging to the sides of fallen trunks was poisonous. He followed Rick into the dimming light.

———

Nathan stepped on a pine cone and his ankle wrenched to the side. He grunted, but kept his footing. Behind him, Wes put a hand out to steady his pack when he stumbled.

"Whoa. You okay?"

"Yeah. I'm all right."

The group ahead of them didn't slow or stop. Nathan hoisted his backpack and continued on. Behind him and Wes, Karina brought up the rear. Protection against stragglers.

"Doing okay there?"

"Yeah," Nathan said. "Not exactly like walking on a sidewalk."

"That's true. Better though, right?"

"Sure. Hey, how much longer?"

"Oh, we've got a ways to go yet. We're not quite halfway."

Nathan lowered his voice and turned his head to Wes. "Shit. I gotta pee."

"We can take care of that," Karina said.

Nathan made a mental note: no city sounds to mask a quiet conversation out here.

"Hey, Rick," she shouted. "Hold up. We got a ten-one hundred."

"Holding," he called back. Even though he was only thirty yards ahead his voice sounded a mile off. These woods, Nathan noticed, they do strange things to sound.

"Take your pick," Karina said.

Nathan saw her wave an arm to the trees all around.

Wes laughed. "The world is your toilet, man."

"Anyone else need to go?"

Ron raised his hand then stepped off the path into the trees.

Nathan felt self-conscious now, all eyes on him. He moved off the path on the opposite side as Ron. Ten steps away and he felt isolated. The trees blended together to make a screen and the heavy breathing of his hiking party was swallowed by the forest around him. He walked another fifteen paces in case anyone had a thought to go explore while they were stopped, then stepped up to a tree trunk and unzipped his pants.

He stared at the bark while he urinated and only when he stood still and looked closely did he see the movement of dozens of small bugs. Passing over the rugged bark in a crooked line the insects moved with purpose in their steep ascent up the side of the tree. Nathan wondered if some animal would make use of his pee. Do insects feed off urine or only feces? Damn, he knew nothing about nature.

***

"Roll out," Rick called.

Sean pushed himself off a tree where he had stopped to lean. He was afraid to sit and not be able to stand again with the weight of the backpack. He imagined having to ask Maia for help up.

What he'd found interesting about the trees at first quickly faded into monotony. Everywhere Sean looked was the same. No definition, no distinct markings. He wondered if Rick was up in front spotting subtle differences in the tree trunks or was he following the path worn into the forest bed over years of hikers.

Maybe experienced mountain men could tell the difference, but Sean was as likely to pick a zebra out of a herd as he was to tell you one pine tree from the next.

After another half hour of hiking his feet started to ache and the sounds of the forest changed. A gentle rushing started in low and gained volume.

"Hear that?" Rick called. "That's the river saying hello. And welcome."

Hippie bullshit aside, Sean was glad to get a break from the endless stretch of dense trees. As close as the river sounded when he first noticed it, there was another ten minutes of walking until they reached a break in the forest and could see the river.

Sean knew he was supposed to be relieved to come to the river, but what had been a gentle hush over the forest floor now showed itself as a fast moving river churning white water over rocks.

"Okay." Rick unclipped his backpack and let it fall to the pine needle carpet below. He had to raise his voice to be heard over the water.

"This is your first test."

Sean could see by the faces of the others that they were intimidated by the fast moving water as well.

"You can see our campsite on the far side of the river." Rick pointed and on a flat clearing were tents already set up, a ring of rocks around a campfire pit, a hammock strung between two trees. "All we have to do is get there."

Rick smiled. He clearly loved this part of the trip. His first chance to get the city folk outside their comfort zones.

"You can see the rope bridge set up for you."

He pointed upstream to a thin rope strung across the rushing river, with two ropes a few feet above it for hand holds. The ropes were anchored to trees on either side of the river but it wasn't anything Sean would call a bridge.

"That looks like a tightrope," Lara said.

"Nah, a tightrope doesn't have hand guides."

"Plus, you'll be clipped onto the lines," Karina added.

"Now everyone get close and I'll go over the details. You all are gonna be fine."

Sean watched as Grady stepped forward, his eyes on the ropes as if he were daring them to a fight.

The group made a semi-circle around Rick as he explained.

The logistics of the traverse were simple enough. Walk slowly, balance with your hands, stay out of the water. Rick went first to both demonstrate and to be there on the other side to help everyone off the ropes.

Maybe it was because of the concerned looks from some of the group, but Rick did go out of his way to explain the speed and volume of the river.

"It's been a really good year for snowpack, that's why

the river is higher than normal. Everything you see here was snow only a few days ago. But, yeah, it's running high and it's running fast so your feet might get wet, but you'll be hooked onto the guide rope and as long as you follow my instructions you'll be fine. I've been doing this six years and we haven't lost anybody yet."

He smiled but the joke was lost on the crew of tech workers and computer geeks.

They all donned belts with hooks on them to which the carabiners were clipped. Karina helped everyone get suited up and helped them balance with their backpacks throwing off their normal equilibrium.

Grady stepped forward to take the first pass after Rick.

"Actually, let's have Maia go first."

Grady looked like he might try to argue for his spot, but he backed away.

Sean was grateful for the open sky above them. The flat canopy of trees during their hike had already gotten him feeling closed in, not what he expected from a walk in nature. But any peace from the open sky above was blotted out by the jet engine noise of the river. Every instruction of Rick's and Karina's had to be shouted.

A chaos of white foam rolled over rocks buried beneath the water. Chair-sized boulders lined the river bank. The rope bridge started at a flat area spared of a heavy rock, but the options were limited. This crossing point was obviously chosen out of necessity and not ease of passage.

As Rick made his traverse his hiking boots dipped into the water several times. He let out whoops of joy as the icy mountain water splashed into his shoes, smiling the whole time to show everyone how fun it was.

Sean was unconvinced. Aside from Grady, no one seemed eager to take on this first task. Like him, they were probably wondering what could possibly be in store for the next five days if this was their introduction to the wild.

Grady moved atop a rock half submerged in the rushing water an arm's length away from the rope bridge. He stood by and watched as if he had advice to hand out on this task none of them had ever done before. Sean saw the jagged edges of the rock like the heavy head of a tomahawk pointed downriver. He had the short, crazy thought that maybe an Indian had carved the stone three hundred years ago as a way to catch fish in the river. If it weren't the size of a bean bag chair it would make a great arrowhead.

With Rick safely standing on the other bank of the river, Maia put one foot on the rope. She hesitated on the second foot. Karina did the same big smile technique to try and fool her into thinking this would be a big laugh once she was out there. Sean had never seen Maia hesitate on any task before.

"You got it, girl," Karina said.

Maia let out a sharp breath. Sean saw her knuckles whiten as she gripped the rope and set her second foot down on the tightrope stretched across the river. Once she committed, she moved swiftly and exactly like Rick had instructed. Her feet shuffled instead of lifted, her hands never came off the ropes, she kept her eyes forward toward her goal on the other side.

When she reached the far side she yelped with genuine joy. Sean wondered if it was the call of someone who felt lucky to be alive.

My God, what a city boy, he thought. It's obviously

easy to do and only seems difficult because it's foreign to us.

"Sean, you're next."

He almost asked Karina to repeat herself. It was Grady's stern look that made it sink in. He was next in line. He moved to the water's edge, clipped in his line and felt the cold spray of water hit his face. It was not hard to imagine how water this frigid had been snowfall only a few hours earlier.

Karina pointed the way and repeated the instructions but Sean heard only the rush of water. Now, with one foot over the water, he swore he could hear the rocks knocking together under the flow. Even if the whole group worked together they couldn't have lifted the heavy stones, but the force of the river knocked them around like pool balls.

"You got it, buddy?"

Grady held out a steadying hand as if Sean needed his help.

"I'm good."

Grady stepped back atop his rock and shrugged *if you say so.*

The water soaked his pants up to his knees. The river got even louder halfway across when he was fully surrounded. Maia shouted encouragement from the other side, her adrenaline still buzzing, but Sean could hear only white noise. A branch that had fallen from some tree perhaps miles away passed by under him, nearly clipping the rope. He stalled mid-river as it went by in a blur. He turned upriver, taking his eyes off his destination. The endless flow coming down off the high mountain seemed like it had a mind to take him with it to where it emptied into who-knew-where.

He focused back on shore where Rick stood with beckoning arms and a wide grin. Sean shuffled, slid his hands, cursed under his breath and made it to land. He immediately shucked his backpack and sat down on the cleared earth of the campsite.

Maia and Rick both applauded, but Sean needed a minute before he could make any sound at all.

Wes was next and he made it with what seemed like less effort and stress than Sean. Sean sat on the bank and wondered if this test was to separate the alpha males from the pack. To let their two guides know who was an asset and who a liability.

Nathan made it across with little drama. He stayed silent with a furrowed brow as he concentrated on remembering his instructions and not losing his footing.

Karina kept Grady waiting. She'd seen his type before. He thought he knew everything already. Had to prove what a man he was. She liked his type. Liked making them wait.

"Lara, you're up next, girl."

As Lara stepped up Grady leaned out from his rock and offered a hand on her elbow.

"Right up here."

She wavered and her foot slipped.

"I got it. Just don't touch me, you screw up my balance."

"I'm giving you a hand."

They had to shout over the river, bringing their buried annoyance with each other to the surface.

"Well, I can do it on my own."

"Fine."

Grady moved onto his rock which shifted under him. He flailed his arms for a moment, then settled, looking around to see if anyone had noticed. He fumed at having to wait.

Lara screamed almost the whole time, but with a smile. Everyone clapped and cheered her on.

"You got it!" Rick shouted over the river noise. "Come to me."

Lara knew exactly what she would do twenty feet from the end of the rope. She kept moving, sliding, and when she reached the end and Rick held out a hand for her to take while he kept the other on a rope to steady her, she leaned forward and fell into his arms, chest to chest, so he had to embrace her and hold her up.

It would have been the perfect story to tell their kids about the day they met, but she knew a week in a tent with this mountain man was all she wanted or needed from him. It was off to a great start.

Ron was up next and Grady knew he was going to be put last. Grady offered the same helpful hand and got the same chilly reception. Ron had remained quiet during the lesson and the wait. His face had gone as white as his knuckles by the time it was his turn.

He started slow. His eyes were closed as often as they looked toward the far shore. His slow steps were more like shuffling in place.

The group shouted encouragements. Rick and Karina knew this was exactly what was supposed to happen. The group was already becoming a team, rallying around each other.

Ken, next on the rope, moved into the ready position and called out to Ron as water soaked his feet.

"Keep going, Ron. Almost there."

Ron was less than halfway, but between Ken urging him on and Rick calling him forward, the momentum was in the right direction. Grady stayed silent.

Sean called out, "C'mon, Ron," to be a part of the team, but his voice was swallowed by the water. He stood near, but not on, the banks. The water still frightened him with its relentless and endless power. He kept looking upriver, thinking surely it would end, but the water crashed downhill relentlessly as if from an endless source.

Sean was secretly glad that Ron was having trouble. It meant he was no longer the slowest or most timid across the ropes. He wouldn't be the target of ridicule around the campfire tonight. Sean knew the pack mentality of a group like this. They liked to select one and single them out, like a pride of lions separating a sick or wounded animal from the herd.

Because everyone else's eyes were on Ron and his struggle to cross the ropes, Sean was the first to see the log. He'd turned his head upriver again and noticed the shape surfing on the rolling waters. At first he thought it was a boat, a canoe of some sort. As it got closer, moving fast around the bend, he saw it was a fallen tree, stripped of nearly all its branches by the assault of the water and the rocky bottom. As it was, the tree was a missile. The larger, splintered end of the tree aimed downriver, the torn shreds of where the tree fell exposed like nerves.

Sean thought about calling out, but he didn't want to panic Ron. He might not be heard, anyway.

The end of the tree trunk shot up as it went over a particularly sharp dip in the river. It crashed down and spun like a pencil in a sharpener. It seemed to aim for Ron.

"Tree!" Sean finally called out.

Nobody turned. His warning was lost in the mix of encouraging shouts.

The tree punched Ron's feet out from under him and off the rope. The tree caught for a second on the rope and the whole apparatus stretched with an audible groan. Sean thought he heard the sound of metal pinging off something.

Ron's legs dipped into the water up to his knees but he held on to the ropes, his arms going from shoulder height to stretch above him. Sean saw the panic in his face.

Rick's smile finally disappeared.

"Hold on." Rick went into fast action. He was back out on the ropes in no time, his carabiner unclipped. Sean had seen it before, someone who had done something a thousand times and urged others to follow all the rules, yet somehow felt the same rules didn't apply to them. Or maybe he was so genuinely concerned for Ron he determined there was no time. Or he forgot. Either way, Rick was playing the part of hero.

Karina stood behind Ken who was still in his ready position. She had the rope bag in her hand, ready to toss.

Ron's hands slid off the ropes. His belt caught and the carabiner held as he grabbed onto his single lifeline with both hands. He sputtered in the icy water that splashed his face. He was waist deep in it now, his legs banging against the rocks.

Rick was nearly to him already, midway across the river.

Sean stood back and watched like it was a nightly news report. He waited for the smooth report's voice, but all he heard was the water roar like a beast.

Grady saw his opportunity.

"I'm going out there."

He moved to step off his rock when Ken put up a hand.

"No. Rick's got it."

"He could use help."

"I don't think the rope can support that many people."

"Four hands are better than two, right?" Grady said. He looked at Ken in the ready position and scoffed at him. "I mean, if you're just gonna stand there."

"I'd go if I thought it would help."

"That's all I'm doing. I know I can help him."

Karina ignored the two men, her singular focus on the man in distress halfway across the rope. Rick reached Ron and held out a hand to him.

Grady pushed off the rock he'd been standing on. It tipped forward, loosened by his shifting weight, and now urged along by the push of water. The tomahawk edge of the stone came down and pinned the walking rope against a flat stone. The sharp and jagged edge cut through the rope strung across the river as Grady slipped and fell to his knees in the water.

The rope they'd been walking on went slack then was taken immediately by the water. It slithered out into the river like a snake on the hunt. Rick tumbled. His footing gone, he spun and landed on his side in the water, his shoulder and ribs striking a pair of rocks. Ron had ahold of his hand and did not let go.

Sean watched it all happen and listened to the river's growl become a low laugh as it swallowed two of the team.

Rick bounced off two rocks. He would have been swept away if Ron hadn't held his grip on Rick's hand. Instead he spun a half turn and his head drove into another rock. Maybe it was one he'd already hit, Sean couldn't tell. He didn't know what he was looking at. Was this part of the training? Had Ron been a ringer, not sent from up north but embedded by the tour company to provide this little piece of theater?

Lara screamed and put her hands to her mouth. She stood on the rocks and looked like she might leap in after Rick if it wasn't for the complete fear making her body shudder.

Nathan and Maia were both at the edge of the river, one hand bracing on the support ropes. Nathan still wore his backpack and he stared at the drama playing out in front of him like he was trying to remember every detail.

Ron was now on his back, his feet pointing upriver. Rick was slack at the end of his arm but Ron wasn't letting go.

Sean heard the scream cut through, but Ron's mouth was shut.

Ken was on his hands and knees in the water. He was still in the rocks, out of the most powerful flow, but his legs were trapped, the ankle to his right foot caught between two heavy rocks that had shifted when Grady's rock tipped forward.

Karina let herself look away from Rick and Ron in the water and came to Ken's side. She lifted him under his arms and tried to get him standing. His leg was twisted, severely. When she tried to right him he screamed in her ear.

Grady scrambled out of the water, and when he saw Ken he could tell his leg was not right. His two feet were pointing in opposite directions. The trapped foot was spun almost a hundred and eighty degrees from the knee it was attached to. Ken's cries of pain made sense.

Karina looked at Grady. "You need to help him. I've got to get Rick."

Grady, so eager a moment ago, hesitated, but Karina didn't wait. She clung to her rope bag and turned her attention back to the river.

Ken squinted his eyes closed at the pain and grit his teeth to keep himself from crying out any more. His backpack still on, it pulled him backward toward the water.

"Move the rock, man. Get my leg out."

Grady tried to see which of the rocks he could move on his own. Step one was to get that foot free.

Sean watched as Ron got dunked under the water again and again, the weight of his pack pulling him down. His grip on Rick was impressive. He could tell Ron saw his hold on Rick as his hold on life, even though Ron's grip was the only thing keeping Rick from floating away. Rick showed no signs of life himself. He moved with the water, his body limp and unconscious.

Maia, Nathan and Lara all hung on the guide ropes, leaning out over the water but afraid to move any further. The crossing rope spun in the river, still attached on the campsite side. It swirled with each eddy and swell.

Sean watched Karina on the opposite shore ready the rope bag. The thing that would save your life, they'd said. She stood in the rushing water up to her knees, but she had nowhere to throw. Rick was a rag, inanimate as the loose rope whipping through the water. Ron had one hand free but one wasn't enough in this water and the chances of him having the focus to catch a half-inch thick rope flying through the air was slim at best.

Sean had said he felt helpless before in situations where he really meant he hadn't wanted to help, but now he knew what true helplessness felt like.

Grady pulled at the rock. Ken stifled a grunt of pain. The rock shifted, but for the moment it only made it worse by putting the full weight of the rock on Ken's toes, crushing the bones into pieces. Grady felt the rock give way from the riverbed and he jerked hard.

The rock rolled away, freeing Ken's foot, but also freeing Grady's momentum. He fell backward towards the water. He might have fallen in deep enough to be taken away downriver had he not hit Karina back to back.

She pitched forward and belly flopped in the water. The current wasted no time in taking her away.

Grady spun and fell where she had been standing, his body landing on the dropped rope bag. The other end was in Karina's hand.

The rope unspooled from the red bag in Grady's hands. Loops of rope leaping from the bag like a party trick. Grady could tell the end of the rope was coming soon. He closed his hands around the bag as the rope snapped taut.

On his backside, his feet propped against rocks and ice cold water flowing all around him, Grady dug in and held the rope.

Behind him, Ken pushed himself into shallower water. His right leg dangled limp below the knee. Tendons were snapped, bones separated and shattered. The ice water did little to dull the pain.

Downriver Karina jerked to a stop and flipped onto her back. The rope had gotten tangled around her as she tumbled across the rocks. She surfaced dazed, but alive, her grip on the rope solid with one hand. As the rope went taut she felt a sting and a tightness. The rope had gone under one arm, formed a loop. That loop was around her neck.

Sean watched from behind Maia, Nathan and Lara as if they were trees in the way. They saw Ron begin to slip from his safety belt. The merciless pounding of the water, the slick wetness and his position facing down-river started him oozing out of the belt. Once he began, he slid out quickly.

He tried to readjust, and his hand loosened on Rick's arm.

Lara screamed again as Rick was taken by the river. He was gone from sight in seconds.

Nathan leaned out farther on the guide ropes.

"Hang on, Ron!"

Ron was trying to grab at the belt. His flailing made the belt slip faster. The four on the campsite side of the river had front row seats to Ron slipping away and moving head first down the rapids. He went under and they didn't see him again.

Maybe out of instinct, maybe as a gesture, Maia, Nathan and Lara all reached out for Ron as he slid away.

Sean heard the same metallic pinging sound and the guide ropes went slack, a fractured bit of metal that held them to the anchor tree flashed by over their heads as it slingshot over the river. Weakened by the floating tree trunk, the pressure of too many bodies on the rope, it had ruptured. All three pitched forward into the river, Nathan with his pack still on, Maia and Lara holding on to each other. Only one rope remained as defense against the torrent.

"Help me," Grady said.

Ken was unfocused, head spinning from the pain.

Grady pulled on the rope, but the current was too strong to reel Karina in.

"You gotta help me."

Ken pushed himself on his hands and got within reach of Grady.

"Hold my waist."

Ken did, but his grip was weak. Grady took what he could get. He pulled on the rope until it gave enough slack he could wrap a loop around his forearm. He leaned forward for another pull. He sat back, letting Ken add to his core strength. More slack, another loop.

In the river Karina felt the rope tighten. Her face was above water, mostly. The water had made her body go numb from the cold already. But as she gasped for breath she knew the sensation might have been from the lack of blood to her brain or oxygen in her system.

Grady reeled in another loop, urged along by the hero's welcome he imagined he'd get back in the office for saving one of the tour guides after disaster struck. He heaved again.

Sean ran to the riverbank. He had no rope bag, no life preserver, no way to help. His three coworkers bobbed to the surface, eyes wide and mouths open and taking in water. They were in shock and paddling furiously.

They weren't taken immediately by the flow. In a tangle of arms and legs, all thrashing against the current, they spun a slow circle and moved in inches out toward the faster flow of water.

Sean reached down and took up the slack rope. It was still attached to the tree on the far side of the river so it gave him something to hold on to. When it was in his hand he stared at it for a second. He hadn't consciously picked it up. His body had made the move to rescue the ones in the water. A strange latent bravery.

He stepped into the water and reached his free hand.

Nathan saw him and his eyes widened. He coughed on a choking mouthful of water but abandoned his paddling and tried to gain some footing on the rocks to reach for Sean.

The water knifed through Sean's pants and stung his legs with the cold. The rocks on the riverbed were uneven and slick with some kind of moss, making solid footing impossible. He saw Lara get pulled by the faster water.

Her legs went first, pointing downriver and moving with the bouncing current. She clawed at Nathan's backpack but her hands slid off. Her scream was drowned in a mouthful of the river.

Sean took another step, reached his arm out until the muscles in his shoulder strained.

"Come on!" he shouted. To them, to him, to anyone listening.

Lara slid away. Maia began to be pulled into the same flow, her legs doing the same dance downriver. Nathan fell forward, his arm outstretched for Sean. He splashed into the water, face first.

Sean let go of the rope and took two long strides forward. His legs submerged into the water up to his thighs. Where he expected a rock he found only a small hollow. The added pressure of the river pushing on more of his body made him tilt forward.

It happened all at once, like a tower of cards falling. Sean fell forward, locked hands with Nathan. Maia was pulled into the deep, fast water but held her grip on

Nathan's belt. Nobody had footing. The three formed a human raft and the current took them.

———

Grady got his hands under Karina's armpits and pulled. Her skin was blue from the cold, but it was the bloating in her face that told him something was wrong. Her tongue was swollen and bulging from between her lips which were a dark maroon color. The skin on her face was tinted dark with blood under the surface, trapped there by the rope pinching off all arteries.

Her eyes looked up at him with webs of burst vessels like tiny blood red lightning strikes.

Grady unspooled the rope from around her neck, tugging at stubborn tangles with numb fingers. He watched as his colleagues across the river floated away.

Behind him Ken screamed again. Grady turned, his backside and legs still in the river seated between two rocks. Ken was trying to move.

"Stay still," Grady said.

"I'm freezing."

"I know. I'll help you."

"You did this to me." Ken angrily slapped the water over his twisted leg.

"I'll help you," Grady repeated.

"Help her up and then you can both help." His words dissolved into a grunt of pain.

Grady knew Karina was dead. The safety rope slithered away into the current. He let her body go and she followed.

"We gotta get to shore," Grady said.

He pushed up and tried to stand. His legs were

numb, his joints locked in place. As he attempted to balance himself he pitched forward deeper into the river. He landed hard, his hands out in front of him, his palms scraping along rocks. His face went under quickly, no time to take a breath.

Ken saw him go in, saw his only hope slide toward the center of the rushing river. Ken leaned forward, reaching out his hands, and grabbed Grady's pant leg.

Grady pushed his face out of the water, drew a gasping breath, and felt his legs tangled. He kicked, thinking he was caught in the rocks, or maybe a fallen tree branch. Anything to restrict his movement meant death.

Grady's boot caught Ken in the chin. He toppled and loosened from his seat in the rocks. His back slid in front of a powerful rush of water flowing over a tall round rock. The flow hit the rock and came down the side in a focused blast that shot Ken's body out like he'd been sitting on a fire hydrant.

Ken slipped past Grady who reached out a hand. The two men clawed for each other, slapping the water, feeling the pull of the river. Their hands were useless, numb, fingers stiff. The sound pounded relentlessly in their ears and the river dragged them into its clutches.

The last two men slid away and into the river's flow.

BACK HOME

THEY ARE LINED up for the photo like a group date at the prom. Responding to media requests, the company's PR department set this shoot up quickly. Allison takes the opportunity to make another speech.

"Of course, all our employees know their jobs are waiting for them, but we want everyone to take the time they need to make a full and complete recovery from both their physical hardships and their emotional traumas."

Sean winces at the camera flashes, hearing the strained written-by-committee tone in Allison's words. Standing for glamour shots feels wrong. These people don't know what went on out there.

Since returning they've been called brave, courageous, heroic. Sean flinches each time the words are used; they are like needles pushing under his skin. He watches Maia put on her brave face—chin up, defiant, solid jaw, Mona Lisa smile that is not cocky but rather assured in her own survival. Was there any doubt she would be one the few to come back?

Grady grins a tight-lipped smugness through his new whiskers. Wes is a little glassy-eyed and unfocused. His attention keeps shifting between cameramen. And Nathan clenches his hands tight in front of him, holding on to some invisible safety line that will keep him from being drawn into the current of reporters and photographers.

"The Synergen Dynamics goal is to provide solutions to any business situation that arises, and we feel these employees exemplify that spirit. They created innovative solutions to real world problems and it saved their lives. Now, I'm not saying we save lives here at Synergen."

Allison demurs with a light chuckle of fake humility.

"But we know these brave people exhibited exactly the qualities we foster and encourage at Synergen Dynamics and exactly what we bring our clients in the tangled jungle of high tech business solutions. Thank you all for coming today."

The photographers stop snapping, knowing this is all they will get from these wounded animals. Sean exhales deeply, his shoulders unknotting now that the assault is over.

Allison turns to them.

"I do mean it, guys. Your jobs are all waiting for you."

"I heard you hired new people," Grady says.

"We needed some temps to fill in while you were absent."

"Absent?"

The tension is back. Sean's shoulders knot up.

"Rest assured the new hires will be transitioned out

of their temp positions once you return to the office, but no rush at all, guys."

She smiles like the mom on the porch watching them head off to prom. So proud of her kids, so sure they will be home by midnight.

"And what about the promotions?"

"We're delaying any decision on that until everyone is back on track and we can evaluate things properly."

"So you gave those away, too?"

Allison clenches a snide comment between her teeth, gathers her smile back for Grady.

"No. We feel your recovery is the most important thing right now. There will be time enough for work related issues later."

Sean lifts his hand slightly to break into the conversation.

"So what's this group therapy session tomorrow?"

"It's not therapy, necessarily," Allison quickly corrects, getting back to the pre-approved talking points. "It's a chance for you all to openly discuss any feelings you have or concerns with a licensed professional. It's healing."

"So, a company shrink?" Grady asks.

"She works for the company, yes."

Maia steps up and puts a hand on Allison's arm. "Can I talk to you for a sec?"

"Yes, of course."

They leave the group quickly. Allison appreciates the old singles bar trick. Same tactic girlfriends use to get you out of an awkward conversation with a lame guy.

"You rescued me," Allison says.

"Yeah, Grady's been...well, it hasn't been an easy transition for any of us."

"I can only imagine."

Allison returns the gesture with a hand on Maia's arm. Genuine sincerity there.

"I wanted you to know, Allison, that I'm ready to go. Whenever you say, I want to get back in there and get to work. Hopefully," she raises her eyebrows, "in a new, and higher, position. But I understand why you want to wait to make any final decisions."

Allison gives her a conspiratorial wink. "I'll let you know as soon as we are ready to move forward. Tomorrow's evaluation will be the first step, but I don't think we'll find any problems in moving ahead."

Maia's eyebrows lower and pinch in.

"Tomorrow is an evaluation?"

"You know what I mean. It's not like a psych eval. It's a...talk. To see where everyone's heads are." Off Maia's concerned look Allison rests her hand back on her arm. "It's a good thing. You have nothing to worry about."

Maia thinks, *that's exactly what she said before we left.*

———

The four men huddle in the corner of the conference room, avoiding eye contact with the photographers as they file out of the room.

Grady focuses on Maia and Allison talking.

"Their periods are probably in sync."

"What?" Sean says.

"Maia. She's got that vagina connection with Allison

and she is using it to the fullest. Trying to box the rest of us out." He lets out a single chuckle. "Huh. Box."

"Anyone sleep last night?" Nathan asks.

Grady ignores him. Wes and Sean shrug. Sean doesn't want to talk to these guys about his awkward night back at home with Kerri. He never talks about his home life, his marriage. Why start now?

"It freaked me out when that cop talked to us."

"They're following up," Sean says. "I mean, people did die."

"I know but...I feel like I'm lying to them."

"Yeah, I know," Wes says. He knows about lying. He knows how it eats at you, infects every conversation you have.

"Maybe we should tell them the rest."

Grady spins. His face is stone and he is looming over Nathan.

"You don't say shit beyond what we all agreed to."

"I know, but—"

"You keep your fucking mouth shut."

His eyes are predator's eyes. Nathan knows the look. Those eyes haunted the woods when they were out there. He thought Grady would leave them behind, but they are here again, staring him down, shutting him up.

"They know everything they need to know. We did what we had to in order to survive."

The heat between the four men huddled close could light dry tinder.

The conference room door opens. A man enters, unfamiliar, eyes scanning the room. Allison looks up.

"Can I help you?"

"Are you in charge of the investigation?"

Allison breaks away from Maia and crosses to the man, her assistant follows a few feet behind her on alert, already texting security. The new man in the room is over six foot, high and tight hair, athletic and professionally dressed.

"What investigation?"

"Into what happened to my husband."

The room is run through with an icy chill. The man is angry, but calm.

"I'm sorry?" Allison says.

Wes speaks up from the corner of the room.

"Ken." Eyes turn to him. "He was with Ken."

The man pulls back his shoulders, stands a little taller. "That's right. We've been together for nine years, married for three, and I'm here to find out what happened to him."

Allison switches into sympathy mode. "Did the police not contact you?"

"They did. Fed me a line of bullshit about a tragic accident. No details. I want to know what happened to Ken."

His façade cracks. Tears form in the corners of his eyes.

"Okay, um..."

"James."

"Okay, James. We will get you all the information we have. We're all still reeling a bit. What happened out there was tragic. But these people can all tell you, Ken fought with all his might."

James turns to the men, seeking answers. He finds furtive eyes, looking away. Only Grady meets his eye, stone cold and stoic.

Detective Kettner stares at piles of paper spread out over a wide table. Statements from the survivors. Interviews collected in the field when they were only hours rescued. Still wrapped in ranger office blankets, still feeding on clear broth.

Another detective, Morris, passes by.

"Nothing yet from the rangers," Morris says.

"Five dead, no bodies. How in the hell…?"

Morris looks at the piles of file folders in front of Kettner.

"Hoping they'll read themselves?"

Kettner laughs. "Oh, I've read them. A lot to unpack but they made it easy on me. Same story times five."

"I'd kill for a case with no discrepancies."

"Yeah. Careful what you wish for, though, right?"

"What do you mean?"

"I dunno. It's a little bit…tidy."

Morris looks at the files. Photos paper clipped to each statement show people with hollow eyes, dirty faces streaked with lines where tears cut through the grime of a month in the woods.

"Been through a lot, these people."

"Yeah. All been through the exact same thing."

"What are you after with this?"

"I'm not sure."

"I'd be glad it wasn't you. If I spent two days without ESPN or bacon in the morning I'd be ready to hang it up for good."

"We all have the survival instinct. It's part of being human."

"You don't think Facebook and cable TV has bred that right out of us?"

"Nah. Some things are too deep." Kettner turns back to the files. "No, people will do what they need to in order to survive."

OUT THERE

DAY 2

BY THE TIME the river calmed and bent east, forming an eddy of swirling water that gathered the exhausted survivors, they had traveled nearly two miles downriver.

The current had pulled them along swiftly, spinning and churning over rocks. They were disoriented, cold, too tired to appreciate still being alive.

One by one they dragged themselves to shore on a small, muddy inlet. Maia and Nathan touched solid ground first, Sean drifting in behind them. Wes sat with his feet in the water, his backside in the heavy mud, and vomited a stomach full of river water he'd ingested on the wild ride down.

Lara wept on the shore, mud streaking her face, knees pulled to her chest.

Less than two minutes later Grady floated by, one hand on Ken who floated on his back, eyes closed, seemingly buoyed by his backpack alone.

Nobody spoke for a long time. They gagged from the water forced down their throats each time they gasped for a desperate breath. Their heads spun, the sudden stillness not caught up yet with their senses.

Once out of the numbing water the cold caught up to them.

"What the hell happened?" Maia asked.

"Are they dead?" Sean said.

Eyes all around. No Rick. No Karina. No Ron.

They were seven. Of those, four still wore backpacks: Grady, Ken, Nathan and Wes. No one knew how far they were from the campsite. No one knew how far they were from a city, from help.

The collapse of the ropes and the trip downriver had taken only minutes. The sun was still high overhead, but the trees threatened to throw them into shadow any minute. The narrow trench the water cut through the trees offered some sunlight, but soon enough it would be like the hike and even afternoon sun would be hidden behind a wall of leaves and pine needles.

Sean stood and stamped his feet out, swirled his arms to try to get blood back into his fingers. He noticed what rough shape Ken was in for the first time and asked, "Is he okay?"

Grady glanced at him. "His leg is pretty bad."

Ken lay on his back, eyes shut to the pain. In shock, maybe, Sean thought. Or passed out. Whatever had happened to his leg looked bad. It hung at an odd angle from the knee down, like it wasn't attached by anything but the pants he wore.

"I can't move my leg," he said, his eyes now open and wide. "I can't move my goddamn leg."

Ken kept looking down as if to see if his leg was still

there. Each time the gruesome twist of his knee made him look away with a new stab of pain.

"What are we gonna do?" Lara began to cry again.

"Okay, we're alive," Grady said. "That's something."

"I'm so cold," Wes said.

"We all are. We have to get out of these clothes and try to dry them." Grady piled the four backpacks together. "We have four sleeping bags."

"That are soaked," Sean said.

"For now they are. Let's unroll them and try to dry them out."

"We need to start a fire."

"Did you bring a lighter?"

Sean didn't answer. They knew from their orientation that each team member was responsible for carrying part of the team supplies. So, in addition to the small amount of clothing they were allowed, each pack was loaded with a portion of what they'd need for their five days in the wild. Cooking tools, water, tents and firewood were all waiting for them at the campsite, but each of the four backpacks had some supplies in them.

"Maybe there's a flare gun," Sean said.

This energized Wes and Nathan to unzip a bag each until they, Sean and Grady were all unpacking everything into unruly piles.

When each pack had been emptied, they took stock.

"No flare gun."

"No fire starter or matches."

"No water."

"Water we have," Grady said, pointing a thumb over his shoulder at the river.

"I'm freezing," Lara said. "We need to get warm."

"If we can't make a fire we'll have to do body heat,"

Grady said. "But for now we still have daylight and if we keep moving we'll be okay."

Sean made a grim face toward Ken.

"What about him?"

"I don't know."

Maia stepped forward and examined the piles of supplies. "Is there a first aid kit?"

"No."

"Okay," Grady said. "Let's see what we do have. We might be out here all night waiting for a rescue helicopter or something. Let's work with what we do have and not worry about what we don't."

"What if one of us looks for a path or a trail out of here?" Nathan asked.

Grady turned to him. "I gave you a plan. Let's do it."

"Yeah, but, what if there's a—"

"Just count the stuff from the bags."

Nobody argued. They were too tired, too scared. Sean remembered his projects with Grady, how he took over and left Sean out in the cold with none of the credit. This could end up being the same thing.

Maia crouched near Ken, ran a hand along his forehead. It was cold and clammy from the water.

"Ken? How are you feeling?"

"I'm fucking dying."

"No, we all made it."

"I'm still fucking dying."

———

Lara had been sitting by the river as they took their inventory. She sat with her chin on her knees, damp clothes still clinging to her as she shivered. The sunlight had gone beyond the trees. She could see through tiny breaks in the tree line, but they were shadowed wherever they went.

"How long before they find us?" she asked to no one.

"It won't be long," Sean said. "They probably check in each night or something. Send some sort of all clear, don't you think?"

Nobody answered.

Lara asked the group, "Do you think Rick or Karina had, like, a cell phone?"

"Maybe a satellite phone? Or a radio to talk to a ranger station or something. This is all national forest so they have patrols and stuff." Sean knew he was talking out his ass. They were on government land but with cutbacks he had no idea if they had rangers here or air patrols or anything. Lara seemed like she needed some confidence, though.

"Holy shit, guys, look."

They looked up to see Lara pointing across the river. A tree had fallen long ago and its branches hung over the banks and into the water. Caught in a tangle of spindly grey fingers was Karina's lifeless body.

Feet rushed to the water's edge, hoping to see movement from their guide. Grady hung back, the only one to know she wouldn't be stirring.

"Is she dead?" Sean asked.

"She looks like it," Wes said.

"She is," Grady said.

Eyes peeled away from the form in the river. Grady felt the need to explain in details he could control.

"She fell on our side of the river. She was trying to go in and get Rick, I think. She must have hit her head, I dunno. But I saw her before she floated away and she was...I think she was dead."

Nathan had kept his eyes on Karina.

"She's not moving."

"She's got a backpack on," Sean said. "Maybe we should try to get it."

"Maybe it's got a flare gun," Maia said.

"No," Grady said. "She's way over there. Besides, why would they even have a flare gun if they had radios and stuff?"

"Okay, the maybe she's got a radio."

"After being in the water like that? That thing is toast—if she even had one. Don't you think Rick would have had it?"

"Why?" Maia said, stepping toward Grady. "Because he's the man and he's in charge?"

"He just seemed like the leader."

"Because of his dick?"

Grady's voice rose sharply over the water. "Because he was out in front—*leading*."

"Well, they seemed pretty equal to me." Maia turned her back on Grady.

"What about the rope?" Sean said.

Among their supplies had been a length of cord. They had no way to measure but it seemed like at least fifty feet of narrow lashing they assumed would be used to demonstrate something like knot tying or weaving.

"That little string?" Grady scoffed.

"We can try to loop it around the pack, drag her across."

"Like a lasso?" Wes asked.

Sean shrugged. "Yeah, I guess."

He knew it wasn't a great plan, but he was trying to toss out ideas.

"Forget it," Grady said. "You'll never make it."

"What about wading across?" Nathan said.

"Did you already fucking forget what happens when you go into the river?"

"It's much calmer here." Nathan didn't sound convinced by his own argument.

Grady's voice rose again. They weren't listening to him. And if they managed by some miracle to hook onto Karina's backpack, they'd see the rope burns around her neck, they'd see the bulge in her terrified eyes.

"I said forget it."

"So fine," Sean said. "You don't want to try then don't. Some of us might want to, though."

"Yeah," Wes said. "Who knows what's in that backpack?"

"More fucking energy bars. Something useless."

"Look, Grady—"

"Guys."

Lara pointed again. Across the river Karina's legs pivoted, her body rolled gently with the current, bobbing on the buoyancy of her backpack, then the current picked her up and she slid out of sight.

"Okay, look," Grady said. "If we're gonna be here all night we need to get serious about staying warm and finding some kind of shelter. So let's get to it."

He clapped his hands together twice and edged into the trees. The others hesitated, then slowly followed.

BACK HOME

THEY SIT in a semi-circle facing the doctor. No, not a doctor, several of them noted when they met. Ruth Peterson, licensed therapist.

She started by asking about their feelings about their experience. It has not gone well since then.

Everyone is cagey, unsure how much to tell. How much others have let slip. How much is really bad or wrong. Who wouldn't do what they did to survive? Why should anyone be blamed for any of it?

"One thing many people in your situation deal with," Ruth says, "is what they call survivor's guilt. It's the feeling that someone died, but why them and not me? Has anyone experienced any feelings like that?"

"What other people have been in our situation?" Grady asks. He's been the most tense during this session. His anger is a raw nerve and it's not healing over since he returned. He can't sit still. It's like his skin has been peeled away and even the slightest breeze sets his body thrumming.

"I mean people who have been through a similar trauma."

"And I'm saying who else has been through a similar trauma? I guess I missed that day in the news."

"Plane crashes, terrorist attacks. Things like that."

"You know what she means," Sean says.

"Yeah, well," Grady bounces his leg, cracks his knuckles, "I don't feel guilt. I made it. They didn't. Maybe I had more fight in me."

Nathan speaks with his head down, his eyes on the carpet. "Ken's leg didn't exactly—"

Grady erupts. "So now that's my fault?"

Ruth tries to regain control of the group. "Nobody is assigning blame here, Grady."

"Bullshit. They all started pointing fingers the minute we got to shore. Somehow because I was with Ken I broke his leg. None of you saw it. Nobody saw a goddamn thing because you were all running around shitting yourselves over Rick and Ron. You don't know what I was dealing with trying to save Ken. And the girl guide."

"Karina," Maia says. "She had a name."

Grady stands. "Sorry, Maia. Maybe if I'd known her more than an hour before she went and did a swan dive into the rapids I'd remember who she was. I had kinda bigger things on my mind, though."

"Sit down, please." Grady towers over Ruth. The clipboard where she's been writing her notes is her only defense if he cracks. "We're all here to help one another. Nobody blames anyone for what happened. This is part of what everyone deals with after a traumatic incident."

"Well, you can deal with it without me." Grady moves for the door.

"Please, it's important that we talk it out."

"Go ahead and blame me for the whole damn thing once I'm gone. I don't care." He leaves the door wide open after he's through.

"Well." Ruth crosses her legs, tries to assume an air of authority. "That was unfortunate. Shall we continue?"

———

The session lasts another forty minutes. They all talk about the fear they felt, the relief of being rescued, about staring down possible death. It all sounds like they are reading from a script. Like no one is revealing their real emotions. It serves the purpose. Ruth has filled the sheets of paper on her clipboard and time is up. They are dismissed.

Out front the four remaining survivors gather.

"I feel like it should have felt better to talk about it," Sean says. He and Kerri have discussed couples therapy, but she falls more on the Grady side of things when it comes to talking to strangers about personal issues. Sean has always liked the idea of a neutral party to talk with.

"Yeah, that was weird," Maia says.

"When it comes down to it," Sean says, "we're kind of the only ones who can talk about it, really."

The others nod.

"We need to stay in touch," Nathan says. "I mean, you can call me any time."

"Yeah, me, too."

"This sounds like AA," Wes says with a smile. He immediately pulls it back, afraid he's opened a vein. "I mean not that I'd...speaking of, who wants to go get a drink?"

"Nah, I've got to go home," Sean says.

"Yeah, my parents are still in town," Nathan says. "Wes, how long are they making you stay here?"

"Another couple days, they said. Until it's all sorted out is how they put it, whatever that means. I'm in no rush to get home. Can you imagine the questions everyone will have?"

"Yeah. Shit. You'll have to rehash the whole thing all over again."

"Let's promise to support each other here," Sean says. He puts his hand out and Nathan shakes it. He turns to Wes who shakes, then Maia.

"What about Grady?"

"He's having a hard time."

"You could say that."

"He was the one who was so adamant about keeping...some stuff to ourselves," Wes says.

"Everyone's got a different way of dealing with it."

"I just want to get back to work," Maia says.

"I'm not sure if I do," Sean says.

Nathan gives a derisive scoff. "Yeah, I'll take all the time off they'll give me."

Maia keeps her focus on Sean. "I need something to take my mind off it, y'know?"

"I can see that. I just have a lot of other stuff to deal with."

Wes spins his car keys around his finger. "You sure nobody wants to join me?"

"No, thanks, Wes. Have a good night."

With a wave Wes walks away to his car.

"I'm out, too," Nathan says. "We're gonna be okay, right?"

"At this point," Sean says. "We've said what we're going to say. Everyone feels so bad for us it's not like they're looking for dirt to dig up. We'll be fine if we keep it together."

"Unlike Grady," Maia says.

"He'll come around."

"I hope so."

"Okay. G'night," Nathan says. He walks away to his car.

Maia lays a hand on Sean's arm.

"Is your wife...not dealing with it?"

Sean is taken aback. He doesn't recall ever discussing Kerri with Maia.

"Things are fine."

"Sean." She gives him her best I'm-here-for-you look. "I know they're not."

"How do you...?"

"I could tell for a while now. And you've let a few things slip. Plus, I've been there. Not married, but I was in a long term relationship that faltered and we tried to keep it together way past the expiration date. I know how it is. I know what you're going through."

"Oh. Well, thanks. I mean, it's fine. We have the average issues. No big deal."

"It's a big deal, Sean. You need someone right now. If you went through all that to stay alive and you come home to, what? A cold shoulder? How fucked up is that?"

"It's not like that. Things have been...I mean it didn't start with this."

"I know. But if this doesn't bring her around, what will?"

"Look, I appreciate this, Maia. I do. But we'll be fine. We'll work it out."

"I'm just saying." Her hand caresses his arm. "If you need to talk. If you need a friendly shoulder."

The vibe from Maia is charged. He doesn't think he's reading into it. Sean tries to make a joke. "I thought the therapist was my shoulder to cry on."

"I'm here for more than crying, Sean." Her hand squeezes his hand. "Whatever you need."

"Thanks, Maia. I should get going."

She pulls her hand away.

"Is this what your wife does to you? Ignores your offers to make a connection?"

"What? No. I need to get home. I appreciate your support, Maia."

"Maybe you're not the only one who needs a little support."

Now he's done it. Sent someone close to the edge who didn't need a push to get there. Sean shuffles his feet, stammers a bit. Cheating on his wife is the last thing he needs, no matter how attractive he finds Maia.

"Maia, if you need to talk to someone they've offered—"

"You met her. Would you talk to her? Besides, I need a real friend. Not some company shrink. Never mind, Sean. You have someone. I don't. Simple as that. I hope you appreciate it. And that she does, which I doubt."

Maia turns and walks away. Sean thinks for a second about following, but what message would that send? He watches her go.

Detective Kettner rubs a finger along a patch of whiskers he missed shaving. Morris sits across from him, the stack of statements between the two.

"Trouble is, we have reports of five dead but not a single body. I don't even know how to fill out the report."

"Maybe if you could file the paperwork you could put this behind you," Morris says.

"Maybe. But still, I got next of kin waiting on something from me. I got reporters crawling up my ass."

"What do the rangers say?"

"They know where the group tried to cross the river, but these office people have no idea where they were when they got out of the water, where they were when they were rescued, what direction they walked. So the rangers have about two hundred thousand acres to search. They didn't give me a very encouraging timetable."

"What'd they say?"

"There was a lot of *ifs* in there. And then they mentioned animals. Did you know they spotted a half dozen wolves in the area in last year's census? And brown bears are making a comeback, too, I guess."

"Fine time for that."

"It'll be the first time my evidence is eaten."

"Did they say how many hikers go missing every year? Gotta be some of them are never recovered."

"I didn't ask. But I bet you're right. You know me, I hate loose ends."

"How do you get through life, Kettner? The whole world is a loose end."

"Maybe that's why I like this job. I'm a loose end tie-er."

"Well, in the meantime, we have other cases to tie up."

"You're right."

Kettner scoops up the files, opens the bottom drawer in the file cabinet next to his desk, and drops them in, kicks the drawer closed with his foot.

A man approaches his desk. James, Ken's partner.

"Detective Kettner?"

"Yes."

"My name is James Heath. They said you were in charge of the investigation into the people that were lost in the woods."

"We gave all our statements already. You'll have to read about it in the press."

"No, my husband was Ken Horton. He's one that didn't make it back."

"Oh." Kettner shares a look with Morris, who offers no help. Kettner motions to the chair beside his desk. "Have a seat."

"I'm checking to see what you know about what happened to Ken."

"Everything we know has been given to the press. It's still very new and we don't have a body yet." He catches himself. "I'm sorry, it's just that the rangers haven't recovered any...remains because the area is so vast and there is very little direction."

James sinks a little in the chair.

"Okay. I understand."

"Do you have any reason to think something happened other than what you've heard?"

"No. I haven't heard anything besides he survived

the first accident but died due to a broken leg. I've never heard of anyone dying from that before, have you, detective?"

This time his glance with Morris gets a raised eyebrow.

"No, I haven't. But like I said, there's still a lot we don't know."

"Exactly."

Kettner studies James' face, seeing the hurt there. And something else. It's in the eyes. Doubt. It's like looking into a mirror.

———

Wes pauses on the sidewalk outside the bar. It's a shorter pause than last time, and no one is there to draw him in. He goes in alone. It's a different bar, but really they're all the same.

He sits on the first stool he finds empty, ignoring the other quiet midday drinkers inside. The bartender walks slowly over to him, raises his chin to ask what he'll have.

Wes thinks about it.

"Jack and Coke." His old standby. The one that got him in trouble, that got him behind the wheel on the drive toward ruin.

"Holy shit," he hears next to him. "You're the guy from the TV."

Wes lifts one corner of his mouth in a shy smile and gives a three fingered wave.

"Brother, you got the mother of all bar stories. Let me buy you a drink."

OUT THERE
DAY 3

IN THEIR PILES of rations they counted: thirty-six energy bars. One bag of dried beans. Two bags of beef jerky. A fishing line and hook, no bait and no pole. A length of cord. Two battery powered head lamps (both working). A mosquito net. A compass.

Each of the four packs came with a tube of lip balm, insect repellant, hand sanitizer.

They had four changes of clothes for the men, none for the women since they'd shed their backpacks on shore before the river took them.

None of it helped them get any sleep the first night.

About fifty paces into the trees they'd come across a fallen log with a depression next to it which made a good pocket for them to sleep lined up like spoons in a drawer trying to steal body heat from one another. They laid out the sleeping bags, still wet, in a makeshift roof from the top of the fallen log to the ground. Several times during the night one bag or the other would slip and land on them like the wet tongue of a cold beast.

By morning nobody had slept more than a half hour at a stretch and they all lay collapsed by the riverbank.

There was no shore here, really. The water carved out a sharp U in the tree line, then shot out and kept going. Rocks and thick mud made a thin barrier between water and the trees, but it wasn't much.

Sean pulled a big yawn and felt his shirt again. A little bit drier than before. Definitely warmer. They day was beginning to heat up and he welcomed it.

"Where are they?"

Lara sat on a rock looking out over the river like it was a long driveway and she was waiting for Mom and Dad to pick her up. Nobody answered her.

The water seemed to have slowed. It sounded to Sean less like a passing train and more like a fountain in a public square. He had a slow realization that the reason those fountains were put there was to replicate this supposedly calm and relaxing sound.

Even the relatively short distance into the trees where they made camp the night before had dampened the sound of the water considerably. The curtain of trees absorbed sound and the floor of the forest was covered in a thick carpet of rotting vegetation that swallowed their footfalls as well as the river noises.

With dawn came some hard realizations. They'd all had time to think about what happened. They'd all been awakened by nightmares and flashes of memory from the day. Processing had begun. So far that morning no one had talked about it, but Sean knew they were all thinking some version of the same thing. No help was coming. Nobody knew they were in trouble. Nobody would know until they were due to come out of the woods and didn't show. Five days from now.

Everyone had been too exhausted and too full of river water to want much food last night, but in the morning people would get hungry. They needed to ration. But to do so would mean admitting they needed to plan to stay out there for a long time.

Sean tried to do the math in his head for the supplies they had, but he was too tired.

"So what do we think?" Wes said. "Is the river water safe to drink?"

"It makes me nervous," Sean said.

Maia stood, took a moment to find her balance. "They said it was all snow runoff. That's as pure as water gets."

"Yeah, but it's been running off for how long? Anything could have gotten in it."

"It's moving really fast." She stood over the rock and looked into the eddy. "And it's so clear."

The others looked into the water and agreed.

"We should at least get it from where it's flowing fastest, not this still part here."

"Okay," Nathan said. "Until Wes said it, I didn't realize how thirsty I was."

"It's safe," Grady said like an announcement.

"Yeah, I think it'll be fine," Sean said.

"No, I know it's safe. I drank from it this morning. If it was gonna make me sick it would have done it by now."

"You already drank it?"

"Yeah. I was thirsty."

"I think with things like that we need to be making group decisions."

"Oh yeah? You think that?"

Grady wasn't going out of his way to mock Sean, but

he felt it the same.

"Besides," Wes said. "We all swallowed a ton of it yesterday when we were floating down here."

"Yeah, that's right," Maia said. "And that was like, eighteen hours ago or something. We would have all gotten sick already."

"Okay. You're right," Sean said. "But don't you think in the future we should be making group decisions?"

Grady stood with a small, flat stone in his hand. He flung it, sidearm, across the eddy where it skipped into the middle of the river.

"Don't you think people can make their own decisions?"

"I'm just saying."

"And besides, how long do you think we're gonna be out here?"

"We don't know. That's the point."

Thoughts of thirst were all muscled out by thoughts of how bad their predicament really was.

"They're coming though, right?" Lara said. She'd finally turned away from the river and faced the group.

"Of course," Grady said. "They won't just sit back and think *well, that was too bad* when we don't come out when we're supposed to."

"Exactly," Sean said. "We're not expected out for another five days. It's possible no one will think to look for us until then."

"That's crazy," Lara said. "Don't they know we lost our guides?"

"And we're not at the campsite?" Nathan added.

"We don't know," Sean said. "That's the point. We need to expect the best, but plan for the worst."

Grady scoffed and threw another rock. "I think the worst has already happened, don't you?"

"For them. Not for us."

Wes gave a look into the woods, toward their camp. "Maybe for Ken."

Ken was laying down in the depression under the log. He'd managed to get several hours of fitful sleep, moaning and making half words in his partial sleep state. The idea of moving him didn't seem like an option to anyone as they started to wake and move back to the river bank.

"Speaking of, someone should bring him some water."

There was one plastic water bottle that managed to stay in the webbed bottle holder on the side of Grady's backpack.

"I'll go," he said, drawing the bottle from his back pocket. He walked upriver about twenty yards where a break in the grasses and bushes along the water made an access point at a fast flowing part of the river.

Wes and Nathan followed him, planning on bending over the water and drinking straight from the source. No ice cubes required.

Sean hung back, waiting for Grady to finish. He felt compelled to keep some distance.

Maia went to Lara and rubbed a hand on her back.

"How are you doing?"

"Not great. Are they really not gonna miss us until we're late?"

"I was thinking it, too. I think Sean may be right."

"Jesus Christ." Tears started to come to her eyes and her voice wavered.

"Stop it, now." Maia rubbed harder. "We've got to keep it together. If we come off as weak or unable to deal with this, they'll stick us on the sideline. We'll be sweeping up the dead leaves before you know it. Playing house."

"I just want to get out of here."

"No shit, we all do. But we have to stay strong. They're already getting out their dicks and the measuring sticks. You heard Grady and Sean. They can't help it. They all want to be Tarzan out here. The big man swinging from a vine. Well, I'm no Jane. I don't need any of them to rescue me. I can rescue myself."

"Jesus, Maia, how can you be so calm?"

"Because the other option isn't an option. Just think of this like another office. We can't show any weakness, we can't act like a victim, we can't give them any excuse."

"You really think after all this that they'll—"

"Look around you." Maia waved a hand at the trees. "We're in the fucking jungle. You watch. They'll turn into gorillas before our very eyes. They can't help it. We need to sit back and let them beat their chests for a while. But remember who does the hunting in a pride of lions."

Lara had no answer for her. Maia scowled.

"The females."

"They do?"

"Yes," Maia said. "And then the males come up and get to eat first, anyway. Not out here. Not in my pride."

Maia watched the men carefully as she turned away from Lara. Grady had filled his bottle and gone into the woods to give it to Ken. Wes was on his knees drinking from the river with Nathan and Sean in line behind him. Maia went to the piles of rations and took two energy bars. She palmed them and returned to Lara.

"Here."

They each hunched over their prize and ate quickly, tossing the wrappers into the water where the current whisked the evidence away.

"I'm thinking this isn't the best spot," Grady said.

"Why not?" Sean stood beside the shelter adding more branches to the covering.

"Look how low it sits. If it rains, we'll all be sleeping in a puddle. Besides, sleeping on the ground like that we're like a buffet for the bugs."

"Where else do you want to go?" Nathan asked.

"Not sure. We should scout around."

"You really want to waste all that time and energy trying to find the perfect camping spot? This isn't a vacation."

Grady took a step toward Sean. "I fucking know that. That's why I want to move. I want us to have the best chance out here."

Sean looked at his fellow team members. Nobody offered help.

"Then shouldn't we stay put? We've already built this shelter."

"You call this building?"

Grady reached up and yanked a pile of branches off the roof.

"Hey."

"Grady, come on," Wes said.

"This is shit. A bunch of sticks leaning on a dead tree? We can do better."

"I'm a systems analyst," Nathan said. "Not a construction worker."

"Just do what I say and we'll be fine."

Sean saw what this was. Grady asserting control. He wanted to move so they would all listen. He wanted to pick the new spot because he didn't pick this one.

"We left behind a perfectly good campsite, you know," Grady said.

"And if we ever had a map we left that behind, too."

"We could hike back up, follow the river."

"All of us?" Sean said. "Some of us can't even move."

Wes stepped forward, inserting himself into the conversation. "They say in a survival situation, staying put is the best course of action."

Grady gave him a narrow-eyed stare. "They say? Do they? Who says that?"

Sean broke in, not wanting the conversation to be derailed by Grady's spite. "Look, a hike for who knows how far into the woods, uphill I might add, just isn't in the cards, Grady. I mean, what about Ken? We shouldn't move him."

Grady looked down at the prone man, eyes shut and leg limp.

"He can stay here."

"What? No he can't. We have to look after him."

"We'll bring him what he needs."

"I don't know, Grady," Wes said.

"Then you can stay here with him." Grady took another step toward Sean and Wes.

Sean stood his ground, but was ready to turn and run if he needed to.

"At night we need each other's body heat. It's gonna be the only way we stay warm enough."

"Not if we build a better shelter."

"And you know how to do that?"

"Yes."

"Like you knew how to cross the river without breaking Ken's leg?"

Grady shoved Sean, two hands in the chest. Sean went backward, legs spinning to catch up.

"Hey, hey, hey," Wes said. He held his hands out in a calming gesture the way he would at a snarling dog.

"That girl guide didn't give me a chance to cross the river, asshole. Maybe if she did we wouldn't be here right now."

Sean didn't fight back. He knew he would lose. This was one of those moments Kerri would have crucified him for. *Stand up for yourself*, she'd say.

Maia and Lara stepped into the clearing.

"What's going on?"

"This little bitch is trying to run things," Grady said. "He won't listen to reason."

"Grady wants to move the camp," Nathan said. "Find something better."

"We should stay in one place," Lara said. "They can find us easier that way."

"He's being a bully," Sean said.

"A bully? What are we in fucking grade school?"

Maia stepped between them. "Back off, Grady. Maybe you two should cool off. Take a walk."

For a moment it seemed like Grady might shove Maia in the same way. But he exhaled and then turned.

"Who wants to come with me and look around?"

Without waiting for an answer Grady walked off into the woods.

Nathan followed. "I'll see if there are any better spots. You never know."

Sean felt an adrenalin dump through his body. His muscles ached like he just ran a 5K. The branches he held were trembling slightly in his shaking hands.

Two hours later and Grady hadn't come back.

Maia sat with Ken, a wet strip of cloth torn from a T-shirt laid over his head. She felt like a nurse. She dared the thought—she felt maternal.

Ken spoke in a shallow whisper. Maia wasn't sure if he wanted no one else to hear or if he was too weak to speak up.

"You gotta watch them for me," he said.

"Who?" She bent down closer to hear him.

Ken reached up and slid the wet cloth off his forehead.

"Grady, all of them. They want to leave me behind."

"Nobody is leaving you." She patted his hand, wondering if that's what mothers did.

"I can make it until we're rescued. I have to. For my family. For my little boy."

"Oh, you have a son?"

"Two and a half."

Ken smiled and closed his eyes, drifting back home for a moment on the memory.

"That's sweet. We'll get you home to him and your wife."

"Husband," he said.

Maia tried not to let her pause run too long so he wouldn't notice her surprise. "Really? What's his name?"

"James."

"And your little boy?"

"Femi. It means adored by God."

"That's nice."

She put the cloth back on his head where she saw beads of sweat forming again.

"We adopted him from a woman, a girl really, and it turned out our ancestors were from the same region in Africa. The Ivory Coast. She said she wanted to give him an African name and we picked that one."

"Well, I like it."

Ken put a hand on her wrist and squeezed harder than Maia thought he had the strength for.

"I need to see them again. Don't let them leave me out here. I can make it."

"Don't worry. I won't let them leave you. You heard Sean stick up for you. It's too many of us against Grady. Don't worry."

On cue Grady stepped out of the woods, Nathan on his heels. Nobody asked if they'd found another camp and neither man said a word. They sat down on the ground, breathing hard from the exertion and lack of calories. Everyone went about their business, ignoring each other.

BACK HOME

SEAN COMES DOWNSTAIRS, yawning. Kerri is in the kitchen pouring coffee into a travel mug on her way out the door to work. Her job was supposed to be temporary. A way to keep them paying bills while Sean climbed the corporate ladder. When he landed his job at Synergen, Kerri thought the need for her to continue in the office at the small clothing importer would end. But Sean started at the bottom, and they needed her salary to afford the house she insisted they buy. To keep both cars they need to get to opposite ends of town.

Every day she has to leave for the tiny, windowless office is an insult and proof that her husband hasn't kept up his end of the bargain.

She scrapes her keys out of the bowl, rattling the keyring in case he wasn't already awake.

"Not going in today?" she asks, though she knows the answer.

"They're giving us time." He yawns again. "I've been thinking about other options, too."

"Options for what?"

"For what to do with my life. I kinda feel like I've been given a second chance, and I need to make something of it, y'know?"

She rolls her eyes at him. These nights in the bedroom have been chaste. Inching closer to a connection, but held up at her border wall.

"Well, while you figure it out and try to find yourself or whatever, this is paid time off, right? And did you ever get an answer, are they going to pay you for the time you were on their little retreat?"

"No one has mentioned it."

"Did you call the lawyer?"

"Kerri, I'm not suing the company. It wasn't their fault."

"Not their fault? Who sent you out there? And I still say you at least have a case against the tour company. Those two amateurs they sent out with you nearly got you killed."

"It wasn't their fault either. You weren't there."

"You could all get your stories together and have a class action suit. Even a settlement would be in the millions."

"Kerri, we talked about this."

"No, I talked and you said no. That's just you being... being you."

Sean yawns. Too early for this shit.

"I'll talk to them about the payment for our time."

"I'm telling you, mention that you've called a lawyer and they'll settle. It'll be less money but that's fine, it'll get here quicker."

Sean looks at the clock on the wall. His desire to set something right is flowing through his hands like water. Maybe he'll find some place to volunteer, do charity work. Maybe he'll stay on the couch all day and not shave.

"You're gonna be late."

Kerri purses her lips and makes no move to kiss him goodbye. Not like she used to, not that long ago, Sean thinks. But a lot can change in a short time.

Grady and Maia arrive in the lobby at the same time, ride the same elevator up.

"Giving it a go, too, huh?" Maia says.

"I'm rattling around my apartment all alone. I'm bored. It's amazing how much time you have to do nothing when you don't have to worry about finding food."

Maia nods. She knows Grady better than that.

"Wanna keep tabs on the promotion, huh?"

"Who? Me? No. I've got that in the bag."

The elevator dings as they arrive on the third floor. Grady doesn't wait for Maia and pushes past her out the door. A quick flare of anger is tamped down by her voice inside reminding her that she has asked not to be treated any differently. Grady is the kind of asshole who wouldn't wait for anyone.

Allison greets them by the bullpen of desks.

"It's so great to see you two back in the office."

Work attire at Synergen has never been too formal. Business casual. Maia has always worn more fitted suits than she needs to, closely matching Allison's wardrobe. She takes a page from the dress-for-the-job-you-want manual.

Grady's clothes fit looser on him than when he left. His tightly trimmed beard is new, too.

Nobody tries to be obvious, but the office has stopped working and is taking sidelong glances and quick looks at the returning survivors.

"I have set you both up with someone to get you up to speed on the newest projects."

"Our replacements, you mean," Grady says.

"The people who have been filling in for you," Allison corrects, "are here to help in any way. Both projects are early in the timetable so there's no crunch yet."

A short woman with a tight pony tail approaches.

"Hi, Maia. I'm Tiffany."

Maia shakes her hand and it feels like the girl might ask for her autograph.

"Hi."

"Welcome back."

"Yeah. Thanks. Good to be back."

The small talk is painful. Maia wants her to ask already, get it out of the way.

Allison gestures them toward Maia's old office.

"I'll let you two get started. Grady, let me take you down to meet with Miles."

"I remember where my office is."

Grady walks away from the women. For a second it looks like Allison will follow, perhaps scold him for his curtness, but she remains still. Not worth the trouble. She got the report on the counselor session. She knows he is edgy. *Potentially volatile*, is what the report said. Allison knows not to antagonize him. Let the new guy deal with it.

Allison puts on a smile. "Okay, well, Maia I leave you in good hands."

"Thanks."

Tiffany takes a small step back and lets Maia lead, it goes unspoken that she, too, knows where her old office is.

———

The offices are small. Only a slight upgrade from the bullpen. On the walk there Maia feels eyes on her, the way she felt unseen forest creatures watching her at night. These predators have only sharp curiosity, not teeth. She is now a mini celebrity the way a viral video star is. Someone who survived a near death experience and got a week's worth of news coverage and an appearance on *Ellen* out of it.

She knows this is temporary. She will blend in again, and soon. The cycle of distractions flows as fast as the river out there. Something new will come along. She will no longer be the one with the best story.

She had forgotten how small her office was. There is room for her desk, a chair opposite and not much else. She notices the potted plant is missing. Then she notices more. Her photos, the plaster cast of her dog's paw the vet gave her when she had Stella euthanized, her mardi gras beads, the trophy her bar trivia team won—all gone. And why wouldn't they be?

There is an awkward moment when Tiffany pauses just inside the door. Maia has made to sit behind the desk and neither woman wants to assume the right to that seat, so they shuffle feet for a few seconds before Maia adjusts course and sits in the guest chair.

"If you want to..." Tiffany gestures to the seat behind the desk.

"No. It's okay." Maia sits. "Do you know what they did with my stuff?"

"Oh, no. It was all gone by the time I...I think HR has it. Or maybe the police took it all."

Tiffany looks like she just dropped a racial slur at Thanksgiving dinner.

"I mean, they filed missing person's reports so the police, they came and took stuff. For the files, I guess."

"It's okay. I'll figure it out."

"Okay, yeah, sorry."

"Tiffany." Maia leans in. "This is weird. We both know it. But let's get down to work and it will get more normal as we go, right?"

Tiffany exhales and smiles. "Right."

"Do you have questions? I guess we should get that out of the way."

"I do, but, it doesn't seem appropriate."

"Honestly, it's all right. The company therapist says we're supposed to talk about it."

"I mean, I've read about it in the news."

"Has there been a lot of coverage?"

"Since you got back, yeah."

It strikes Maia that they were gone long enough that a full news cycle had passed, maybe two.

"When we were gone?"

"At first, yeah. But you know how it goes. If there's not new updates people lose interest." Tiffany catches herself again. "Not that I...I mean no one at the company lost interest."

"It's okay. I know how it goes. Life goes on. We have to, too. So let's get to work, okay?"

"Okay."

Maia thought maybe they should have another meeting. Fill the conference room with employees and let them get out all their questions. Let she and Grady give a blow by blow account of what happened out there.

Their version.

It starts her thinking. People want to know. There is interest here, but it is waning. She has a story to tell and people who want to hear it. That can be monetized. Survivors write books. They are the subjects of documentary films, or maybe her experience is fodder for an Academy Award winning performance. Amy Adams with dyed brown hair. Or, hell, keep it red. Maia always wanted red hair.

Yes, this thought sparks in her mind much more than a new account for software solutions. Tiffany begins to run down the proposal for a company based in South Korea that wants to break into the U.S. market and how they need to adjust their user interface for an American market. Maia barely hears any of it. She wonders if her face would be on the book jacket or maybe a wide photo of dark woods.

THERE AND BACK, she thinks. That's a good title.

Allison steps out of her office when the voice can't be ignored any longer. Someone is shouting, an argument in full bloom.

She follows the eyes of the workers in the bullpen. She turns left. The voices get louder and she knows she is headed for Grady's office. She knew it was too soon for him. *Potentially volatile.*

The door is open and Grady's back is to her as she approaches. He is looming over Alex, the man sitting behind Grady's old desk.

Territory. A man is nothing without his territory.

Grady came to the door and Alex stood, but never offered to relinquish his chair. He might as well be sleeping in Grady's bed.

"I can remind you how temporary you are," Grady says.

"What the hell does that mean?"

"It means I'll ask you one more goddamn time to get the fuck out of my seat."

"Look, I was hired and they gave me this office. Whatever happened before I got here doesn't concern me."

"I happened before you got here. I don't concern you?"

Allison stops at the open door.

"Gentlemen, is there a problem?"

"Are you fucking kidding me?" Grady says.

"Grady." Allison means it to sound scolding, but she has no more to follow it with.

"He won't give me back my office. He's an asshole. And he's getting his shit-stained ass all over my chair."

"That's enough."

Alex throws his hands up. "What is all this? I haven't done anything wrong."

Grady whirls on him. "You're ignoring me, for one

thing."

"You made an unreasonable request. Now you're insulting me and—"

"I said that's enough."

Alex sinks into his chair, embarrassed that his emotions got the better of him. Grady shows no shame.

"This is how you welcome us back? With scab workers rubbing their asses on our chairs?"

"Grady, I explained the situation to you. Maybe it's a little soon for you to have returned."

"You mean you haven't had time to clean up the mess you made here? You think I wouldn't notice that some other ass-wipe has been farting into my chair cushions for a month?"

Allison glances over her shoulder to see eyes look away. She thinks about calling for security.

"We can make other accommodations if something isn't right."

"Get him out of my office. Get him new accommodations. Easy as that."

Allison is in a difficult spot. Corporate lawyers have been adamant that nothing can happen to make these employees even think of the word lawsuit. They can't be let go, can't be made redundant. They are not to be antagonized or pushed too far. They can't be made to return to work too quickly. But this was Grady's idea to return.

No security, she decides.

"Why don't we try this again another day?"

Grady waves a hand around the tiny office. "He doesn't have much shit. He can be out by tomorrow. Looks like you cleared away all evidence I was ever here. Just get me that stuff back and we will be good to go.

What do you say to that, Allison? Does that work with your Synergen plan?"

Now she wants to slap him.

"This is my space. Mine."

"Technically, it's the company's," Alex says.

Grady reaches out with two hands, grabs the front of Alex's sweater, and hauls him to his feet. It is only two steps to the back wall, and Alex is pinned there with Grady inches from his face.

"We can settle this," he says. "I don't give up what's mine that easy."

Allison moves into the office. "Grady, please."

She puts a hand on his shoulder. Grady spins his neck to her, his eyes sharpened stone like two arrow-heads. She pulls the hand back, but it has broken the spell between him and Alex.

Alex struggles against Grady's clenched fists, but he is a smaller, weaker man.

Grady shoves him into the wall and lets go. He turns, lets Alex fall to the floor behind the desk.

"I want his shit out of here," he says as he passes by Allison out the door.

Again Allison thinks of following, but if Grady is headed for the door she doesn't want to slow him. She goes to Alex, thinking how she can spin this to the lawyers.

On his way to answer the phone Sean realizes he hasn't brushed his teeth today.

He hasn't interacted with anyone since Kerri left for work this morning, so why bother? Being out of the habit of tooth brushing while in the woods is staying with him.

"Hello?"

"Hi, is this Sean?"

A woman's voice he does not recognize. She sure acts like she knows him, though.

"Yes."

"This is Corey Clark from CNN. How are you doing?"

"I'm...fine."

"Well, all of us here in the newsroom were so happy to see you all get rescued. I'll tell you we were glued to this story from the day it broke. I bet it's nice to be home, huh?"

Sean looks around his house. It feels empty, hollowed out. It offers him less shelter than the sunken ground beside a fallen log in the woods where he'd made his home. Every cheerless room and overpriced finish builds on the sadness this house represents.

"Yes. Sure is."

"Listen, Sean, I really think America would love to hear your story straight from you guys. They've seen enough of me talking about it." She laughs. Sean can picture her too-white teeth, her rouged cheeks and thick mascara. He's seen her on TV now and then. Her standing with a microphone at an inauguration, in a hurricane, outside the Supreme Court.

"Yeah?"

"You're dang right they would. And I think we are the network to tell it. What I want to know is—when can we set up a satellite link and get you on the air?"

"I don't know if—"

"What I really want to know is—who do we make

the check out to?" She laughs again. It sounds the way too much perfume smells.

"Check?"

"Oh, we would absolutely compensate you for your time. And for the exclusive rights to cover your story, of course."

She throws that one in like a used car salesman.

Sean is confused. She's offering to pay him for an interview?

"Can you do that? I mean is it—"

"Oh, it's perfectly legal," Corey cuts in. "We do it all the time. And I think this is a story with legs. We'd love to get you on the air as soon as we can. After that I think we'd be looking at follow ups, an hour long documentary, maybe a return to the woods where it all happened."

"Is everyone doing it?"

"We haven't been able to reach any of the others. You're the first one, in fact. Isn't that exciting? Eventually we want to talk to everyone who came back from that terrible tragedy."

Her voice has shifted gears down into fake sincerity.

Sean stammers a bit. "We...we already spoke at the press conference."

"And you did great. What we're looking for is something more in depth. It's what we do here. We want to give people the full story. America has questions, Sean. About you and your bravery in the face of tragedy and, let's be honest here, near certain death? I mean, how *did* you make it out there? No. Wait, don't tell me yet. Wait until we're on the air." She laughs again.

"I'll have to speak to the others."

Reporters. They try to trap you with their questions.

They want the ambush, the exclusive. It worries Sean. Are they after a real story or are they after something more than what they already know from the statements they released? Would all five of them be able to stand up under questioning like that? The police asked basics. But reporters, they're paid to dig up dirt.

"Of course, of course. And I'll be calling all of them, too. The sooner we can get your story on the air, though, the more interest there will be. And, the higher the interest the higher the ratings. The higher the ratings, the bigger your check."

"As long as we don't talk to anyone else."

"We call it an exclusive. Just think how many people would tune in to that, Sean."

Good for her, he thinks. *Makes no difference to me.*

"I'll have to let you know."

Group decisions. A democracy. All for one.

"Of course, of course. You can call me back directly on this number. It'll get right to me. And Sean, think about who you want telling your story. Do you want a bunch of news talking heads, or do you want America to understand the truth of what went on out there directly from the source? I can guarantee the others will want to be in on this. We want to hear your side of things. America wants to."

"Okay. Yeah, I'll call you."

"Okay then. I'll be talking to your fellow rescuees. I'll let them know you say hi."

Sean noticed how she never said survivors. She was already spinning the story.

A check, though...

Allison thought she put this all behind her, but as she walks to her car her mind is filled with the problem of Grady and his little outburst. All day she thought about calling the lawyers to ask for advice, but she didn't. Not yet. Why alert them to a problem before it becomes something real?

Grady had a right to be upset. Maybe not that upset, but she understands where the instinct comes from.

She thought she'd done her mourning. When the group of young executives didn't return, the company had started to move on. It was her biggest test as a leader and a manager, and she passed with flying colors. She proved expert at the right amount of sympathy mixed with stiff-upper-lip forward looking. She'd eulogized them well and never missed a chance to conflate them with the best of what Synergen Dynamics had to offer.

If people could see Grady throwing a goddamn tantrum in his office because somebody moved his toys, the Synergen image might take a hit. No, keep it to yourself, Allison, she thinks. He'll get over it.

But good Christ, what is he gonna do when he doesn't get the promotion? For that she'll have security on hand. A rep from HR, too, in case there is ground to fire him. And also a generous severance package in case he wants to quit. They'll gladly help him out with a golden parachute rather than risk him tarring them with bad PR. After all, these five employees now synonymous with Synergen Dynamics are the faces of the company.

It's why she suggested giving them *all* new titles, raises and company cars. She was shot down.

She assumes the rest who haven't shown up back at

work yet, won't. They'll take whatever package they're offered. Not have to work for two years, probably, then come back to the work force anonymously. Right now everyone was up in their business. It's a distraction for the workers and for clients.

But as long as Allison manages the heroes, it means more eyes on her and that's a good thing. If Grady can keep his goddamn temper in check, that is.

Seven thirty and her car is the last in the row. The black Audi sits waiting for her. Only eight more payments on her lease and she can get that Tesla she wants. No, that she deserves.

Her heels click and reverb off the cement. The low ceilings of the parking garage are lined with exposed pipe, each thick concrete column is splashed with brightly colored numbers and letters to mark the rows and sections. Some graphic design school grad had been paid a stupid amount of money to pick a font that was "forward thinking."

Her keys are still in her purse. No more of that clumsy rooting around in the bottom of the bag for a key fob business with cars that recognize when you step close. She picks up her pace, a glass of pinot noir waits for her at home.

Something heavy hits the side of her head, right above her ear. She stumbles to the side, an acrobat on high heels, she doesn't fall. The car is still there, ahead of her, but it is blurry now. And a warm orb of pain is growing from inside her skull.

Something hit me, she thinks. The blow comes again, a little higher this time, and she falls. Her purse goes sprawling, knees hit concrete, hands out to stop her fall slap the ground and send shockwaves of pain up her arms.

She's making a sound. Not a word, just a sound, but she's unaware she's doing it.

Her car beeps its greeting. She is close enough. She feels blood flow across her cheek, fall in drops off her nose.

A metal half circle falls to the ground in front of her. It makes a high pitched clang off the hard floor, reminds her of the bell at a boxing match. When it stops moving she can see it is the letter D. She recognizes it...she thinks. It looks like the D from the sign out front, the one in die cut letters bolted in to the stone marker by the circular driveway in front of the building.

Feet step into view.

Something didn't hit her. Some*one* did.

The person doesn't say a word. They look like men's shoes. She thinks she is going to be raped. That's what this is. But he makes no move to touch her. She can see his hands find her purse and dig out her cell phone. It drops to the concrete floor and the glass shatters. A foot comes down and the heel grinds the phone into the floor. It comes down twice more, nearly splitting the phone in two.

Allison tries to move. She makes that sound again. There is more blood. So much more.

The feet vanish. She feels pressure on her feet, her ankles. The weight grows until her ankle bends. The pain is sharper than her head, more focused. After putting his full body weight on her ankle, he pushes down and snaps the bone.

Her scream echoes in the garage.

She can hear the footsteps walk away.

OUT THERE
DAY 6

SEAN LAY on his back looking up at the greedy trees. They were greedy for the way they stole the light before it reached the ground. Hungry leaves formed a shield above them and kept them in dim shade for all but a couple of hours a day. He watched a light breeze make them sway in a mocking dance as the sunlight stayed behind the wall.

So far they had avoided rain and the days had been warm. Put one in the pro column for global warming.

They had managed to parse out their meager supplies in anticipation for the day of their probable rescue. The day everyone would realize they are gone. The day they were supposed to return home.

It hadn't been easy to live on three quarters of one energy bar and one strip of jerky a day, but Maia found a clump of berry bushes not too far away and Wes took a chance and sampled a type of mushroom that grew on the trunks of dead trees all around them and found them to be edible. It hadn't been ideal and they were hungry, weaker, slower—but alive.

Ken was a problem. He'd been laying down for nearly the entire time they were there. Grady and Sean had gotten into a routine of helping him stand so he could step a few feet away and pee, but even with a man under each arm, Ken struggled to hold himself up and he grunted and cringed in pain whenever his leg was moved. He had no control over it. The lower half of his leg hung like a broken branch on one of the trees that boxed them in.

Whenever they would move him or return to the shelter after soaking in as much warm sunlight as they could beside the river, they all shared looks of silent concern, but no one had talked yet about what to do with him since nobody knew exactly what that would be.

Sean always thought the forest would be quiet. People talked about the placid feeling of calm and peace when they took to the outdoors. He found it a cacophonous place of unrelenting tones. The water filed the air with white noise. The insects called in waves of rising and falling songs. Birds talked over each other like rude guests at a party. It was constant. There was no peace.

The birds especially had seemed curious about the newcomers to their habitat. They perched in branches overhead and chattered warnings. Sean knew nothing of birds but some of the ones who stopped by wore beautiful plumage in reds and blues. He understood why people took up bird watching. He also understood the old cartoons where someone, starved in a life raft or on a desert island, would look at a bird and start to see a fully cooked Thanksgiving turkey.

Palm-sized birds began to seem like three course meals to him.

And then the fish. They'd unwrapped the fishing line on day two and had been casting about in the river ever since, but hadn't so much as seen a fish float by.

"There's no point, anyway," Grady said. "Not without fire. What are we gonna do, make sushi?"

Fire was another issue but everyone had been able to excuse it away knowing that this day would be their rescue. Right now rescue crews were gearing up, helicopters taking on fuel, teams of volunteer hikers were massing at the trailhead to start the tree-by-tree search for the lost. Surely that was happening.

There had been a weak attempt at rubbing sticks together early on, but it didn't last when it provided more blisters than smoke.

The group managed to stay warm by lying with more branches and pine boughs over their shelter, the sleeping bags unzipped and dried out and then laid over them in a giant shared blanket at night, and the collected body heat of all seven members of the group.

The men's whiskers had grown out now to beyond merely a weekend scruff. The women ignored their legs. Everyone ignored their stringy hair, oily skin, lengthening nails.

The river provided quick washing up, but it was too cold to sustain a full bath. Faces were kept relatively clean, underarms scrubbed to avoid the most offensive B.O. Ken stewed a bit in his own smell, but Lara took the responsibility of soaking a bandana in water and rinsing his face each day.

She seemed the weakest, not only because of a lack of food. Her spirit was the most fragile. Her fear the closest to the surface. She talked more about getting rescued, about her hunger, about how scared she was than anyone else.

Sounds in the night caused her to flinch and kept her from sleep. Her eyes were rimmed in dark circles and her skin sallow. Sean worried about her almost as much as Ken.

"So today, right?" Lara asked. "Today was the day we were supposed to be done so they'll look for us, right?"

"They should," Sean said.

"They will," Maia said. She seemed to understand Lara was looking for certainty and that anything less might send her into another panic.

"I wish we could build a signal fire or something."

"Our luck we'd start a forest fire," Sean said. "I think there are heavy restrictions on fires in this forest."

"I'm not that concerned with restrictions right now. Let them give us a ticket after they find us."

"Wouldn't do us much good if we all died in a fire."

"You think it matters whether we burn to death or starve to death? Both have the same outcome."

Sean saw the argument going nowhere so he dropped it. Lara didn't need to spin any more wild thoughts on how they might die out there.

"I saw a possum, I think." Nathan joined Grady at the riverbank. Wes was close by and wandered over to join them.

"Where?"

"In the trees, past the shelter. I was checking on Ken."

"How's he doing?" asked Wes.

"Where was the possum?" Grady cut in. "If we could catch it, that's a ton of food."

"It was back in there," Nathan said with a wave of his hand at the world of trees indistinguishable from one another. "How are we gonna catch it, anyway?"

"I've got my knife," Grady said and drew his pocket knife from his front pocket, flipped open the blade with his thumb. It was something, but it was less than impressive.

"It scurried away. I don't think you could get close to it."

"Maybe set a trap," said Wes.

"Do you know how to do that?"

Wes shrugged his shoulders.

"If you see it again, call me," Grady said.

Maia had walked around the bend in the river searching for more berry bushes. In their six days nobody had ventured more than a few hundred yards from their shelter. The trees quickly became a maze with no outlet and anything other than the river as a guidepost sent them in circles. And, as each day wore on, the energy they had shrank the distance they could walk without panting for breath and needing to sit. Even the salads she usually had for lunch and her small but sensible breakfasts kept Maia in more calories than she was getting out here. She vowed to never again complain about starving herself.

Maia realized she'd never truly been away from everything before. Her nature had come prepared and packaged. Being truly alone out here in the woods gave her the same feeling as being in a totally dark room or trapped in a too-tight space. It stole her breath, it made her feel like falling and drowning at the same time. She knew this was how phobias started. She knew she wasn't the only one.

As long as she kept the river on her left she knew where she was.

At another curve in the river she found another eddy moving in slow swirls. Low trees dipped branches into the water like a strainer collecting dead leaves, branches, pinecones in the sieve. She wondered if maybe this calmer water would be a better fishing spot. Unless they hoped for a salmon moving upstream, the water where they were was too swift for fish.

She noticed something tangled in the branches.

She couldn't spare the energy to run back to the others. Shouting was enough.

"Guys! Come here!"

She walked back almost halfway before they heard her over the water.

"What is it?" Sean called back.

"Come here," she repeated.

The group followed her voice and she walked back to the spot where she'd seen it, but kept her eyes down.

"What is it?"

"There." She pointed.

In the tangle of branches a few feet off the shore was Rick's body.

"Jesus Christ," Wes said.

Lara began to sob and turned away.

"Holy shit," Grady said as he started to move toward the shore. Rick's body was a few feet into the current. He reached once but missed.

"How did he end up here?" Wes asked.

"He must have gotten caught on something and hung up for a few days then floated farther down. Or maybe he's been here the whole time. Have any of us been down this far before?"

No one answered. All eyes were on Grady in the water.

"Why do we need to get him?" Sean asked.

"What?" Grady barked from the water where he stood knee deep.

"What are you gonna do with him if you fish him out?"

"Someone will want his body, don't you think? He's gotta have family somewhere."

"Yeah, Sean," Maia said.

"Give me a hand." Grady held out his left arm toward the shore. Nathan stepped up and braced himself on shore before taking hold of Grady's arm so he could lean deeper into the water. He got a hand on Rick's boot and guided him in to shore.

Rick was face down and for that Maia was grateful. Then Grady flipped him over. Rick's head had a deep dent in his right temple where he had hit the rock. His skin was a pale grey, eyes clouded over. He was stiff, arms and legs straight.

"Grady, do you have to turn him over like that?" she asked.

Lara buried her head in Wes's chest, afraid to look up.

"I'm seeing if, y'know..."

"If what? If he's alive. Come on."

"You think Ron and Karina are somewhere along here?" Sean asked.

"They've gotta be somewhere."

Wes spoke over Lara's shoulder. "Maybe they're so far downriver someone found them days ago. That would start them searching for us, right?" He patted her back, encouraging.

"Or maybe they're hung up somewhere back there," Grady said, pointing upriver. "If he didn't float all the way down until now there's no reason to think they did."

"Isn't that an argument for letting him go?" Sean said. Off Grady's look he said, "I mean if someone picks up a body floating by they'll know there was trouble."

"So use him like a signal flag?"

"I don't know. I guess so."

"No way," Grady said. "He's still a person. And besides, and I know no one is gonna want to hear this but shut up and listen for a second. We have to consider the possibility, we have to at least consider it, that it might still be a long time before anyone finds us."

The look on Nathan's face was pure crushing defeat. "But today is the day we were supposed to come back. They *have* to know we're gone by now."

"I know that. But think about how far off we are from the campsite. Nobody knows to look for us here. And think about where we are. No trails. No signs of life. We're in a place where people never go. There's no access. Maybe they send a raft down, I don't know. I don't see how they could get a raft down the trail to even make it to the river. And those were some class five rapids we went through to get here."

"So what's that got to do with Rick?" Sean asked.

Grady climbed out of the water, shook off his legs to dry them a little and get some feeling back after the icy dunk.

"This could be a source of food if we get to that point."

The river kept them from total silence but nobody said a word. Above, a bird screeched as if lodging a protest.

Lara said quietly to Wes, "I want to go back to camp."

Wes nodded and turned them both and walked away.

"You've got to at least see that the possibility is there," Grady said.

"It's been a week," Sean said.

"And we're starving. We ate the last of the jerky today and the bars were gone last night."

"But, he's been dead a week."

"And he's been soaking in cold storage. That water is only a few degrees above freezing. It's colder than your fridge at home, I guarantee it."

"You can't be fucking serious," Maia said.

"Okay, fine," Grady said. His tantrums had become more frequent, more angry and less pouty when he didn't get his way. "Talk to me in a few days when all you've had to eat is fucking fungus off a dead log. We're humans. Meat eaters. We need protein to survive. That's why other people have had to do it when push came to shove and they wanted to survive. And that's what I intend to goddamn do—survive."

"No, Grady," Sean said. "We're not going to sink to

that. We'll be rescued, we'll figure something out. Anything, but not that. It's not even up for discussion."

"Sean, I swear to fucking God you need to stop acting like the goddamn law out here."

Sean looked from Nathan to Maia. "Back me up, guys."

"Sorry, Grady," Nathan said. "But that's too much, man."

"Abso-fucking-lutely not," Maia said. She crossed her arms over her chest.

"I'm not saying I want to do it," Grady said. "I'm saying it's better to have the body there when the chips are down than not to."

"This discussion is over," Sean said. "Let's get the rope and tie him off so when we're rescued…" He gave a pointed stare at Grady. "We can turn him over to the proper authorities."

"At least I'm taking some fucking initiative. That's what this exercise is all about, isn't it?"

Sean swung around, his face heated and his voice loud and firm.

"This isn't an exercise anymore. This is way beyond that. Are you still worried about your goddamn promotion? I don't give a shit what you think of me or my leadership skills, we are not stooping to that level. So forget about it and let's move on."

Grady stepped forward, his chest out. "You wanna get loud with me?"

"Oh, for fuck's sake, Grady," Maia said. "You lost this one. Back off and forget it."

Sean pushed past Grady and headed back to camp for the rope. Maia and Nathan followed.

BACK HOME

WES WAKES up to a familiar feeling. Not welcome, just familiar.

His head is pounding, mouth dry, muscles sore. His hotel room looks unfamiliar. He walked here last night, somehow. Got his key card in the door. A functional drunk, that's what he always was and apparently still is. He remembers. He never was a blackout drunk. Maybe once or twice there near the end.

Right now it's the memories that are doing it to him. He remembers the long nights under a canopy of trees, the lean-to shelter of branches and dead logs. The insects crawling on them in the night. The changing smell of Ken's leg as it ripened with time.

He remembers.

The fights and power struggles between Grady and Sean. Grady and Maia. Grady and everyone.

He remembers walking Lara back to the shelter after Grady made his insane proposal to keep Rick like some side of beef in a meat locker. He held her up, weak-kneed and leaning on him. She leaned into him. He stood strong.

They made it back. Ken was sleeping. He walked her past the log, deeper into the woods for some space, a place to calm down amid the drone of bugs and the calls of birds. Away from Ken and what he represented —looming death.

He remembers leaning on a toppled tree. Her face in his shoulder. Her tears hot on his skin as they soaked through his filthy shirt.

He remembers leaning into her, his lips tilting toward hers. Her pulling back. The look of horror a deeper shock than her reaction to Grady's proposal. He remembers apologizing and leaving her there on the log, rushing back to the riverside and throwing rocks in the water.

He never heard her mention it to anyone.

———

His eyes fight to stay open against the glare of mid-morning sun. This is a hair-of-the-dog moment but he won't give in. That's how it starts.

He rotates his body and his feet hit the carpet. He knows it has already started. But he can still stop it. Maybe if he gets home.

He calls his sponsor. An answer this time. A woman.

"Is Gordon there?"

"Who's calling please?"

"This is Wes. I'm his...I'm a friend of his."

"This is Emily, his daughter. I have some bad news, Wes. My father..." He hears her swallow the words.

She's not yet used to saying them. "My father passed away on Tuesday."

"Oh, my God."

"Yes, it was quite a shock. I'm sorry."

"No, I'm sorry. I didn't know."

"There will be a memorial next week some time. Would you like to be on the invite list?"

"Yes. I mean, I may be out of town. But hopefully not. Do you mind if I ask how it happened?"

"How did you know my father?"

"Just friends, like I said."

"Was it through AA?"

He pauses. "Yes."

"Then you should know he had started drinking again. I don't know what exactly set him off but after almost fifteen years..."

"Oh, I'm so sorry."

"He suffered a brain aneurism. They think it was brought on by the drinking, or at least worsened because of it. It happened when he was very drunk and he couldn't make a phone call or anything. I'm sorry, this is probably more detail than you wanted."

"No, no, it's okay. I'm sorry for your loss."

"Oh, my God. Wes, I just realized. Was my dad your sponsor?"

"Yes, but, it's okay."

"And did you need him? Are you in trouble?"

"No, no. Not at all. I was just checking in. I'm fine. Just fine."

"Okay. If you need anything..."

"I'm fine. Thank you, Emily. I'm sorry again about Gord—about your dad."

Wes hangs up. He feels a long way from home.

———————

They're eating at the same time, if not together.

Sean stands at the kitchen counter eating out of the paper container his Chinese food came in. Kerri is at the dining table having a reheated meal of ravioli.

"So I got a weird call today," Sean says. Small talk. This is how marriages work. You make small talk.

"Yeah?"

Not ignoring him is good.

"A news reporter wants to interview me for a story."

"About being lost?"

Sean fights the instinct to get sarcastic. *No, about the face of Jesus in my toast this morning, what do you think?*

"Yeah," he says.

"Cool."

"Yeah, I don't know if I want to do it."

"Why not?"

"It seems like they're going to make a big deal and it's already too much. I don't want to lose our privacy, y'know?"

"You really think people are gonna care for more than a week? We can't even pay attention to wars for more than a month."

"You're right, but still. It seems icky to take money for something like that. Feels like exploitation."

Kerri sets down her fork.

"How much money?"

"She didn't say. But it's to be exclusive to their network, which also seems shady."

"That's not shady. What's wrong with it?"

"I don't know. I doesn't feel weird to you for a

supposed news organization to go offering money to people for a story?"

Kerri pushes away from the table. The small talk is gone, and as unfamiliar as that mundane task felt, the rising anger in her voice sounds very familiar to Sean.

"It's not weird. It's how things are done. What's weird is that you would turn down an offer of free money. Is that what you're going to do at work? Turn down the promotion because it *pays* too much?"

"This is different. I earn that money."

"You earned whatever they want to pay you by being out in the fucking wilderness for a month on your own."

"Exactly. It wasn't only me out there. I need to find out what everyone else wants to do."

She stands. Never a good sign.

"I fucking swear, Sean. This is why you haven't made more of yourself. You don't know how to take advantage of opportunities. We're drowning here and someone throws you a lifeline—"

"We're not drowning."

"It feels like it."

"You're being dramatic."

He knows he shouldn't have said it. She hates to be told how she is acting, how she's feeling. The only thing worse is to tell her to calm down.

"And you're being a fucking idiot."

"You don't have to get nasty."

"You don't hear me otherwise. Listen to yourself. You have to ask what everyone else wants to do? Take a fucking stand, Sean. Think for yourself. Ask for something. Or when someone offers you something, take it, for God's sake."

"What do you want from me, Kerri?"

"I just told you. Damn it, you don't listen."

She's moving past him, leaving her plate on the table. She moves by so fast he can feel a breeze. She's headed for the stairs. If she makes it there the conversation is over for the night. She won't come down. This will be left to simmer overnight.

"Fine." The power in his voice startles him. Kerri stops walking. "You want me to take action? Is that it? Here I am, then. I wanted that job and I did everything in my power to get it. Believe it or not I want to stay with you and I'm doing my best for that, too. But maybe I need something more than a promotion. Maybe I need a whole change. I need to make something of this opportunity in front of me."

"So take the goddamn money, Sean."

"Not like that. I need to earn it. I need to put something out in the world to make up for what's not there anymore. The lives of people, real human beings, Kerri, who aren't here anymore."

"How is that your responsibility?"

"It just is."

"Well it isn't mine. And what you do affects me. Don't forget that."

He shoves off the kitchen counter, meets her in the living room. They stand like two boxers in center ring.

"You don't get to tell me how to deal with what I've been through. You don't get to tell me how to do my job. We're supposed to encourage each other. To support each other. But all you do is tear me down and I'm fucking sick of it."

Sean finds himself only inches from her, not sure how he got so close. The hot anger in her eyes has moved to fear now. She flinches. He realizes she thinks he might hit her.

His mother used to say—"Temper, temper." Her hot blooded boy. He kept it in check, forced himself to cool down. Learned how to control it. *Temper, temper*, he reminds himself.

"I thought about you out there, you know. I thought about how bad I wanted to be back here with you. But I knew there was a chance nothing would change. I mean, I honestly thought you might have already found someone else. I did. I know we're a fucking mess right now. But I fought hard to come back to you. Not for a job. Not for a payout from some news show. But for us to have a life that we used to talk about together. But this shit, after all I went through? This is a slap in the face. How selfish do you have to be to make this about you?"

"How is it selfish if all I'm trying to do is make our life better for the both of us? How is that making it about me?"

"You don't get it."

His shoulders slump and he turns away. Facing the kitchen counter lined with Chinese takeout containers he has never been more depressed. Something about the tableau is the saddest thing he's ever seen.

"Yeah, right," she says. "I don't get it."

With his back to her he can hear her feet on the stairs. Tonight he will sleep on the couch. This round is over. He doesn't know who won.

OUT THERE

DAY 7

THERE WAS a break in the trees directly overhead that Ken could see out. It was like a skylight in a tall ceiling but to Ken, it felt like the south end of a deep well and he was on the bottom looking up. He hadn't moved much since they set him down beside the dead tree a week ago. The pain in his leg had gone from a thousand knives to a single, thumping dullness. Now and then he felt short stabs of pain but he knew they were ghosts sparks running along the nerves in his numb lower leg.

Sean stepped next to him, briefly blocking his light.

"How are you doing, Ken?"

The earth pressed at his back. "Dirt. Dirt and water. Whole world is just made of dirt and water."

Sean studied him, not knowing what to say back.

"That's really all there is. Dirt and water. We die, we get planted and go back to the dirt. The water evaporates and then falls back as rain. Everywhere you go, all over the world, dirt and water."

"You need anything?" Sean asked. There was a look of concern on his face.

"Nah, man. I got my dirt." He patted the ground next to him. "I can hear the water." He paused and they both listened to the far-off river. "That's all there is so that's all I need."

"Okay. I'll check back with you in a bit."

Ken could tell Sean was happy to walk away. He'd probably go tell the others that Ken was losing it. His mind was not the thing Ken was worried about. His calf muscle had turned dark and mottled. Pooled blood. Like a corpse.

They'd kept him fed and hydrated. Berries and mushrooms. Leaves that Nathan found were edible, if not delicious. But this lying down was making him crazy. His back itched and his muscles were sore from doing nothing. He was at the mercy of the ants which crawled over him like he was no more than another rotting log on the forest floor.

Through the break in trees would come a shaft of light. Any time now. Each day around this time the sun sat at the right angle and pointed a beam of light like a finger down in his eyes as if to say, "You awake? You awake? Are you dead yet?"

Ken wanted to stand, he wanted to help, to contribute. He wanted to be rescued and see if his leg could be saved. The hope of rescue was still alive in him, the hope for his leg was fading.

"You're not gonna like this," Sean said.

Grady, Lara and Wes looked up from the water's edge where they were sitting, many feet apart and in their separate worlds.

Sean held his shirt in a pouch with something weighing down the center.

"What?" Wes asked.

"I found these under a big pile of rotting leaves and stuff."

The others stood and made their way through the low ferns and bushes of the water's edge to Sean. Sean held out the shirt to show a writhing tangle of white blobs.

"They're grubs. Pretty big ones. I heard they have a lot of protein."

Lara put a hand over her mouth.

"Nice score," Grady said.

"We eat them raw?" was asked.

"No other choice," Sean said. He hadn't tried one yet and was hoping someone else would volunteer for the job. He expected Grady would if only to prove how unafraid he was.

"Looks like more than a dozen."

"Yeah, fourteen, so two each," Sean said.

"That's breakfast."

Nobody reached for the wriggling pile, they watched them squirm and roll their eyeless bodies over each other.

"Should we get the others?" Sean asked.

Grady cupped his hands around his mouth and called out, "Maia! Nathan! Breakfast!"

Upriver, Nathan stood from where he'd been hidden in the tall bushes.

"What'd you get?"

"You don't want to know," Sean said.

This is what survival is, Sean thought. Doing things you know you need to do, no matter how unpleasant.

Man survived for thousands of years on food like this, right?

"What the fuck?" Maia's voice carried from down-river at the eddy.

Everyone perked up, full attention.

Wes started running first. "What is it?"

"Who did it?" Maia called out. Her voice was far away but the anger carried.

The group started moving toward her. Sean held his pouch of grubs in front of him, careful not to spill the even portions. He'd thought about taking an extra one or two for himself right when he found them, but couldn't bring himself to pop them in his mouth. After he'd picked up his fourteen, he left behind another dozen, perhaps. Each one he'd picked up like it was electrified. Grabbing quickly with fingertips and dropping them in his shirt.

Grady brought up the rear of the group.

When they reached Maia she stood beside the hanging branches where they'd found Rick the day before. Sean's stomach tightened wondering what else she found in the strainer of trees.

"He's gone," she said.

"Rick?" Wes peeked over the edge of the river and into the empty space.

"Someone cut him loose or untied him."

Maia held up the end of the rope they'd used the day before to tie his ankle to a short tree close to shore. A simple knot around one leg kept him in place in case the hanging branches let go.

"The current took him," Grady said.

"All of a sudden? He was here for who knows how many days before we found him. Why last night?"

She shot accusing glances at Grady.

"This rope could have been cut with a knife, Grady."

"That rope is barely strong enough to tie my shoes. What made you think it was gonna hold a whole human being?"

Sean didn't have the heart for another argument. He tried to move the conversation forward.

"Did you look downriver at all? Maybe he's still nearby."

She hadn't and the group fanned out to check the bend in the river. Where it turned, though, the ground sloped away and the river picked up speed. If anything came loose from the strainer, it would be swept away easily.

Nathan tried to offer a positive spin. "Well, maybe he'll be found. Like we said."

"Kinda like you wanted, Sean," Maia said. She sounded like a prosecuting attorney.

"I didn't untie him." Sean spun toward the group spread out around him, eager to defend himself. As he turned the grubs fell out of his shirt pouch and fell into the long grasses growing by the riverbank.

"Shit."

"Fuck. There goes breakfast," Grady said. He stepped to Sean and bent down with him to try to gather the grubs. "Happy with yourself, Maia?"

"Someone did this," she said, not backing down.

"Yeah, the river. Get over it. Help us find these grubs or we go hungry today. Everything else is gone."

Everyone got on their knees to hunt for the grubs wriggling through the grass.

When they got back to the shelter Ken was pushing himself up on his arms.

"Get me the compass."

He was eager, sweating with the effort of pulling himself along. He'd built up a small pile of dried leaves and pine needles and surrounded it with a small trough of dug out dirt.

"Ken, are you all right?" Lara asked.

"Where's the compass? We don't have much time." Ken looked overhead to his shaft of light.

Nathan dug into one of the backpacks and found the compass, unsure what Ken wanted it for but sensing his urgency. He handed it over.

Sean watched as Ken twisted it in his hands, cracking the plastic case and breaking it in two. He's lost it, Sean thought. The pain or the isolation had gotten to him and broken him. He was witnessing a man go mad. Sean had thought about the possibility that someone would lose it. Grady seemed to be the least stable, the most likely to crack, and the fact that he had a knife frightened Sean.

Ken looked to the sky and held the clear face of the compass in his hand. He calculated the angle, then put the small disc into the beam of light. Like a lens it focused the sunlight into a sharp point and Ken aimed it at the pile of dried tinder.

At once the group knew what he was trying to do.

Sean remembered a news magazine show he'd seen about the dangers of Christmas trees gone dry and he knew how volatile dry pine needles could be. This might work.

Sweat dripped from Ken's forehead as he adjusted the angle, kept the lens focused on the same spot in his pile. He swallowed down the pain in his leg as a tiny curl of smoke began to rise from the pile.

"Get small sticks," Grady said. "Small stuff to get it going and bigger stuff to keep it lit. And rocks. We need to build a ring around it otherwise we'll burn our house down."

Everyone stood watching the rising smoke, waiting for the first glimpses of orange fire.

"Go," Grady commanded.

Wes and Nathan moved off into the woods. Maia reached to the tree next to her and began snapping off branches.

"We need dry wood. Dead stuff already on the ground," Grady scolded her.

She looked as if she might argue back, but she knew he was right. She stepped away into the woods and Lara followed her.

Grady pointed at Sean and his pouch of grubs. "Find some sticks to use as skewers. We're gonna roast those little fuckers over an open fire, baby."

Before Sean turned away he saw the first lick of fire sprout from Ken's pile.

They had a slightly nutty flavor. Sean overcooked his, wanting to make really sure it was dead and free from any bacteria. When it popped in his mouth the grub spit hot goo that burned the roof of his mouth. He chewed quickly and swallowed.

Everyone's faces were a mixture of relief to get some needed protein and revulsion at the method they needed to do so. When everyone's second grub had gone down, they sat in silence, both grateful that it was over and frustrated that it wasn't nearly enough.

"You said you saw more?" Grady asked.

"Yeah. And I'm sure if they were there, there's a ton all over the place."

Nobody seemed all that excited about the menu, but a steady source of protein could get them through a few more days if they needed. The mental boost from seeing fire and having something in their stomachs which they'd provided for themselves gave the entire group a lift.

In no time the fire was built up and rung with stones from the river. A stack of wood lay in wait and everyone had praised Ken for his brilliant thinking. Who needed a goddamn compass, anyway?

"I can watch it," Ken said. "You give me a pile of sticks and I'll keep it fed."

The task gave him a noticeable boost. He wasn't merely a burden on them anymore. The smile on his face was betrayed, though, by a sheen of sweat and his heavy breathing. Still, the others vowed to keep his stockpile filled.

Lara stared into the fire, the small taste of protein set her mind to thinking of food. "I wish we could eat those little lobsters."

"What lobsters?" Nathan asked.

"In the river. Over by the bend where Rick was...over where we were this morning."

"There's no lobsters in a river, Lara."

"I dunno. They looked like lobsters. A bunch of them."

"Do you mean crayfish?" Grady asked.

"I don't know what that is."

"They look like tiny lobsters. They eat them in cajun food."

"I don't eat cajun food. It's too spicy."

Grady stood, his frustration with Lara out in the open.

"Lara, you're lucky you got lost with a group. You'd be dead already if you didn't have us to carry you."

"Hey," Maia said. "That's uncalled for, Grady."

"I don't give a shit. Sean," he pointed like a military commander, "grab the mosquito net and come with me."

Sean found himself obeying the command, but he didn't like it.

Maia moved closer to the shelter. "I'll stay here with Ken." When she looked down Ken was asleep, flat on his back. The exhaustion of building the fire had taken its toll on him. She looked down and saw that his leg was twisted, the foot pointing in an unnatural way. She examined him closer and saw his sleep was something deeper.

"Ken?"

She lightly touched his shoulder. Sweat beaded on his forehead. He didn't move. She shook him and said his name again. Worry came to her voice and she gave his shoulder a sharp push. "Ken."

He jerked awake, looking at his surroundings in a daze. After a moment of orientation he cried out in pain and his hands shot to his leg. When they touched it he shrieked again and drew his hands back.

"Help me," she said to anyone who would listen.

Sean and Wes stepped in and adjusted Ken. His leg flopped into alignment but not without yelps of pain from Ken. When they set him down he shut his eyes again and lay there panting like a dog. Sweat coated his face and the smell of stale body odor wafted off him.

Maia ran her hands along his head to try to calm him.

"You guys go, I'll be all right."

As they left for the river the rest of the group shared concerned looks. Ken didn't look good.

BACK HOME

THEY DON'T KEEP Maia waiting for long. A woman in a navy blue skirt suit clicks across the polished wood floor on high heels with her hand extended out like she's holding an invisible leash.

"Maia, sorry to keep you. I'm Amy."

Maia shakes the book agent's hand. The office is all high ceilings, exposed beams and pipework, natural wood finishes. Display shelves of books line the walls, a few Maia has heard of.

"Come in," Amy says and leads her to an office with glass walls. As she passes by an assistant's desk she asks for two waters.

Maia sits on a couch with modern straight lines and Amy sits in a stiff armchair across from her. Brightly colored coffee table books on photography and architecture lay open on the table between them.

"So I recognize you from the TV coverage," Amy says. "I bet you've been getting that a lot lately."

"Yes. It's weird."

What she thinks is—*barely. I haven't been out of the*

house much. I don't want to see anyone. When people look to me all I see are their sharp fangs and yellow, predator's eyes these days. But she doesn't say it.

"I am so glad you got in touch. That's so funny that you know Glenn, too. Small world, huh?"

"It is. Unless you're trapped in the woods. Then it seems like it will never end."

Amy laughs a small, tentative laugh, unsure if it was meant as a joke or not.

"Well, I'm glad you're here. I have to tell you I am *very* interested in your story and I know the reading public will be, too."

Maia likes this woman. She oozes business. Her short, severe haircut says she doesn't mess around. Her suit looks expensive, her shoes certainly are. Good signs.

"What I want is to nail down an exclusive deal. Do you know if we can copyright the story or anything? I want this to be my account and not have it be clouded by anyone else's fuzzy memory. Do you know what I'm saying?"

"Absolutely." Amy knows she can't totally ensure that, but she will find a way to figure it out. "If we can get something signed then we can start that process rolling."

"But, like, if someone wants to make like a movie about it or something, they have to come through me, right?"

"Okay, you know *Unbroken*? The Lauren Hillenbrand book about the guy in World War Two?"

"Right. Angelina Jolie did the movie."

"Yes. So that was that guy's life, right? Well, guess who got paid because she wrote the book?"

"Exactly. That's what I want."

"How about *Lincoln*, the Spielberg movie? A movie about Abraham freakin' Lincoln and who gets paid— the author of the book. If you own the book, you own the story."

Maia smiles. "Yes. Okay, good."

"What we need A.S.A.P. is the book, of course. But we don't need that to sell it or to pitch to Hollywood. All we need from you is a short summary and a contract giving us the authorization to get out there and start pitching it on your behalf."

"Where do I sign?"

Let the others whip out their dicks and get out the rulers. Let them fight and break each other's heads over a corner office. Maia has a plan.

"One thing I'll tell you right now," Maia says. "I don't want to let this go for anything under six figures."

Amy smiles a shark's smile.

"I like the way you think."

"Thanks for meeting with me, Sean."

Nathan keeps his hands stuffed deep in his pockets. The square is busy with people walking to and from the restaurants, the theater on the corner, the coffee shop and bar offering live jazz on weekends. It couldn't be more opposite from the woods.

Sean takes a seat on a bench next to Nathan. They go unnoticed by the crowd. Cabs sweep them with headlights every few seconds, their own private light show.

"What's up, man?"

Nathan looks like he hasn't slept. His eyes are sunken. He already lost weight out there. They all did. He had more to lose, perhaps. His face had filled out since college, work had eaten into his time and running got dropped from his routine. Now he looks like a meth addict with better teeth.

"We said we could talk to each other, right?"

"Yeah. Anything. What's up?"

Sean sees the first tears. They brim at the edges of his eyes, threatening to fall.

"I don't know. I don't think I can do this."

"Do what? There's nothing to it. We get back to life."

"I can't. Not after...everything."

"It sucks. It does, I know. But we gotta do it."

Nathan wipes away the tears. He's regained himself a bit. He takes a moment to watch the traffic, the cars and the people. They hung out a little bit, when Nathan first started at Synergen. But they hadn't seen each other socially in a while. Nathan knows a little of Sean's marriage problems, but he hasn't pried. Maybe if he'd been a better friend it wouldn't be so awkward now to bare his soul to Sean.

"Do you still see it? When you try to sleep?"

"Yeah. I see it. I hear it, too. The bugs and the birds."

"And the water."

"Yes," Sean says. "It never stops."

Nathan lifts his chin to the street in front of them. "It's different than this. I don't know how but it is."

"I know what you mean."

The truth is, Sean barely thinks about it. He works hard not to. He tamps it down like the fresh dirt on a new grave. To keep whatever is buried in its place. But Nathan needs him now.

"I want to talk about it," Nathan says. "I can't tell my parents, though."

"Yeah."

"Did the news lady call you?"

"Yeah, she did. What'd you tell her?"

"I told her I didn't know. I don't. I don't know what to do. If I talk to her, what do I say?"

"You tell her what happened."

"I tell her everything?"

Sean waits. He keeps his eyes on the square. A trio of pigeons pecks at the ground for crumbs. If they'd had dumb birds like that out there they could have caught them, no problem.

"I don't think you should."

Nathan laughs, then sniffs, his nose clogged with unspilled tears.

"I didn't think you would."

"Look, you don't owe me anything."

"I was an asshole to you. I'm sorry."

"It wasn't your fault. You weren't yourself. None of us were."

They sit side by side, not looking at each other. Being ignored by the people passing by. Nathan coughs a single laugh. "Maybe we were finally being our real selves. That's what I'm worried about."

"That's nuts."

Nathan draws his hands from his pockets and rubs them together. His hands are bony. Sean swears he can hear the knuckles clack together like dice rolling in his fists.

"Is it? I'm holding it in but it's like a goddamn cork in a bottle, y'know? Everybody says don't bottle stuff up. Someday it's gonna blow. Everyone says it."

His voice rises. People continue to ignore them. A taxi honks at a guy on a bicycle.

"And what then?" Nathan asks of no one. "What happens when it bursts? Do I tell it all? What would anybody do with a story like that?"

"Nothing. It's our story. Nobody else would understand."

Sean can feel his own pressure build. Everything he hasn't thought about, everything he's been pushing down while he deals with Kerri, with the news lady, with Grady and his therapy session freak out. He realizes his hands are clenched into fists.

"Nathan, you'll be fine. Each day it will get easier. Eventually the news people will quit calling. We can go back to life. Our lives."

"What about the ones who didn't make it out? What about—"

Sean cuts him off before he says any names. They are blank, faceless ideas. Not real people. That's what helps keep it down. Keep it out of his thoughts.

"We have to live our lives. We have to go forward. That's what kept us alive out there. Not looking back, looking forward."

Nathan sits and wrings his hands. Sean listens to the traffic. Maybe not so different from the river, after all.

"You're right. I know you're right."

"Jesus, Nathan, think about what it would mean. We'd all be…"

"I know." Nathan turns to Sean. "I am sorry. The way I...I don't know what happened. I guess Grady...I guess I needed some leadership. Someone to follow."

"It's all right."

"No, it isn't. That's what the fucking nazis said. Just following orders."

"Don't get—come on. Don't do that."

"Okay, sorry. But still."

"We all had our moments out there we're not proud of." Sean fixes a gaze at Nathan until he looks up and locks eyes. A cab passes and sparks of light glint off Sean's pupils, reflect in Nathan's trembling tears pooled in the corners of his eyes. "All of us."

All other sound fades away. Sean's ears are filled with the rushing of the river over heavy rocks. He keeps his eyes on Nathan, his fists in balls. Nathan nods. The motion loosens tears that roll down his cheeks and drip from his sharp jawbone.

Being outside has taken on different meaning. Grady walks straight, the sidewalk offering no obstacles, no turns. No trees to step around. Above him is black night sky, a few willing stars poking through the darkness. Open and unobstructed, yet less visible.

The sounds are different, the smells. Bird calls replaced by voices in languages both familiar and as foreign as the birdsongs.

Grady walks because why go home? Nothing there. Since he returned he's realized how much nothing there is here. His survival is handed to him. He passes a small market, food enough for a year or more. Water trapped in bottles. Food sealed in plastic. The motivation for survival is gone. We're all walking in a straight line with no turns, no destination.

Nathalie has called him a few times, first looking for an apology, then offering one herself. He's ignored them.

He passes a couple of men under a street light, smoke drooling from their lips and carrying their words to him as he passes.

"Hey, man, looking for smoke? You need smoke?"

Grady ignores them even as a hot ball burns in his chest. Territory. He knows it is theirs, but he wants to make it his own. For no other reason than that he can. But he knows, he still knows enough of how to behave in this world stripped of its survival instinct. You can't do that.

Two blocks later and he sees a woman. She stands, blinking like a neon sign, offering up her body. Even *that* is offered up for the taking. Grady turns away from her, or maybe him. They hand us our food. Hand us our mates. What else is there left to fight for? The job? That's why we end up in glass skyscrapers fighting for territory, seeking out reward, looking to dominate. It's our instinct relocated. Put into steel boxes.

The job. It's where he has to put his effort. It's the only territory left to conquer. And it will be his.

A car cruises slowly by his side. He looks up and the woman is gone, vanished into the camouflage of bricks and mortar. The car is a police car. Grady keeps walking.

"You looking for something, buddy?"

The cop leans out the window, his partner driving slowly to match Grady's pace.

Grady ignores them.

"A neighborhood like this," the cop says, "people like you only come here looking for two things. Drugs and pussy."

Grady continues to walk straight. No obstacles.

The cop is annoyed. He's not used to being ignored.

"Hold up there, pal."

The car comes to a stop. Grady does not. The passenger cop is out and walking swiftly to catch up. The driver cop scrambles out, fumbling with his hat.

The cop puts a hand on Grady's elbow, stopping him. Grady feels the white hot ball in his chest again. This is not the cop's territory. He wants to think it is, but it is not. It is up for grabs.

"Hold on, buddy. Let's see some I.D."

Grady faces the cop, notices his gut hanging over his gun belt. The driver cop approaches behind him, boxing him in. Both acting like they own the street.

"Did I do something?" Grady asks.

"Yeah, you fucking blew me off."

"Maybe that's what he's here for," says the driver. "To get blown."

They laugh. The sound cuts. The ball heats up.

"Maybe you'll have luck with one of the he-shes down here, but with me you gotta show some fucking respect. And some I.D., so come on, pal."

"You keep saying that but you don't act like my pal."

The cops share a look. *Can you believe this guy?*

"You high, pal? Huh? You come down here for a little something-something? Maybe spark up as soon as you got your rock?"

They do not exhibit good leadership skills. They do not deserve this job. They did not earn this territory.

The driver cop steps closer to his partner. Grady sees his arms tense, ready to move. Ready for Grady to react. The cop eyeballs him for weapons.

"What's this?"

The driver cop reach for Grady's shirt. Grady tenses, his body a coiled rope. The cop tugs at his shirt.

"Is that blood?"

It is. Allison's blood. He didn't get much on him, considering. He should have changed his shirt, but he didn't.

"You hurt, pal?"

"No," he says. "Not me."

"Okay. Turn it around, buddy. Hands behind your—"

Grady chops with the side of his hand, catches the passenger cop in the neck. With his other hand he clamps on the wrist of the driver cop who is pinching the blood-stained section of shirt between his fingers.

Clutching at his throat, one cop staggers back, heel slipping off the curb, and falls into the street. A dog barks madly nearby.

The driver cop tries crossing his left arm across his body to reach for his gun. Grady spins him with the arm he controls, keeping him off balance and away from his weapon.

"Motherfucker," the cop says with a spray of saliva. They dance like this, twisting and pirouetting on the sidewalk, for half a minute. The cop on the ground is gagging, trying to force air in his lungs.

Grady shoves the cop against the car. When his back hits, the air *whuffs* out of his lungs. The gun is there. Grady can reach it. But men fight like men. They best each other with strength and cunning, not weapons. They dominate.

He spins the cop's arm and makes him punch his own face. It isn't hard, but humiliating. Grady drags him down the hood until his face smashes the plastic casing of the side mirror. With a grunt the cop goes limp for a second. More blood gets on Grady's shirt.

The passenger cop is almost pushed up to standing. Grady kicks at him, catches the top of his head, knocks him down again.

He's won the territory, but who would want it?

Grady turns and runs, fading into the same camouflage of bricks and mortar. The city swallows him. The dog continues to bark.

OUT THERE
DAY 10

LARA WOKE UP CRYING AGAIN. The group peeled itself apart like a giant creature emerging from a cocoon. Each night they seemed to fuse closer together while they slept. The caked-on dirt of their clothes, the foul smells from their bodies made them a part of the decay of the forest floor. They fit right in.

Ken most of all.

No one could deny it—he smelled the worst. And they knew it was because of his leg. He hadn't complained much. He said it had gone numb, only a dull throb at his knee where the sensation suddenly dropped off like the rest of his leg wasn't there.

It smelled like rot. Nobody wanted to discuss it.

Sean stood up and walked away to urinate. Water hadn't been a problem. The river provided as much as they could drink and the fast moving current gave them clean, clear water. Since Lara's discovery of the crayfish and Sean's foraging for grubs, their protein intake had been stable for the past few days.

The food seemed to do little for Lara's mood, though, which grew darker with each passing hour. She was quick to tears. Her talk became drained of hope. The first week she speculated and questioned when they would be rescued, now she questioned if they would be.

Maia did her best to keep her spirits up but much of this came in the form of 'tough love' pep talks where Sean could overhear her berating Lara for showing weakness. He doubted that did Lara any good.

That morning she stayed in the shelter, huddled in on herself and crying.

Sean moved through the woods, thinking about more foraging but taking a moment to be in his surroundings. Even with each person getting three cray-fish a day and a handful of grubs, plus the few remaining berries they could scrounge, they were still far under their normal calorie intake. Walking made him tire more easily, made tempers shorter. Sean had taken to walks alone to avoid Grady, who had a burst of anger to match each of Lara's crying jags.

They were both on edge in different ways. And Sean found it easiest to avoid them.

He stopped to regard a spider web strung between two trees. A sliver of sunlight caught it from behind and turned the drops of dew clinging to the silk into scat-tered diamonds. The spider, he thought, was doing the same thing they were. Living in the woods, trying to get along. Doing what he knew to do. But he was adapted for this environment. He could create beauty while hunting for food. He could create the tools he needed from his own body. He was self-sufficient in a way the humans were not.

Sean watched the light playing across the tiny sparkles on the silk. He wondered if these were the moments he would remember from this. If it would be only the hardships or would he be able to retain some of the beauty?

He wondered if he would be alive to recall any of it.

When he thought like that, like maybe they wouldn't make it out, he thought of Kerri. He wanted to make it work with her. He wanted to provide.

Each moment out here when he came up against a task he could not perform, another way he found he could not provide for himself or the group, he knew what Kerri saw when she looked at him. She saw him fail at getting a raise or a promotion, and in her eyes it was the same husband who couldn't catch a fish, who couldn't make a shelter any more stable than a leaning row of branches against a fallen log. She saw a man who couldn't find his way out to safety.

If he made it, he knew she would either have her worst fears about him confirmed or he could prove to her that he was capable of providing.

Overhead he heard a bird. He tilted his head up and saw the bird only a few branches up, sitting on a nest. The bird gave trilling calls that bounced off the surrounding trees and then faded. It stood, looked left and then right—then flew away leaving the empty nest.

Branches made a crude ladder to where the bird had been sitting. Sean thought of eggs. If he could bring back eggs to the group...

He started to climb.

"Budget cuts, that's the problem."

Three men in matching tan work pants, hiking boots and brown short sleeve shirts with RANGER patches over the breast followed a trail through the woods. Leading them was a man in a tie-dyed T-shirt, with a ponytail and a walking stick.

The second ranger in line behind the walking stick kept up a steady patter in his ear.

"You know how many we got for this whole parcel?" He didn't wait for an answer. "Three. For eight hundred sixty seven square miles." He scoffed and said, "Three," again like it was the lowest number you could possibly say.

"You got your government to thank for that," he went on. The man with the walking stick picked up his pace, trying to outrun the rant. "Bunch of bureaucrats who don't give a whip about the national parks."

"This is a state park," said the hippie guide.

"The money all comes from the same pipeline. And they went and shut off the spigot so they could hand out more tax breaks and sell off more land for mineral rights."

"Well, I'm not one to get into any sort of political debate. You're preaching to the choir on that one. All I want is to get our campers back."

The last ranger in line spoke up, "Three days late, you said?"

"Yes."

"I tell you what," the lead ranger said. "Our search and rescue capabilities have been severely compromised by the cuts. I wrote a letter to that son of a bitch senator last year and all I got back was some form letter thanking me for my input and God bless America and all that crap. I just about went down there myself and—"

"Holy shit."

They'd reached the river. The trail opened up where the crossing line was strung across the water, the campsite on the far side. The four men lined up on the riverbank.

The severed line from the rope walk snaked along in the water, endlessly slithering since the accident more than a week ago. They could see the tents and supplies on the other side in disarray. Two of the tents were torn with long shreds down the sides. Two others had collapsed.

A round tin container of food supplies was tipped over and empty.

"What the hell happened here?"

The guide from the tour company leaned on his walking stick.

"Bears, more than likely. Must have smelled the food." He scanned the riverbank left and right. "Doesn't make any sense why they didn't tree the food supplies, though. They know better than that."

"I don't see any bodies," said a ranger.

"Or blood," said another.

"Must have run off," said the lead ranger.

The guide tapped the remaining rope on the cross over with his stick.

"Weird that the rope walk is broken."

"Maybe they cut the line after they came back across so nothing could follow them?" one of the rangers said.

The lead ranger slapped him on the shoulder. "Bear couldn't cross on that rope, you idiot."

"A bear wouldn't need to," the guide said.

They kept staring at the decimated campsite. The rushing of the river filled the air.

"How many did you say there were?"

"Ten total, with the guides."

"That's three times as many people as I have to go look for them," the lead ranger said. He kicked a loose rock into the rushing water. "Goddamn budget cuts."

———

Grady noticed Sean wasn't around the shelter. He motioned to Nathan, who joined him at his side.

"I saw that possum again last night," Nathan said. "I think I counted four babies with it. All these little red glowing eyes in the dark." He gave a slight shudder. Grady ignored him.

"Let's do it now. Grab one."

Nathan looked around the campsite. Wes was there not too far off. Lara still inside sniffling, Maia off having a morning pee. Ken was on his back, eyes closed, looking ashen and weak next to the grey coals of the dormant fire.

"Yeah? Do it now?"

"Yeah. Let's go."

Grady seemed to like having an order obeyed. Nathan went to the shelter and pulled down one of the sleeping bags from the roof structure. Dead leaves and bits of soft branch fell in on Lara. She crawled out brushing dried leaves and pine needles from her hair.

"What happened?"

"Nothing, don't worry about it," Grady said.

"Worry about what?" Maia said as she entered camp.

"The roof caved in or something," Lara said. She squinted against the daylight, her eyes red and puffy.

"No, it didn't," Grady said. "We're just taking one of the sleeping bags."

"What for?"

"I'm making another shelter a few hundred yards upriver. It's a better spot but you guys don't want to leave here so, we're going on our own."

Nathan stood with the sleeping bag hanging limp in his hand.

"You can't take part of the shelter and leave," Maia said. Her tone was one she reserved for rude baristas and sales clerks.

"Why not? You guys don't want to leave and it's not like you have a monopoly on the supplies. We're only taking one."

Maia walked over to the shelter, stepping over Ken as she did. Ken opened his eyes and looked on, unfocused, at the discussion going on overhead.

"Now there's a big hole in the roof."

"So patch it up with some branches. Jesus fucking Christ, do I need to do everything for you?"

"You're not doing anything." Maia gestured to Nathan. "You're making him do it all."

"He wants to come with me because it's a better site and because this place is becoming untenable."

She mocked his vocabulary. "Untenable?"

"Look, you might not want to say it but this place stinks to high heaven. Nobody is going far enough away to take a piss or a shit, this many people and their B.O. is deeply unpleasant and let's be frank, Ken's leg smells like week old meat left out in the sun."

"Grady," Maia scolded.

Grady pointed to Ken who had no reaction, his face dull and blank. "He doesn't care. He doesn't even know."

"You can't take part of the shelter away."

"I can and I am." Grady stood on the highest ground of the clearing. He looked down on Maia and Lara, who stood behind her. He looked down on Wes who had drifted back toward the commotion. "You want to try to stop me?"

Grady put a hand on his front pocket where his knife sat clipped. Nobody spoke or moved, the forest around them went on about its day.

"We're only taking one," Nathan said.

Grady kept his eyes on Maia. "Go ahead and go, Nathan. I'll catch up."

Nathan started to move, hesitated, then marched upriver near the bank, dragging the sleeping bag behind him.

"You want to take an inventory, Maia? Make sure we don't take more than our fair share? 'Cause I'll tell you right now, I'm also taking coals from the fire. You gonna deny me that, too?"

"I really don't think we should split up," Lara said.

Grady locked gaze with her. "And I really don't give a shit what you think."

She began to weep again. She fell into Maia and clung to her back, sobbing.

"Grady, you're an asshole."

"No, Maia, I'm a leader. Something you'll never be."

"Fuck you."

"I bet you'd like that, wouldn't you?" He turned and started walking the way Nathan went. He nearly bumped into Sean coming back to camp.

"I got eggs," he said proudly.

Grady chuckled. "Eggs?"

Sean held out a hand with three tiny eggs, each only slightly bigger than his thumb in pale brown shells with freckles on them.

"Better than grubs, right?"

"How the fuck are you gonna cook them?"

Sean paused. He didn't know. Everything they'd been eating since they made fire had been on a skewer. Grubs, crayfish, even mushrooms. Eggs, though...

"Even if we just swallow them like *Rocky*."

"Like *Rocky*?" Grady mocked.

Sean could tell he'd walked into more than just a discussion about eggs.

"What's going on?"

"Nothing. I want to see you eat one of the eggs, *Rocky*-style. Go on."

Maia stroked Lara's hair. "Grady and Nathan are making their own camp and taking some of our stuff with them."

"What?"

"Go ahead, Rocky," Grady said, goading him. "Drink up."

On the spot, Sean didn't know what to do. He didn't see Nathan around, the others looked weak and defeated.

"Where are you going?"

"Wouldn't you like to know?" Grady said.

"We shouldn't split up."

"That's what she said." Grady pointed to Lara. "You guys are so much alike."

Sean felt the barbed insult sting. It felt like talking to

his wife. He wasn't man enough. He wasn't a provider enough.

"So go on, Rocky Balboa. Drink a raw egg."

Sean thought about hurling the eggs at Grady's face, seeing them crack and slide down. But it was food. Food not to be wasted. He thought there must be some way divide the three small eggs evenly, but now with two fewer team members it would be easier. But with Grady taunting him, he needed to swallow one by himself, give the other two away.

Sean leaned his head back, took an egg in his fingers, opened his mouth and tapped the shell against his teeth. The shell broke, dropping tiny fragments into his mouth. He didn't give Grady the satisfaction of spitting them out.

But nothing flowed. No gooey protein dripped out, clear surrounding and yellow yolk. The egg kept its shape, but bits of shell continued to fall away.

Sean took his hand away so he could see the egg. Grady was already laughing. In his hand was a tiny oval of wet feathers. A baby chick, still too small to break out. Somewhere between an embryo and a bird.

Why hadn't he thought of that? These weren't eggs on a farm. This was nature with real, fertilized eggs.

Sean nearly gagged.

Grady's laugh reverberated off the trees.

"You don't even know how to fucking harvest an egg."

"Shut up, Grady," Maia said. "If you're gonna go, then go."

They could hear Grady's laughter long after he disappeared into the woods.

That night they moved in close to each other, bodies near to one another for heat, missing the other two.

Lara had finally fallen asleep out of sheer exhaustion. She'd spent most of the day crying on and off. At one point Sean reminded her to drink more since she was losing so much fluid. Holding a conversation with her was becoming more difficult.

Ken had been slowly moved farther out of the covering due to his smell. They extended the roof of branches to shelter him, but it amounted to nothing more than a drape of dying leaves resting over his sleeping form. It reminded Sean of a funeral pyre awaiting a match.

Sean lay there thinking he should try to wash his clothes in the river tomorrow. Even a simple rinsing was better than nothing. He scratched at the lengthening whiskers on his cheeks. He'd never had anything he could describe as a beard before, and he was getting close. Grady already looked like a junior lumberjack and Nathan and Wes each had dense, dark growth. Sean suffered from his Asian heritage and was slower to fill in a full set of whiskers.

Next to him Maia stirred.

"You awake?" she whispered.

"Yeah."

Maia checked around them to see the others were asleep.

"I don't want to go to sleep."

"Why not?"

"I'm afraid to dream. I keep picturing what's going to

happen to us. I keep seeing helicopters lifting out dead bodies."

"That won't happen."

Maia turned on her side to face him.

"I'm not Lara. You don't have to bullshit me."

Sean looked her in the eye. "I think we're going to get rescued. Any day now. They have to be out looking for us."

"How long do they look before they give up?"

Sean didn't want to face these questions himself. He didn't know what to say when he had to attempt to answer them for someone else.

"I don't know."

She set a hand on his.

"Thanks for being honest."

"If I'm really honest, I think Grady is gonna kill me before the forest does."

"He's a little intense, huh?"

"I swear I think he's starting to like it out here."

"That's scary."

She smiled. Sean's eyes adjusted to the darkness enough to see tiny beads of light shine off her teeth.

"If we don't..."

"We can't think that way. They say a huge percentage of survival is mental. It's about not giving up."

"This isn't the office, Sean. You don't need to do data analysis. We might not make it."

He didn't want to argue so he let her speak. He felt she was getting something off her chest. Maybe that was as healthy as keeping hope alive.

"If we don't," she continued, then paused.

"What?"

She kept her eyes on his, looked like she might say something. She leaned forward and kissed him. Sean pushed her back.

"What are you doing?"

"It's just...we might not make it, so—"

"I'm married."

"What if none of that matters anymore?"

She leaned forward again. He let her in closer this time and their lips met. He waited, then pushed her away again.

"I can't. This is—this is nuts."

He threw glances around to see if Lara or Wes were awake.

"I need a little closeness. A little intimacy, I guess. I'm scared, Sean."

"Me, too."

They held hands, clutching tight.

"I don't have anyone at home."

"Maia, we're going to get out of this. We're all going to have a chance to get back home and start over."

He knew he was convincing himself, not her.

"This is not going to defeat us. We've made it this far."

She pushed into him, her lips crushing his. She leaned on him, pinning his shoulders down. Sean pushed up on her, but found his arms weaker than they ever had been. He twisted his face away from her kiss.

"Maia, I can't."

She began to cry. Not mournful sobs like Lara. Angry tears.

"You can. You won't. You won't let someone else feel

what they need to feel. You won't put anyone else's needs in front of your own."

"Maia, that's crazy. It's—"

"I'm crazy now?"

Her voice rose. Behind him, Wes stirred. Sean slid toward the opening of the shelter.

"I'm going to put more wood on the fire."

"Fuck you, Sean."

Maia turned her back on him. He left the shelter, crawling over Ken as he went.

Out in the darkness of the woods he walked away, breathing in the night air. The wind swirled a bit, a cool tinge to the current. Above him the canopy of trees shook their leaves like arms waving for help.

He heard a sound. The familiar cracking of tiny branches, the crunch of dry leaves. To his left, about ten feet above on a branch, he saw two shiny coins of eyes looking down on him. The possum that they had seen on and off for days. It watched him, tracking his movements. He stood twenty feet from it, wondering what it thought of the stranger in his home.

He heard the claws on the bark as it climbed higher into the tree. Once the tiny reflectors of his eyes turned away, it became invisible to Sean. Only the sound of his climb betrayed his presence there. Much farther away he swore he heard a wolf howl.

Sean gathered an armload of wood, hoping Maia would be asleep by the time he got back to the shelter. With Grady and Nathan gone there was space now for him to sleep behind Wes, putting a body between him and Maia.

The wind picked up and the sound of the leaves blowing overhead rivaled the rushing of the river. That night, for the first time, the rains came. Grady had been right. The depression in the earth where they made their shelter acted like a bowl. By two a.m., they were all awake and trying to fashion the roof into umbrellas to hold off the rain. There would be no more sleep that night.

BACK HOME

KERRI HAS MOVED OUT. She left no note.

When Sean responded to Nathan's text and left, she packed some things—enough to get by—and left. He doesn't know if he is supposed to follow her. To find her and ask for her back. To make promises and lies. He doesn't leave. Sean sits on the couch and stares at the blank TV screen, power off, seeing a ghost of his own reflection in the flat black surface.

In truth, it takes him nearly half an hour to realize she's left after he gets home. He thinks she has simply retreated upstairs and shut herself in. When he goes up to change his clothes for another night on the couch, he discovers she is gone.

Maybe it's for the best. He can't give her what she needs. By knowing that and seeing how clearly he has failed her, he also knows she can't give him what he needs. He feels no anger. Not now. He knows it may come later. When she asks for too much in a divorce. When she wants half of everything he has worked for. Half of what wasn't enough in whole for her.

If she had left him before he went on the retreat, would he have made it? Would he have slipped under the water of the river and not fought for breath?

They all followed beacons out there, something pulling them home. Sean thinks so anyway. Except maybe Lara, which is why she had such a hard time. Grady and Maia focused on the job. The rewards awaiting them when they go back. Ken had a husband to keep him going when the pain tried to crush him down.

Wes, Sean doesn't know. He wants to know more about Wes. He needs to know in that moment. What light did he chase? And Nathan. Not his parents. They seem to annoy him. Not the job. He never thought he could get it. What drove him, or was he pulled behind Grady in his wake?

He gets out his phone, sends a text to Wes.

WHAT GOT YOU THROUGH IT? WHAT WERE YOU LIVING FOR?

He texts Maia. Nathan. He doesn't text Grady. He sits in the dark to wait for a response.

Maia writes back right away.

WHAT DO YOU MEAN?

Sean: OUT THERE. WHAT WAS HERE THAT KEPT YOU GOING? WHAT WAS YOUR LIGHTHOUSE?

Maia: NOT GIVING UP. NOT BEING DEFEATED.

Sean: STRONG.

Maia: Bet your ass.

He knows she works hard at the persona. He knows there are cracks under the veneer. There have to be. Everyone has them. Even stone gets worn down by the river over time.

Sean: My wife left.

Maia: I'm coming over.

Wes reads Sean's text from the floor. He wanted to reach the bed, but hasn't made it. He looks at the tumbler tipped over on the carpet. No spill. Nothing left to spill. His last one, his nightcap from the lobby bar. Not supposed to bring the glass upstairs, but no one noticed.

Nobody recognized him in the bar. He drank there, anyway. Bought his own. Came back to the hotel, company dime. One more, then upstairs.

Now he's on the carpet, three feet shy of the bed. Good enough. Been in worse places for a night. He smiles, then laughs. He looks at the text again.

What got you through it? What were you living for?

His laughter stops. The smile slides off his face like dripping paint. His rebuilt life is his answer. Everything he constructed out of scraps and rubble from a life he bulldozed down, or nearly did. He saved it before the final brick fell. He built it back stronger, he thinks, and taller.

Built trust back stone by stone. Built responsibility back board by board. He is his own architect. He lives in his own construction.

That's why he can't answer Sean. Why he can't say it out loud or type the words. Everything that kept him alive out there he has torn down again back here. The rope he pulled to climb out of the deepest well has been knotted into a noose by his own hand. He knows he has to unknot the rope.

But tomorrow. Tomorrow. Right now, the carpet will do.

———

Sean hears the knock. The room is still dark. He thinks it might be Kerri, but then why would she knock. It's Maia, here to help. Help he didn't ask for. Or did he?

He answers the door.

"You didn't have to come."

"We said we'd support each other."

"Still. You didn't have to come."

"Did anyone else?"

Sean hangs his head and lets her in.

"I saw Nathan earlier," he says. "He's having a hard time keeping things to himself."

"Like what, he might tell the police?"

"It seems like he might. I don't know. I talked him down." Sean moves past her. "Can I get you something to drink?"

"Wine?"

"Sure."

He goes to the kitchen where he knows there is an open bottle of white in the fridge.

"How are you doing, Sean?"

"I'm not thinking of telling if that's what you mean."

"No. I mean your wife moved out on you. And now. I mean, that's shitty."

"It wasn't only about now. It's been coming."

"Yeah, I could tell. Still, though."

Sean hands her a glass.

"None for you?"

"No."

He sits on the couch. She sits next to him and sips. The house feels like an empty cave waiting for the bears to return for hibernation. Kerri's only been gone for a few hours, only took a few things, but the house feels like the roof has fallen in.

"I was thinking of skylights," he says.

"In here?"

"Upstairs. In the bedrooms. I think I started to like seeing the stars while I slept. Is that weird?"

"No. I liked it, too. You won't see many stars here, though."

"No, I guess not."

"Already moving on, huh?"

"No. What do you mean? You think she won't come back?"

"Well, you're already redecorating." She sets her wine glass down on the coffee table.

"I was saying I thought about it."

"And no, I don't think she's coming back. Do you?"

"She didn't take all her stuff."

Maia examines the room. "Did you want her to call a moving van in the middle of the night?"

"No. But...maybe she'll come back."

"Maybe is a big word. Like maybe Nathan will tell."

"I think he's all right now. He needs to adjust."

Maia drops the shoes off her feet, slips her legs under her on the couch.

"Maybe I'll tell."

She says it like a threat on a soap opera. Sultry and with a dare to talk her out of it.

"I don't think you will."

"What if I told you I signed a book contract?"

"A book about what happened?"

"What if I said I was going to tell everything?"

"Everything?"

"It doesn't have to be everything."

Maia slides a finger along Sean's arm. He feels gooseflesh crawl alongside her nail as it carves a line. His bones are still close to the surface, his face still gaunt. Maia looks better but he knows she hides it well. He can see in her collar bones the sunken wells on either side of her neck. It's only been a few days and she is still regaining lost weight. Readjusting to the real world.

"I can leave stuff out," she says. "We can make a deal."

"Did you really sign a book deal?"

"I'm going to write it and it's going to be the record of what went on out there. People will treat it like it is carved in stone."

"Maia I—that's surprising to me."

"You could convince me to leave some things out. So convince me already."

She pulls her shoulders back, opening herself to him. Sean doesn't know what to do.

"Sean," she says, getting annoyed. "You know what this is."

"What is it?"

"Unfinished business." She unbuttons the top of her shirt.

Sean can see it now. She doesn't want him, she wants control of him. She wants to be his boss. If she gets the promotion she will give him orders. She's already doing it. This is a power play.

"Maia."

"Your call, Sean. I have plenty of story to tell without you in it. I mean, of course you'll be there, but maybe you don't have to—"

"What do you want?"

"Oh, come on Sean. Did she keep you that hard up that you don't even know when a woman wants to fuck you anymore?"

Kerri has a key. Kerri could come home. Kerri could get more than half. He doesn't want to, but there's a lot he doesn't want right now. He doesn't want Maia to write that book. But she will. He can scrub his part of the story clean. Can anyone, really, though?

She leans into him, her mouth on his. She lifts his hand and puts it on her breast. He doesn't know what to do. The water is rising around him, sweeping him away. He fights to move in his own direction, but he is swimming against the current.

Feeling his body still stiff and hesitant, Maia breaks the kiss.

"Come on, Sean. The bitch isn't coming back, and she's not the one you should be worried about."

Sean is pulled downriver, gasping for air.

OUT THERE
DAY 11

GRADY AND NATHAN made a passable covering for their first night. When the other group came upon them they were reinforcing the roof, putting in stronger branches to build up walls.

"Well, well," Grady said, straightening up from his work.

He was stronger somehow. Less haggard and worn than the rest of them who looked like last night had stripped another ten pounds from them. Lara had been wearing hunched shoulders and puffy eyes since the first day, but now her entire body looked drenched in her tears. Maia walked defiant, but shivering under her skin which showed in ripples like tiny tremors of weakness. Wes stared at the high ground and thick standing trees of the new shelter area with envious eyes. And Sean shuffle stepped closer, his body trying to stop him from giving in to Grady.

"How'd you all sleep last night?"

Grady's grin showed predator teeth. Nathan

continued to work as if a job foreman would dock his pay if he slowed.

"It's ridiculous for us to be split up," Sean said.

"You mean your camp sucks and you want to come to mine."

"I mean we're stronger together."

Grady peered behind them. "Together, huh? I see you didn't bring your mascot."

"Ken's too weak to travel for no good reason," Maia said.

"So you want to be here, is that it?"

"I want to go home," Lara said, then started to cry.

Grady rolled his eyes to the sky. "Well, first things first, none of that shit."

Lara tried to stop the sobs. Wes put an arm around her shoulder to quiet her.

Grady leaned on the thick branch in his hand. He stood on a bump in the ground slightly higher than the others. They'd come pleading, if not with their words, then in their bodies and damp clothes. Behind their eyes they begged for rescue. To be saved began to mean less than being pulled out of the forest, it meant not enduring another night in the rain. It meant not dividing the group and feeling like a shattered glass.

"A few rules," Grady said. "This whole thing has lacked leadership. We need someone calling the shots and making decisions. That's me."

He stared down the group, waiting for dissent. He got silence.

"You understand that and things will go a lot smoother. We'll have a schedule, jobs, responsibilities. You do them and you eat. You don't, and you go hungry.

Food is the only currency we have so that's your paycheck."

"Grady," Sean said. "You don't have to be so—"

"If you got a problem with it, your crap little camp is still back there. Go bunk with Ken until he kicks off. You want to stay here, you accept my terms."

"I'm saying we can all make decisions about what—"

"You made your decision. Where did it get you? Soaking wet. Look at you. You look like a bunch of wet dogs. I wouldn't slow my car if I saw you crossing the street. I'm offering you shelter. I don't have to. Take it or not. Fuck if I care."

Wes stepped forward with Lara in the crook of his arm.

"Can we get her next to the fire? She's freezing."

Grady waved them on. "Go ahead. Plenty of heat to share."

He gave granite eyes to Sean and Maia. He reveled in the moment, the numbers tipping in his favor. Sean exhaled deeply through his nose.

"We have to go get Ken and figure out how to move him up here."

"You have to get the rest of the sleeping bags and supplies, too. All those packs, what rope is left. There's a break in the bushes for water up here closer. I haven't seen any crayfish so we'll need to keep making the trek down there for those, but I bet if we look close we can find some other food sources close by."

Nathan had never stopped working.

"Fine." Maia said the word hard, like a hurled rock.

"Let's get Ken and bring him up here," Sean said.

"Okay," Grady said, stepping off his taller pitch of

earth. "One quick thing." He brought the branch around and swung hard at Sean. It caught him in the chest, emptying his lungs and putting him on the ground. The others flinched but did not step in to help. Nathan kept working on the roof.

Grady stood over Sean. "That's the last goddamn time you question me."

He kicked dead pine needles up as he stepped away from Sean, piercing his face. Sean fought for air. He felt like he was back in the river.

They brought Ken up to the new campsite using a sleeping bag like a stretcher. The first time they walked between camps it didn't seem that far, but with Ken in tow the uphill climb felt like miles.

They were farther from the river now, but could still hear it. The shelter had grown twice the size since that morning, and now that the sun was setting, they all looked forward to a warmer, dryer night inside. Clouds dotted the sky and wind gusted but no one could tell if it would rain or not.

Grady passed out assignments. Wes on thick branches for the structure. Sean on firewood.

"Lara, you and Maia should take whatever clothes we have down to the river and wash them. It's warm enough, guys who are working you can strip your shirts off."

He began to pull his dark stained shirt over his head.

"What the fuck, Grady?" Maia said. "Doing the laundry?"

Shirtless he stared at her. He'd lost weight. They all had. He maintained an athlete's build though, somehow making the isolation and hardship work for him. He stood still, letting them remember the lesson he'd given to Sean. He waited her out until Maia's anger was redirected into her work.

Sean returned with an armload of mid-sized sticks for the fire.

Four sturdy trees formed the back wall of the shelter. Sean had to admit it was an ideal setting. Nature had done most of the work for them. When they arrived with Ken he asked to be leaned against a tree, sitting. He complained of back pain. Sean lifted his shirt to check and found it red and angry with sores. He'd been on his back too long, the wet ground seeping in and letting bacteria fester. He needed medical help. He needed it a long time ago.

During his transport he hadn't cried out in pain. He grunted, moaned and sucked air between his teeth, but the sharp pains had ended when all feeling left his leg.

"We should check it out," Sean said. "Just to see."

The unspoken words in the traded looks between the others were: *But what can we do if it's bad? It's going to be bad. I don't want to see how bad it is.*

Sean asked if he could roll Ken's pant leg up.

"I can't feel much down there, anyway. I wouldn't be surprised if you found nothing at all. Just a big blank space."

"Do you need something to bite down on or anything?"

"Nah. I'll be all right."

Ken gripped the sleeping bag in his fists while Sean gently rolled his pant leg up.

The leg didn't look like flesh. Grey on top, dark wine stains on the bottom. Pooled blood. Blood that wasn't flowing any more. And the smell. Without a word, Sean rolled the pants back down.

"Not good, is it?" Ken asked.

"You need a doctor. But we knew that."

"Who ever heard of dying from a broken leg?"

"You're not dying."

"Bet you wish you had a mirror to say that into."

They hadn't had time to forage much. Dinner was a few mushrooms and some leaves. They took turns walking single file to the water's edge, carving a trail as they went. Grady felt like an Indian chief leading his tribe.

At dusk Grady was fifty yards from camp gathering stones for the fire pit. He wanted to build it out to have a separate fire for warmth and one for cooking. He heard movement. He turned to see the neighborhood possum staring at him with beady eyes. He froze and realized the possum had, too. Curious, maybe a little less frightened than the first time he'd spied on the intruders, the possum went still in hopes that he could avoid being seen. But Grady already clocked him on a branch about ten feet off the forest floor.

The animal was the size of a small dog or a very fat cat. Thirty pounds at least, he figured.

In his hand was a rock filling his palm, his fingers wrapped around it like a baseball. He took a small step forward, careful not to stir the noisy ground cover. The possum stayed still. Grady took another step. He was on the mound and the possum at home plate, maybe closer. He took two more steps. The animal's eyes reflected what little light was left breaking through the trees.

His pockets held two more rocks, but Grady knew if he missed he wouldn't get a second chance. He drew his arm back, tried to remember high school fastball coaching. He threw the rock and ran after it as soon as it released.

The rock struck the possum on its shoulder, narrowly missing its head. But it was stunned. It fell from the branch. Grady was moving at full speed, his hand snatching the knife from his pocket. He thumbed it open and landed on the animal with the blade out like a claw.

The knife plunged into the base of the possum's skull and Grady felt warm blood flow over his hand. He leaned over the top of the animal, his weight holding it down as it thrashed twice and then went still. Grady felt the body heat on his chest. He felt the last breath go out of the animal under his weight.

His own heart pumped against his ribcage. Adrenaline flowed. He stood, lifting the possum by the knife blade and holding his prize in front of him. Lines of blood like tears flowed down his wrist.

Grady howled into the fading light.

"Holy shit, dude." Nathan smiled, wide-eyed at the prize carried before Grady.

Grady held out the catch for everyone to see and to marvel at.

"Is that what that yell was about?"

"A hunter should be allowed to celebrate his kill."

"Oh my God," Maia said, practically drooling.

"That's so much meat," Wes said.

"We should ration it," Sean said.

Grady side-eyed him. Not his place to make that call.

"If you think so, Grady." The words tasted bitter in Sean's mouth.

"Get some skewers ready. We'll see how much bounty this guy has to offer."

Grady set the possum down and pulled the knife out. Drops of blood flung off the blade and dotted his face. He went to work skinning the animal. The others watched as he tore into the flesh, slit it down the middle, spilled guts on the ground. He worked sloppily, with no regard to how much mess he spread around. He seemed to revel in the blood.

"Maybe we can use some of what we're not going to eat as fish bait," Ken offered. He was sitting up straighter at the proposition of meat on the table.

"What do you mean what we don't eat? We're using all of this animal."

"I meant like the heart or something."

Grady reached into the pile of organs on the ground, plucked out the heart like he was picking fruit. He held it between his thumb and two forefingers, about the size of a large strawberry. Looking Ken in the eye Grady put it in his mouth and let blood drip from his chin.

Nobody said a word. Grady chewed, though it was clearly tough. He didn't show any signs of stopping or gagging. He forced the heart down his throat and drew a deep breath before continuing on his butchery.

BACK HOME

TALK at the office is all about Allison and her tragic assault. This bigger story has pushed Grady's temper tantrum to second page news.

When he arrives back at work the office is murmuring like birds chattering in the trees. He bypasses his old office, heads straight for Allison's.

He stops at the desk of her assistant, Kelsey.

"Until we work out this office situation with my old space and the new guy, I'll be setting up in here."

He moves past her.

"I don't think—"

"This is what Allison and I talked about on my way out yesterday." Grady sets down his shoulder bag on her glass topped desk. He turns back to Kelsey. "It's awful, isn't it? Do they have any leads on who did it?"

The power of office gossip distracts her like a shiny object.

"No. They took her wallet, though."

"Probably some drug addict."

"She's still in the ICU."

"Oh, my God," Grady says. "Did we send her flowers?"

"Um, no. I don't think so."

"We should do that. Can you coordinate a bouquet gets sent to her room? I know she loves tulips."

Habit kicks in and Kelsey takes the order. She has a task now. A task for her real boss and a task that makes her feel like she's doing something.

Grady doesn't know that Allison likes tulips. He doesn't know anything about her flower preferences, when her birthday is, the real color of her hair if she doesn't keep her monthly appointments at her two-hundred-dollar-a-pop salon. He does know where her wallet is. It's under three feet of half-eaten Italian food behind an Olive Garden six miles from where Allison got attacked.

He turns back to her office, lets the door glide shut behind him.

Territory. You want your own? Move camp. Set up somewhere new. Act like you belong.

"I'm not going in today," Maia says.

Sean in on the couch. She stands in front of the coffee machine waiting for a fresh cup. He feels snakes inside him. Coils of confusion and anger, fanged with shame. He expects Kerri to come in any second for the rest of her belongings.

"I'm going to ask for a sabbatical," she says. "They can't deny it, right? That's what you're on, right? Still getting paid." She doesn't wait for him to answer. "I'll collect a paycheck the whole time I'm writing the book and then I won't need the job once it comes out. I'm not allowed to discuss the payday, but it's gonna be huge."

She brings her coffee into the living room, steam rises from the rim of the cup.

"Will you relax?" she says. "You're good. I'll paint you like a little saint. Hard working, never-say-die attitude."

"Don't you think Grady is the one you need to worry about?" He finally looks her way. "Or are you gonna make the same deal with him?"

"Grady? Ew. No. He's too crazy."

"And I'm not?"

"We all did things we didn't think we were going to do. We all did things to make it out there."

"And last night? In case you didn't notice, we're not out there anymore."

"You liked it." She smiles as she sips.

"Maia, if you write that book—"

"I'm going to write it."

"When you write that book, Grady won't let it go. Nobody will. Did you even ask Nathan? Wes?"

"I'll deal with it. There are ways to tell a good story, one people will still want to read without, y'know, all the other stuff."

"What about one people will believe?"

"People believe us now. All I have to do is get it on paper."

She sips again, the steam curling around her face like smoke from the cauldron of a wicked witch.

"So what have you been doing with your days off?"

"Nothing yet." He pauses, wonders if he should say

what he's thinking. "I might go volunteer some place. Find a soup kitchen or something."

Maia goes wide-eyed as she looks at him over her coffee. "Really?"

"Yeah. I just feel like I need to, I don't know, balance the scales or something."

"Alleviate the guilt. I get it."

"No, it's not guilt. It's...it's..."

He knows what it is, and she named it.

"I think that's good. It's nice."

It's not enough, he thinks. It will never be enough.

A thin file folder slaps the desk in front of Detective Kettner like an open palm across the cheek.

"They found two of your bodies."

Kettner turns his neck away from his paperwork so fast his neck jolts with pain.

"They did?"

"Floated down to the reservoir," Morris says. He's holding a half-eaten danish in one hand. Fingerprints of icing are on the outside of the folder.

Kettner snatches up the file, quickly scans the one page report and flips to the photos.

"The girl guide and one of the company people?"

"Yeah," Morris says. "Ron something. And Karina. Two out of five."

"That's a step." Kettner flips through three pictures each of Karina and Ron, their bloated bodies look like rubber, clothes mostly torn off from their trip down-river. "Ended up right where they were supposed to, huh?"

"Yep. End of the line." Morris bites his danish.

Kettner flips back to the M.E.'s summary report on page one.

"Take a look at the notes on her," Morris says around a mouthful of food.

Kettner studies closer. "What?"

"His is death by drowning. Hers, not so much." Morris has a sly smile on his face. He knows his partner wanted something like this. Kettner goes back to her photo.

"Look at her neck," Morris says, swallowing. "Ligature marks consistent with strangulation."

"I'll be damned."

"Nobody mentioned that in their statements, did they?"

Kettner studies the photo of Karina. The redness has faded into a mottled purple, but he can see the bruises and lines around her neck. Ron has contusions on his head and his torso that make sense from bouncing off a bed of rocks for twelve miles down to the reservoir. He had water in his lungs consistent with drowning.

Karina has contusions, as well, and some water in her lungs, but not the same as someone whose primary cause of death is drowning. And her eyes. Bloodshot, burst vessels. More signs of strangulation. But how? And who?

Morris finishes his danish. "Kinda makes you want to see the other three now, doesn't it?"

"I thought finding them was supposed to bring closure and wrap up this case."

"Hey, I'll admit when you're right and I'm wrong." Morris gives a broad smile to his partner.

"Music to my ears."

"The music to your ears was the word strangulation, you sick bastard."

Kettner turns back to the file. "Yeah, but combine it with your words and it's a goddamn symphony."

OUT THERE
DAY 12

KEN WOKE WITH A FEVER. He rolled side to side on his back, moving as if he was on a boat in high winds, moaning like creaking floorboards. Sweat dripped off his forehead, off the tip of his nose. Lara served him water from the lone plastic bottle they had.

The others stood out of earshot.

"Something's gotta be done about it," Grady said.

"Do you think the move made it worse?" Maia asked.

Nobody knew. Head shakes all around.

"What can we do?" Sean asked.

Nathan ran a hand through his greasy hair. "We need to know what the problem is. Is it just a fever or does it have to do with his leg?"

"I looked at it," Sean said. "And it's bad."

"If it's dead," Grady said. "It could be poisoning his blood."

"Could be gangrene. I don't know what that looks like, though."

"That's because none of us is a doctor," Maia said. "Which is why we should wait until we get out of here."

Sean could see Ken writhing in the distance over Maia's shoulder.

"What if we don't have time?"

Grady folded his arms. "It has to come off."

"His leg?" Wes said.

Grady nodded. The others said nothing. What could they say? It was crazy.

"We don't have a way to do that," Sean said. "Even if we wanted to."

Grady unfolded the knife from his pocket, held it out to the group.

"That's not exactly surgical equipment," Maia said.

"It's all we have and it'll have to do," Grady said.

"Hold on, hold on, hold on." Wes searched for words to argue. "You want to amputate someone's leg outdoors with no anesthetic and no antibiotics and the only tool you have is a pocket knife?"

Grady didn't close the knife as he spoke firmly. "Do I want to? No. Do I think he's gonna die if we don't? Yes."

Maia stepped out of the circle. "He'll die if we do."

"He might."

"This is fucking nuts." Wes also stepped away from the circle.

"I'm saying we do it," Grady said.

"Let's wait," Sean said. "He's only been like this for today. Let's wait a little while, okay?"

Grady's nostrils flared, the knife wavered in his hand. He exhaled. "Fine. We'll see how he is later today."

Grady thumbed the knife shut and walked away.

Maia stepped next to Sean.

"He's out of his goddamn mind."

"I hate to say it, but he might be right."

Nathan finally spoke up. "It might kill him if we let it go unattended."

"There's tending to it and then there's cutting it off."

"I think Grady knows what's best."

Nathan turned and followed Grady.

"Great. Now's he's out of his goddamn mind, too." Maia looked at Sean. "And I'm starting to worry about you."

They ate the rest of the possum around noon, saving a few small scraps for dinner that night. They'd charred the meat well done over the open fire. Nobody flinched at the idea of eating a rodent they all despised. The meat was chewy and tasted metallic, but they savored it.

Maia brought back three more crayfish from the river, saying they seemed to have moved on or else they'd eaten them all. They'd need to find a new source.

"I saw babies with that possum. They're out there and they're not far," Wes said.

"How do we find them?"

"I don't know. Maybe they'll come out looking for her. We can set a trap."

"Great," Sean said. "Do you know how to make one?"

Wes was quiet.

Lara picked clothes off a low branch where she'd hung them to dry. She'd gone through all the clothes and washed everything, letting people rotate into the cleaner reserve clothes from the packs. Maia refused to do any washing, though she went with Lara to the river and helped her lay out the wet clothes on the branches.

Saving her own for last, Lara stripped off her shirt and stood by the river in the sports bra she'd worn since day one. Maia watched her dip her shirt in the river and then slap it on a rock by the shore the way she'd seen villagers in Africa do it.

Lara's ribs were sharply visible, her bones jutted up above the waistline of her pants. Maia noticed a small tattoo of a butterfly on her right shoulder blade.

"Drunk night in college?"

Lara looked over her shoulder at Maia. "Huh?"

"Your tattoo."

"Oh." Lara reached back and touched it. "I forget about it."

"I never got any. Guess I was always studying in school."

"I got it after school. My boyfriend at the time wanted one so I went with him. He kinda talked me into it. I knew my dad would be pissed."

"Did he get the same one?"

"No, he got a skull with a snake crawling out of its mouth. We didn't last long after that."

Maia smiled. "At least you have that to remember him by."

Lara's face went dark. She was always on the verge of tears or a bigger breakdown. Maia thought she'd been giving her a moment of lightness, but she saw now she might have pushed her into one of her bouts of depression.

"It's a reminder, all right. It reminds me how easily I'm pushed to do things I don't want to do." When she looked up Maia saw tears brimming in her eyes. "Like this trip. This goddamn trip. I never wanted to be here. I never wanted to come."

"I'm sorry, Lara, I didn't mean to upset you."

"It's not you, it's me. I let people manipulate me. I give in and roll over. I wish I had your strength."

"You do." Maia stood and went to her at the riverbank. "You've made it out here this many days." Maia realized she had no idea how long they'd been out there.

"This is making it?" Lara slapped at her protruding ribs. She whacked the shirt against a rock, then threw it down to the dirt. "I'm dying out here doing someone else's laundry."

Maia was torn. She normally had no patience for anyone else's weakness, especially another woman. But she knew Lara needed something out here. She needed a lifeline, a glimmer of hope. But Maia had none to give.

By early afternoon Ken had vomited up his possum and water.

The group formed another circle and Grady drew the knife again.

"We need to do it."

"It's crazy," Maia said.

Nathan raised his hand. "I vote yes."

"It's not a vote," Grady said.

Sean tried to put steel in his voice. "Ask him."

Grady cocked an eyebrow.

"Ask Ken what he wants us to do. We'll all go with whatever he wants. It's his body. His life."

A moment of silence hung dark in the circle like the oncoming night. Grady folded the knife and said, "Fine."

They stood around Ken, who lay still on the ground. Sean thought it looked like they were preparing for a human sacrifice, and it might turn into one. The chances of doing this without a major problem were so small he couldn't even figure the odds.

So the rest of the group could see, Sean started to roll Ken's pant leg up to expose the injured leg. As he worked slowly, Grady stepped over him and put the knife inside the pant leg, pulled his arm up and out, cutting the fabric from cuff to knee. Sean held his tongue and he pulled back the two flaps of fabric.

Lara looked away. Nathan and Wes both covered their noses from the smell. Sean stood back. It looked worse than before. Darker. Dead.

"Take it off," Ken said. "Just do it."

Grady turned to the group with a smug satisfaction. "Here we go."

Grady gave the orders. They used a length of rope to tie off Ken's leg above the knee. They pulled it tight, cutting off as much blood flow as possible.

Sean and Wes stoked the fire and kept wood on hand. Grady wanted high, hot flames. He heated the blade over the fire.

"This will sterilize it and I'll need it to seal off the wound when I'm done."

"But we don't have any needle or thread to sew him up," Maia said.

"That's why I need the heat. The heated blade will cauterize it."

"You're going to burn it shut?"

"You got a better idea?"

She had no answer. The fire crackled and rose as Sean fanned the flames.

"The fish hook," she said. "That's like a needle. And the fishing line could be thread. Let's use that."

"It'll take too long."

"Jesus Christ, Grady, let's at least try. You can't burn him."

"He'll have passed out way before I get to that part."

"I think it's a good idea," Sean said.

Ken pitched his body side to side, riding the high seas again.

"Let's pick something," Wes said.

"Okay," Grady said. "But if he's losing too much blood then I'm going in."

Maia went to the backpack where they kept supplies and got the fish hook and line. Sean put a hand on her arm as she came back.

"Can you do this?"

"How can I answer that? I have no fucking idea. I can't sit back and watch a guy get burned like that, though. This whole thing is barbaric enough."

Sean let her go.

"Okay, Nathan, Wes, you guys get on him and hold him down. He's gonna buck and kick so you need to keep on him until he passes out, which is gonna happen."

The two men straddled either side of Ken.

"We got you, buddy," Wes said.

Ken nodded.

"You ready to do this?" Grady asked.

Ken swallowed hard, his mouth and body dry from the sweat. "You do what you gotta do. If it doesn't work out, don't blame yourselves. I know you're trying."

"Thank you for saying that," Maia said.

Lara broke out in sobs.

"Get her out of here," Grady said. "We don't need that shit while we're doing this."

Maia nodded at Lara. "It's okay. I'll come get you when it's done."

Hand over her mouth to stifle her sobs, Lara turned and ran downriver.

Grady pulled the knife from the flame, his hand wrapped in a wet T-shirt to keep the heat at bay on his hand. "Here we go."

"Give him this to bite on," Sean said and handed over a short stick from his kindling pile. Nathan put it between Ken's teeth.

Grady pulled his T-shirt over his nose to fight the smell and nodded at Nathan and Wes, who each held down one of Ken's shoulders. He nodded to Maia, who held the fish hook and line in one hand. Sean slowly fanned the fire.

Grady bent over Ken, keeping his back to the man's face. He put a hand on the lower leg and found it cold. He tried to find a line to cut, a mark of where the flesh was dead. He figured he could cut right below the kneecap, try to work the shin bone free from the femur and make as clean a cut as possible. The area around the knee was misshapen from where the rock had crushed it. It gave Grady a jagged line to follow, and he hoped once he got under the flesh, the bone would already be separated.

He leaned forward hard and pointed the tip of the knife into the flesh. He sucked in a breath and pushed down.

Ken tensed and tried to thrash but Nathan and Wes bore down. He made a deep, animal noise through the stick.

Thick, almost black blood pooled around the knife, and Grady thought for a moment that he might catch whatever blood poisoning Ken had, but it was too late now. The blade bit down and sank the knife to the hilt of its five-inch blade. Still holding his breath he knew he had to work fast. Grady sawed.

Sean watched him, saw the red tint come to his face from the exertion and his held breath. Sean watched him for signs. For the same bloodlust look when he gutted the possum. He looked for signs Grady might be enjoying this.

The knife blade came out and Grady repositioned it and plunged again. Ken arched his back and Nathan put a knee on his chest.

Grady pulled the blade toward him. The rope tie was holding well. There was less blood than he expected. He realized the blood had stopped flowing to much of Ken's lower leg, the reason it was dying while still attached.

But it was barely attached. The flesh splayed open and Grady could see white bone through the dark blood. Under the knife blade a tendon snapped in two with a pop. He didn't have to worry about trying to uncouple the shin bone from the femur, the job had already been done by the rock. Shards of sharp bone fragments floated up on the sluggish blood.

He cut down, repositioned, cut down again. Let loose his breath and sucked in a new one. Held it.

He pulled the knife out and held it over the flame. The smell of the blood cooking filled the air.

"Can I start?" Maia asked, though she didn't look eager to do it.

"Let me get it all the way off. Almost there."

Ken went still. The stick fell from his mouth. Wes put two fingers to his neck to check for a pulse. "Just fainted."

"Okay. Last bit, let's go."

Grady pulled the knife from the flame, the blood charred and blackened on the metal. He stabbed and sawed the last piece of flesh and Ken's lower leg fell away. Grady sat back in the dirt, heaving breaths.

Maia moved in. The wound didn't look like anything recognizably human and it helped her. It didn't feel like she was trying to stitch a leg. She curled the fish hook around a flap of skin and pulled. The thin, clear fishing line dragged through until it caught on the knot she'd tied in the end. She found a spot below the cut and dug the hook in again.

She had to turn away to catch her breath to avoid the brunt of the smell. The dead leg, the open wound, the burnt flesh and blood.

Sean stepped away from the fire and picked up the leg. He tossed it aside.

The wound still bled. Maia's stitches weren't closing the two open ends of skin together. The wound was too wide.

"You didn't leave enough skin."

"There wasn't much to work with," Grady defended. "He's still bleeding."

She hooked another stitch.

"You have to do them closer together. Make it tight."

"I'm trying."

Grady leaned over her shoulder. She tried to ignore him. The hook began to slip in her fingers as they became more coated in blood. She hooked the line through again and did her best to cinch the two pieces of healthy flesh together. There was still a gap of open wound.

"Can we leave it like that? If we keep it clean, maybe?"

"I don't know," Wes said.

"Let me do it," Grady said. He held the knife over the flame again.

"No. We can keep it covered and wash it out. It'll heal on its own."

"It'll get infected."

"I can do this." She hooked another stitch and pulled the line as tight as she could. The thirty pound test bit into her fingers as she tightened. The open wound smiled at her like a mouth of pulled teeth. All red meat and bone fragments. She turned away to breathe.

"Let me in," Grady said as he pulled the knife from the fire, the blade blackened again. His hand burned from the heat, the T-shirt dry now and offering little protection.

"No. It will heal."

Sean put a hand on Maia's shoulder.

"Let him do it."

Maia threw down the fish hook. It dangled on the

line from the mess of bloody meat. Ken's blood dripped from her hands. She turned away, crying.

"You're all fucking animals."

Maia walked away toward the river to wash her hands.

Ken awoke with a yell when Grady put the hot knife to the open wound. The sizzling sound chased Maia as she left the camp. Ken fell quickly back into unconsciousness. Grady heated the knife again.

Sean studied the pool of blood beneath the operating site. It was nearly black. Inch by inch, blade width by blade width, the wound became sealed. When Grady had seared the last of Ken's leg shut, he turned the blade and cut the fish hook free. Maia's stitches remained, fused with the ragged stump of Ken's leg.

Grady stood and everyone followed. They all huffed for air, trying to slow their heart rates and not breathe in the smell of cooking flesh.

Grady folded the knife closed, hooked the clip to his pants stained with blood. He pointed to the amputated leg where Sean had thrown it. He gave the order to no one in particular.

"Take that and bury it."

BACK HOME

WES DOESN'T MAKE it to the hospital. The others do.

Allison is in intensive care, but the bleed in her brain has been stopped. When they are allowed in they are given masks and booties to wear over their shoes. They are told five minutes, no more.

Maia enters first, Nathan behind her, then Grady and Sean in the rear. Their feet shuffle across the tile floors, paper booties rustling like leaves. Two different machines beep in separate rhythms, falling in and out of sync.

Allison's eyes open in slits. They are wet and red around the edges. Her hair has been shaved from half of her head. There is a clear tube running from between black stitches. An open portal to her brain. Her bed is tilted at an angle so she can see people more or less straight on. Still the group hovers over her like she is lying on the ground.

"How are you doing?" Maia asks.

Allison's voice is a rasp. The doctors warned them

about this. A byproduct of the intubation tube that was removed last night.

"Alive," she squeaks.

Their polite smiles are hidden behind the masks.

"All's well at the office," Maia says. "Grady and I have been making regular stops in." She decides to ask about the sabbatical another time. The others in the office don't need to know why she isn't there today.

"Everything is on track," Grady says. "You take all the time you need."

The machines mark the time between words.

"Can we bring you anything? A magazine or something?"

"It hurts my eyes to read," Allison says.

Maia nods. She wishes one of the others would say something.

"It sucks they did this to you," Nathan says, his voice quiet behind the mask.

The statement lays flat in the room. Nothing more to be said. It does suck. The faceless they. The drug addicts. Kids. Gang members.

Grady stares at the stitches. Six neat black knots. The stubble on her scalp is shorter than his beard. And she had such beautiful hair. He admires the doctor's craftsmanship, but he knows another artisan was at work here. The one who gave her that scar.

He flexes his hand, feels the power there.

He wants to tell her he has taken her office, but he doesn't.

They shuffle back out into the hallway, peel off the masks.

"Christ, did you see that?"

Nathan can't seem to stop shaking his head.

"I wonder how long before she's back at work?" Sean asks.

"A long time," Grady says. "I've been getting up to speed on all the accounts for the next six months." He offers his eyes to Maia. "Someone is going to need to run point until she gets back. If she gets back."

Maia looks away. Grady sees it as a victory. She's been shunned from the office. His territory now, alone.

"You don't think she will?" Maia asks.

"I don't know, man. A head injury like that...she might never be the same. A lot of people don't go full vegetable, but they're never quite right, you know what I mean?"

Maia puts a hand over her mouth. "Oh, God."

"It's something we need to be prepared for."

"I'm not sure I'm going back," Sean says.

"Yeah, it's hard for some people." Grady eyeballs Sean, waiting for him to make eye contact so he can make sure he was understood. *It's hard for you because you're weak.*

———

Outside the hospital, a woman in a dark blue suit approaches.

"Hey guys, Corey Clark from CNN."

She extends a hand like a politician. No one is eager to shake it.

"What are you doing here?" Maia asks.

"Same as you, visiting your boss, Allison Gates. We're not sure if we're doing a feature on this or not, but I figured I could come down here and check it out and see all you guys at the same time." She checks the group. "We're missing one, though, aren't we?"

"Wes couldn't make it."

"He didn't go home yet, did he?"

"Not for two more days, I think."

"So." Corey rocks on her heels, hands clasped in front of her. "Anyone had enough time to consider my offer?"

Sidelong glances are exchanged.

"I think we all feel like we've said enough," Grady says.

Corey maintains her anchorwoman smile. "But you haven't heard my questions yet."

"It's a very personal experience. For all of us. We'd all like to maintain some privacy."

Corey looks to the others in the group. "Is that true for all of you? You don't want the real account of your experience?"

"It's not that," Sean says.

Corey cuts him off. "That's what you're going to get. This story will be reported on, and soon before it's expired. I could have your first hand, truthful account, or I go with hearsay, park ranger reports, a bunch of facts about how many people get lost in the woods each year. If it were me, I wouldn't want that to tell my story. I'd want to tell it."

Grady steps in front of Sean, breaking her connection with him. "Well, you're not us. You weren't out there."

"So put me out there. Take me on that journey with your words and your memories. Come on, guys."

Sean steps out from behind Grady. "You never

mentioned specifically how much money you were offering."

"We can negotiate that. Why don't you come in and meet with me and my producer tomorrow." She addresses Grady. "And look, if you don't want to be involved, you don't have to be. As long as I have at least one firsthand account, the story will be told and told the right way."

"None of us are doing it, lady."

"Okay, I get it. You're out. But let's let the rest of them make up their own minds."

Maia uses her best business negotiating voice. "There's a matter of exclusivity..."

"Again, all things that can be discussed tomorrow. Ten a.m.? What do you say? I'm speaking with the police at nine about the bodies they found."

A charge like an electrical storm runs through them.

"What bodies?" Sean asks.

"Karina, the tour guide. And Ron. You didn't hear?"

"We've been busy," Grady spits at her.

"What did the police say?" Maia asks.

"Y'know what?" Grady cuts in. "You can fuck off, lady. You really want to make us re-live all this shit? Is that what you want? You want the tears and the break-downs? You want to show shots of the dead bodies? Does that get you more ratings? You're sick, you know that. None of us want any part of your fucking freak show."

Grady grabs Sean and Maia by an arm each and pulls them away. He knows Nathan will follow. They leave Corey by the hospital entrance.

"Let me fucking go, Grady." Maia pulls her arm away. They are in the parking lot under tall stanchion lights.

"Nobody talks to her, is that understood?" He aims a finger at them like a weapon.

"Yeah, Grady," Nathan says. "Understood."

He aims his finger at Sean. "What about you? You sounded like you were ready to sign on the dotted line."

"It's a lot of money, Grady. And we can control the story better if we tell it."

"We told it. It's done. The more it gets retold, the more room for error. You should know that, Sean."

"Look, I just think—"

"Well, stop thinking. Stop doing anything. Be like you were out there—useless and quiet."

Inside, Sean begins to boil. Familiar feelings. *Temper, temper.*

"Or else what?" Sean looks ready to stand up to Grady. Grady laughs in his face.

"Shit. I don't know. Maybe the worst I can do to you is to let you talk. Then I'll talk. Maybe we should all talk. We all have some interesting things to say, don't we, when you really pick out the right stories?"

"What's the matter, Grady? Are you scared? Is this some sort of standoff? Like one of us goes down, we all go down?"

"What if it's not us?" Grady said. "What if it's someone like your wife?"

Sean coils, looks ready to pounce.

"Leave her out of it."

"Then you don't say shit. I don't trust you." He spins to the others. "Any of you. So keep your goddamn mouths shut."

"Nobody is saying anything," Maia says. "Just calm down."

Sean is still fixed on Grady, a wild look in his pinprick eyes.

"You stay the fuck away from my wife."

Grady moves in close, drops his voice low. "I'll cut her fucking throat like that tree rat out in the woods. You've seen me work a knife, Sean. You know what she'll look like when I'm done."

"Enough."

Maia grabs Sean and tugs him away. They leave Grady with Nathan beside him, a silent sidekick.

Sean staggers behind her as he is pulled along. He tries to calm his breathing, remember his techniques for getting back in control. *Temper, temper.*

"You ever consider maybe the wrong people never made it out of those woods?"

"Every day," she says. "It breaks my heart and makes me mad as hell."

"What do we do about it?"

"Nothing. What can we do?"

Sean remembers how many times he asked himself that same question out there. Never did find an answer.

Wes is on his second nightcap. The bartender in the lobby bar studies him, tries to put his slumped shoulders and half-lidded eyes to memory for the next person he is trying to decide when to cut off.

Second night in a row he's stopped off at the bar before going up to his room. Second night he's stopped in already drunk.

"We owed him, and he wouldn't let us forget it."

Wes delivers a monologue. The bartender half listens, finds it hard to follow along.

"He took us in and acted like a landlord or something. Like we all owed him rent. More like a slumlord. One of those guys who gouges you and then delivers nothing."

He takes another fistful of pretzels from the bowl.

"I mean, I thought he was dangerous. I never did trust the guy. Ken was the only one I knew before. Kinda the only one I could trust. And y'know, they'll say he died from his leg. Don't believe it."

"Do you need me to call someone to help you get up to your room, sir?"

"Huh? No, no. I gotta go home. Tomorrow or the next day, they say. I get to go home."

"That's good, sir."

"Yeah. Good." Wes finishes his drink. The bartender has done his best to water it down, much more Coke than Jack.

"Ken's not going home, though." Wes swirls his ice cubes. "Ken's not going anywhere. His leg." He blows air from his mouth, motoring his lips. "That's not what happened. You wanna know what happened? I'll tell you."

Wes points at the bartended with his drink. A half melted ice cube flings over the rim and shatters on the bar. The bartender steps in with a crisp white towel in one hand and scoops the glass out of Wes's hand with the other.

"Okay, time to go up now, sir."

"Yeah, yeah," We says. "I gotta get home. They're letting me go. I get to go."

"That's good, sir."

Wes stands from his stool. Takes a second to balance himself, then screws up his face as if he forgot to say something. He waves it off and walks toward the elevators.

Detective Kettner is at his desk, head down in paperwork. The real police work. The part nobody ever shows in the movies. Good. Kettner would never go see that movie.

Morris walks past. "For you, Steve." He keeps on going. When he clears Kettner's vision he reveals James walking behind him. Ken's husband is back.

Off Kettner's look James says, "Don't worry, detective. I'm not here to give you shit. I'm just checking in. I hadn't heard anything in a while."

"These things take time, Mr. Heath."

"I understand." He puts his hands on the chair beside Kettner's desk. With his look he asks to sit. Kettner rolls his eyes and waves James in to the seat.

"Detective Morris said you found bodies."

"He did, did he?" Kettner makes a mental note to chew Morris a new asshole for that one. "We did as a matter of fact, but neither were Ken."

"But presumably he'd be nearby."

"I make no such presumptions, Mr. Heath. Presumptions are the enemy of police work. The two bodies we found were over ten miles away from the insertion site and had been brought there by the river. According to our reports, your husband was left in the woods after he passed."

James leans his face into his palm, his arm resting on the arm of the chair.

"It sucks not knowing anything."

"I spend most of my time not knowing about the crimes I investigate. Sometimes the knowing doesn't come for months."

James sits up. "So you think there is a crime here?"

"No. I didn't say that. It's what I normally do. This falls to homicide because there are dead bodies and we investigate everything. Don't go around thinking there's something evil at work here, Mr. Heath. What happened was a terrible tragedy, but an accident. The rangers have been hampered in their recovery efforts due to weather. They're hoping the storm system clears and hasn't done too much damage to the sites as the survivors described them."

"I'm sorry, detective. I guess I need closure." James wipes at his eyes with the back of his hand.

"And I respect that. I'll do my best to see you get it. As soon as I hear anything from the rangers, I'll let you know."

"Thank you. I'm sorry to bother you." James stands.

"You mind if I ask you, Mr. Heath..."

James stops mid-turn and faces Kettner again.

"This was a team building trip they were on. Was there any reason they needed team building? Any problems or animosity within the company?"

"Not that I know of. But Ken wasn't from this office."

"Yes, yes, I remember. But he never spoke of any reason for the trip?"

"They did it every year, as far as I understood it. Aren't these questions more for employees of the company?"

"Yes, but sometimes spouses tend to tell each other more than coworkers do. Especially if there is any bad blood between the workers."

James studies the detective's face. "I thought you just told me not to be suspicious."

"Yes, but it's my job to be."

OUT THERE
DAY 16

FOR TWO DAYS Ken woke up screaming. He complained about pains in the leg that weren't there. He complained about fire and ants and cuts as deep as bone. The others stood around him and told him he would be okay. They didn't contradict his phantoms. They assured him of his recovery and their imminent rescue.

Everyone tried to believe it. Everyone failed.

Ken's screams pierced Lara's ears. She put her palms on the side of her head, hummed tuneless songs to keep the sounds of agony at bay. She stepped away into the woods, moving deeper each time.

Sean and Maia took turns calming Ken and keeping him hydrated. They moved him on to his side to avoid him lying on the growing sores on his back. They each took to the task with focus and care. They could tune out most of the screams as fevered nonsense. But when he would cry softly, it was worse.

He would murmur names between sobs. James. Femi, his son.

"My baby boy," he would say. "Daddy will come home."

These soft cries were harder to hear than the wailings of pain like the sawing of his leg had never stopped. The quiet cries and whispered names of his family rang louder in their ears.

———

Grady hunted for the baby possums.

On day fifteen he heard a noise high in a tree. He started to climb, but he was exhausted by the time he reached ten feet off the ground. The branches were too far apart, his muscles too weak. His strength left him as if he had a leak, precious energy seeping out of him with a high pitched tone.

He dropped to the forest floor and lay on his back for fifteen minutes listening to the scratching of tiny claws overhead. He never saw their rodent faces and pink noses. They'd starve to death up there without their mother and he'd starve to death down here listening to them.

He kicked the dirt by the roots of the tree. An earthworm came up with the dead leaves and loam. He reached down and ate it.

———

Sean felt his bones moving beneath his skin. He felt joints grind against each other. He came upon Wes staring out at the river as if it spoke to him, like it might be telling him to come in. To drift away. To be rescued by the current. He left him there, afraid if he joined him the river might talk to him, too.

Sean remembered a time with Kerri. They went to a park and stole away off the trail. In a stand of trees they felt alone, off in the wild. They kissed, feeling cut off from the world. He looked at her and said, "I'd love to go someplace and get lost with you."

She tilted her head slightly, a sly smile turning up the corners of her mouth. It was the moment—that look —when he knew she was falling in love with him.

He scoffed at the memory. A park? Get lost? They'd had no idea. It was a dumb thing to say. He was trying for a romantic movie line, but he had no idea what getting lost actually meant. Now he knew. And he wouldn't wish it on anyone. Not even Kerri.

"We have to face facts."

Grady stood before the group. The night before it had rained again. Not bad, but enough to be demoralizing and make them all cold. The six people seated before him were worn thin, sunken-eyed and blank. Beards were growing longer, far beyond a vacation scruff. Everyone's hair stuck to their scalp in greasy tendrils. Lara's hair had begun to dreadlock in places. Clothes looked ready to split at the seams and reveal the bony bodies beneath.

"If we want out of here, we need to do it ourselves. That means moving."

"Are you asking or telling?" Maia said. "Because since we moved to this camp, you've been doing a lot more telling."

"I told you when you came here this place needed a leader. Are you even keeping track? It's been sixteen days. Two weeks plus and not so much as a sign of a rescue team. If someone needs to step up and be the leader who says it's time to save our own asses, then I'll be that guy."

Lara pulled her knees tight to her chest.

"I don't think we should move. What if they're close? What if we start walking and only move farther from where they are?"

For days Lara had been a drop of water about to fall from a leaf, tremulous and waiting for only the slightest bump to send her splashing apart. Even sitting still, she spun.

"If it hasn't happened by now..." Grady said. "Look, if it was up to me, I could stay here. But I'm worried about some of the rest of you."

"Oh, come on," Maia said.

"Y'know what, guys?" Sean said. "I actually agree with him. I think we need to get out of here and find our way out. It might be the only way."

"We don't know where the fuck we are," Wes said.

Nathan sat behind and to the left of Grady. His vote was clear by his silence and his dedication to anything Grady said over the past few days.

"If we don't know, then they don't know," Grady said. "So we gotta move."

"We can't wait any longer," Nathan said.

"What about a raft?" Wes said. "We have a river here and we've never even tried to make a raft."

"First off, we only have about twelve feet of rope left. Second, we have no idea what's below us on that river. Did you really like the trip down here? You want to make it again over maybe rockier rapids or waterfalls or some shit?"

Nathan said, "We'll all be soaking wet and frozen by the time we pass the bend. I'd rather stay dry and be able to change course if I need to. Once we get in the river, we're committed to it. No turning back."

The bird calls had started to sound familiar. That's what flipped Maia's mind. There in the heavy pause of the conversation she recognized the birds, pictured their plumage, wondered if they were the same birds who'd been living in a tree outside of camp.

"Okay, fine," she said. "But what do we do with all the stuff?"

"We leave most of it. Take only what we can carry in the backpacks, and most of that should be food."

"We don't have enough food to fill one pack," Wes said. "Let alone three."

"So we spend the rest of today foraging, getting as much as we can. Plus, when we move into different territories, we'll find new food sources."

"Fire?" Maia asked.

"We'll take the compass lens, some tinder. We can make a new one if we need it."

"How far do you think it is?" Sean asked.

"I'd be lying if I said I knew."

Maia shook her head and her hair flopped in oily strings. "Fuck me."

"Here's one other thing," Grady said. "I think we should leave Ken here."

Tension gripped the circle.

"No way," Sean said. "He'll die."

"He'll slow us down. We have no way to transport him. We can send help back."

"He's still not over the shock of his leg. And he's been feverish."

"So we'll move fast and send help as soon as we can. Look, do you want to make it out or not?"

Maia made her voice small so Ken wouldn't hear. "He's got a family, for Christ sake. A little boy."

"I'm trying to save him."

"By leaving him alone like road kill?"

"The faster we get out of these woods, the faster we can send someone back to find him."

"We can't even find ourselves out here."

Maia turned her back on Grady. When Grady stepped forward to reach for her, Sean put himself between them.

"Maybe someone could stay behind."

Grady looked over the group. "Any volunteers?"

Nobody stepped forward.

"I don't want to split up," Lara said, the tears already brewing in her eyes.

"The more we stay together and work together, the better chance we have," Grady said.

"As long as we follow your directions," Maia added.

Sean took a mental inventory of the supplies. "We can make a stretcher. We get two big branches, loop them through a sleeping bag and lift it up by the poles. We carry him out."

"You know how hard that's gonna be?" Grady said.

"We're not leaving him behind."

Grady was clearly outnumbered. The look in his eye could have meant murder, but he held his composure.

"You make the thing and we'll see." Sean nodded at the command. "Everyone else, let's gather up what we can keep and try to get some more berries or something for the trip."

An hour later Sean had made his stretcher. Two long branches, baseball bat thick, were supporting a sleeping bag between them.

"Okay, let's roll him onto it."

Sean and Wes took opposite ends with a pole in each hand. Nathan helped ease Ken onto the sleeping bag. Ken seemed half awake, helping where he could but fighting ghost pains in his missing leg and a fever that wouldn't break.

Sean and Wes stood. The makeshift stretcher sagged in the middle until it almost closed over Ken, but they held their arms apart and were able to walk with him.

Even weakened, starving and missing part of a leg, Ken was heavy to carry. They walked him once around the camp as a demonstration to Grady that it could be done. They set him down, both sweating.

"Okay," Grady said. "He can come if you can carry it. I hope he doesn't die on us. And I really hope he doesn't kill us all."

By that night they had the three backpacks ready. One for firewood, which consisted of mostly small sticks and dried leaves and pine needles. Carrying real logs would be too heavy. One for food, which was mostly empty. Lara had found more berries. The little red ones that were bitter and hard and gave everyone heartburn from the concentrated acid. The third pack had the compass lens, the remaining rope, the water bottle, what was left of the fishing line and the hook they saved from the pool of blood under Ken's leg after the amputation.

Grady had picked out a walking stick for himself. He gave out assignments, assuring he would never be responsible for carrying Ken as he was the leader and would be walking ahead forging a trail.

Maia whispered to Sean. "Jesus Christ, all he needs is a pith helmet and a faithful Indian squaw by his side and his fantasy would be complete."

"I think this is gonna be good for us."

"It can't be any fucking worse."

Grady addressed the group.

"We'll leave at first light. Everyone will stop by the river for a full drink of water and then we'll go. Try to get a good night's rest. We're gonna need all our energy for tomorrow."

"What time should I tell the front desk for my wakeup call?" Maia said. Nobody laughed but her.

BACK HOME

NATHAN CAN SEE the police station from inside the donut shop. He laughed when he first went in, wondering if someone thought they could make a dollar off the stereotype, but in the nearly two hours he's been here he hasn't seen a single cop come in.

His styrofoam coffee cup is empty, but he spins it in his hand, up to a thousand rotations or more as he stares at the front of the building.

The shop owner, or maybe the owner's son, made his annoyance at Nathan's loitering known. Two hours and one donut with no refills on his coffee. The man behind the counter huffs and exhales loudly between paying customers, who are few and far between.

Nathan watches. Officers go in and come out. Men in well-fitting suits walk up the steps with purpose. Men in ill-fitting sport jackets hesitate on each step as if it might be their last steps of freedom. Women go in with urgency and come out crying.

He could go in. He could tell everything. He could unburden himself. And it is a burden. Keeping a truth is like carrying a stone. It gets heavier with each step. It gets harder to conceal what you are holding.

The news lady wants to pay him to tell. The police want to reward him to tell, maybe with less punishment. Maybe with freedom.

But the others. His parents.

He's already facing the rest of his life as a man with a footnote attached to him. A small notoriety that is enough to cloud any interaction with anyone he meets. It will come out at a party one night.

"Oh, my God, you're one of those people who were out there all those days?"

He'll get older. There will be some who don't remember the story. He'll have to stand there while someone else tells the condensed version of his life, his only distinctive quality the fact he lived where others died.

But what story does he want told? Is it the one that will get him pats on the back, eager questions, admiring looks? Or quiet pause, uncomfortable silence, physical distance?

Nathan stands up. The man behind the counter says under his breath, "About time."

Nathan steps outside. Traffic is loud after the bubble of the donut shop, the strange drone of an ethnic music he can't identify.

He knows if he was going to go inside and speak to the police he would have done it by now. He knows the detective is in there, but he will remain outside. He knows the rock is getting too heavy to carry.

Nathan looks to his left at the oncoming traffic. He's between a station wagon and a pickup truck parked at meters along the street. Cars pass by at irregular intervals, then stop. The light on the corner two blocks up is red.

A pigeon lands at his feet, pecks at donut crumbs. He could reach down and grab it. It's not afraid. Different from the birds out there, always on alert for danger. Seeing a threat even where there was none. Here, in the city, they could stand to be a little more cautious.

Traffic is moving again. Nathan is hidden between the parked cars. The sound of cars passing is steady and regular like fan blades whirring. The space between grows. Traffic widening out.

He steps forward, eyes closed.

A horn. Tires screech like a cornered animal. Nathan feels the heat of an engine breath hot on his leg, but it stops short.

Muffled behind glass, "What the fuck, dude!"

Nathan stands still. Other cars honk, veer past the stopped car, shout insults.

The car is black, four door and heavy. The engine rumbles, anxious to get moving again. Nathan stares straight ahead. The driver's side door opens and a man gets out. He's large, thick around the middle. A shaved head showing prickly stubble. Tattoos scatter his fore-arms. His T-shirt is black with skulls and the logo of some band Nathan does not know.

The man moves quickly to the front of his car. In the passenger seat is another man, a matched set. The other man cautions, "Vic, c'mon. Let it go."

"The fuck is wrong with you, dude?"

Heat comes off Vic's skull like the engine idling next to them. Nathan shows nothing. The police station is there, waiting, but on the other side of the river of traffic.

Vic examines the front of his car for scratches.

"Get a fuckin' grip, man."

His partner leans out the open window.

"Vic, fuckin' come on. That's a cop shop."

Vic looks up and sees a curious uniformed officer looking from across the street. He thrusts a finger toward Nathan.

"Your lucky fuckin' day."

Vic climbs back in the car. Nathan hasn't moved. Vic backs up, turns the wheel and drives off with a vicious screech of tires. Nathan turns back to the curb and walks away, the police station behind him.

Sean is still hungry. He cooks three eggs and bacon, but it's not enough. The food makes him slow and sleepy, but he wants more. His body craves fat and salt.

It's all a reminder that he is still adjusting. He is still returning to normal.

He rolls that word around his brain. Normal. Can he return? Will he be welcomed back?

A sound at the door. A key in the lock. Sean glances up to see Kerri walk in. She pauses in the doorway, an animal caught in bright light. She continues inside moving slower, her features softer than the last time he saw her.

"Sean," she says.

"What are you doing here?"

"Well..." She places her keys in the bowl, the familiar sound of metal on ceramic. "After I took some time to cool down—time I needed—I didn't want to just leave you without explaining." She holds her wrist with her other hand, contrite and demure. "I didn't want to miss out on another chance for us. Maybe."

Sean feels his pulse moving in his veins, blinks twice to check his eyes, listens for the dying ring of the ceramic bowl. Anything to sense how he is feeling. He gets nothing. Then, a realization.

"I don't want you here."

"What?"

"I think you were right," he says. "I think you should go."

"Sean, I came back here because you've been through a lot. I thought you might need some time to figure things—"

"I do. You're right. But not with you."

He exhales, the words cool in his mouth like mint.

"Kerri," he says, "if I'm going to start over and make any changes, any *real* changes, I need to do it alone. You're a distraction."

He sees the words make her flinch.

"Sorry. That's not it. I just...I need to figure out my next step. And I think it's best I do it alone."

He sees the rising anger in her eyes, vessels going red.

"What next step, Sean? You gonna go work for the Peace Corps or something? Did you make some promise to God and you're gonna go off and become a priest? You've done nothing since you got back. Nothing's different. Nothing at all, Sean."

"I'm working on it."

"Working on it? Give me a fucking break."

She sets her purse down on the counter.

"You can't kick me out."

"You left."

"And now I'm back. This is my house, too."

He waves a hand at the couch.

"You can sleep down here, I guess."

She is horrified.

"What the hell, Sean?"

"I told you. I think it's better if I figure some things out on my own."

She snatches her purse again and whips it over her shoulder.

"You act like what happened out there was such a big thing." She scoops her keys from the bowl. "It's called fucking camping, Sean. People do it for fun. Don't act like what you did was so goddamn life changing. Like you're some kind of a hero or something."

"I'm no hero. I never said I was."

"Well, good."

She stalks toward the door. He watches her calmly. He feels a strange assurance that this is right. He's making the right move. A good change. A tip toward balance.

"I'll call you when I—"

"Fuck you, Sean."

She slams the door.

He would follow her to explain if he could, but he can't articulate why this is right. It's control. A tiny bit. That's the best he can do. He feels a small lever of control and it is a welcome feeling. Maybe he can explain it to her, later.

For now, he is still hungry.

Nathan didn't even know Grady knows where he lived. He's never hung out with anyone from work outside of a work event. Holiday parties, celebrations for landing a big client. But there is Grady at his door, expecting to be let in.

Tiny pinprick hairs stand out on Nathan. Warning signs. The feeling of a predator stalking him. Grady pushes forward. Nathan moves aside.

"I'm thinking we might need to do something about Sean and Maia."

"Do what?" Nathan shuts the door. He feels locked in a cage, the smell of raw meat agitating the animals. Grady gives off a hunter's vibe. Nathan has seen it in the woods. He won't stop moving. He paces.

Nathan is ready to move. Fight or flight—he chooses flight. He knows how sharp this animal's claws are, knows his chances.

"We've got to really put the scare into them," Grady says. "We can't let them talk."

"I don't think they would tell everything. They have too much to lose also."

"I don't care what they say about themselves, but I don't trust either one worth a shit not to sell you and me out to anyone with a checkbook."

"So what are you going to do?"

Grady stalks the floor. Nathan is still, a coiled spring.

"We need to find a way to get them too afraid to talk."

"You can't hurt them."

"Maybe not them."

"I heard what you said about Sean's wife. You can't do that, either."

"You know we can. You know it could work."

"Stop saying we."

Grady stops his movements. He is turned, looking over his shoulder at Nathan. Grady's eyes are two knife-points, but Nathan doesn't care. He knows Grady can smell his blood beneath the skin, but he doesn't mind. If his blood needs to be spilled, so be it. He stood silent too long out there. He became Grady's right hand. He knows that time is over now.

"I went to the police today," Nathan says.

"You did?"

"I didn't go in. I didn't say anything. But I went."

Grady squares up on him. His chest forward. Nathan checks his belt for the knife.

"Do we need to have a talk?" Grady asks. Nathan knows there will be no words. What he means is for Nathan to be silent.

"No. But I'm done. No more. I don't know if I'll tell or not. But it's my choice."

"Bullshit."

"We're home now," he says. "It's over."

"Maybe you forgot a few things."

Grady steps forward and shoves Nathan in the chest. Nathan stutter-steps his feet to remain standing. He eyes the door.

"Maybe I need to remind you," Grady says.

Nathan charges. He can barely see through the tears instantly in his eyes. He hits Grady mid chest with his forearms, pushing forward and knocking Grady back. The predator falls, hits a bookshelf. Chaos and noise. Nathan runs for the door.

He's out, leaving the door open, and running for the stairs. He lives on the second floor, his car is in the parking garage underground. His senses are like an exposed nerve. He runs—a rodent with a hawk diving for him.

Grady is up, climbing from a pile of debris. He follows. Stop him. Silence him.

Nathan passes the elevator, moves for the stairs. His hand in his pocket, gripping his keys. Grady's feet on the stairs like thunder growing closer.

Nathan reaches the parking garage. Fluorescent lights. Concrete floors. The opposite of the woods. Twenty-six spaces, one for each apartment. He is number twenty-one. He runs down the row, feet slapping in small echoes. Sound trapped like he is in a bunker.

Grady is behind him, breathing loud. The hunter wants the prey to know he is close behind.

Grady is faster than Nathan. He passes cars, empty spaces, nears his prey.

Nathan reaches his car, presses buttons on his key fob. Locks the car, then unlocks it. He reaches the hood, skids his shoes as he makes the turn. Grady's arm is reaching across, grabs hold of his shirt. He is pulled back from the door handle. Grady slams him against the hood. Nathan fights back. He throws a wild elbow, catching Grady in the temple. Grady leans back. He tilts forward again, throwing a punch into Nathan's gut. Nathan grunts and falls forward.

Grady has ahold of his shirt and keeps him from hitting the floor.

"Maybe it's not you," he says. "Maybe your parents. Maybe I should go talk to them."

Grady punches again, hits Nathan high in his ribcage, the pain radiates through his veins into each extremity.

Nathan twists, kicks a leg. He catches Grady's ankle. His balance is thrown. Nathan follows through on the kick and Grady loses one leg to the air. He is falling, his grip on Nathan's shirt unwavering and stronger than the seams. The shirt tears and Nathan pulls away.

A car tips its front end down the incline into the underground. Nathan pulls at the door but Grady's body blocks the door from opening. The car pulls into a spot two down from them. A woman gets out.

"Oh, my God."

Nathan does not ask for help. He shoves on Grady with a foot. Grady slides away and stands, he breathes deep and his teeth show through his open mouth. The woman screams. This makes Grady turn and Nathan pulls the door all the way open.

She gets a cell phone out of her bag and puts it to her ear. Grady sees the newer threat. He steps around the front end of Nathan's car and approaches her. She gets no answer on her phone. She digs in her bag again and now her other hand is holding a canister of pepper spray. Grady keeps moving toward her.

Nathan sits behind the wheel, cranks the engine. He watches Grady stalk the woman.

She presses the button when he gets within a few steps. Grady puts out a hand, blocking the stream with his flat palm. The spray collects in his hand, spreads around him like a halo he walks through. None of it reaches his eyes like in her training class.

He reaches her and puts his palm flat against her face. She screams as the pepper spray stings her eyes and her lips.

Nathan chirps the tires as he drives away, leaving his neighbor to her fate.

Grady turns away from the woman as Nathan passes by inches from the back of his legs. The fine mist of pepper spray in the air is making his eyes water. He knows he can't rub them with his hand covered in the stuff.

The woman has fallen to the ground. He leaves her and rushes to his own car, but he knows he can't catch Nathan.

The phone rings on Detective Kettner's desk. He picks it up on two.

"Kettner."

It is the coroner from Arapahoe County, where the group got lost. He's found another body.

"No shit?"

"No. A male. According to the files we got on the missing, this is Rick, the guide from the tour outfit. Physical description matches, several tattoos. Body's waterlogged, of course, but easily identified."

"You fished him out of the reservoir like the others?"

"No, he was caught up about a half mile upriver, tangled in some weeds."

"One more down, two to go."

Kettner snaps his fingers twice to get Morris' attention. Morris joins him at his desk. Kettner shows the quick scribbled notes he took. Morris nods his approval.

"The thing is, Detective, this one isn't so straightforward."

"Oh, no?"

Kettner snaps his fingers again for Morris to get on another line.

"Well, the reason he got hung up like that is there was a rope tied to his foot."

"A rope you say?"

"Yeah. Frayed end like it'd been cut or maybe got clipped on a rock or something. Hungry beaver, I dunno. We're looking at it now but after so long in the water..."

"A homicide man's worst enemy, water."

"M.E.'s, too. Anyway, it's not only that."

"Do you have a report you can send me?"

"I haven't written it all up yet. I called you right away since this is...unusual."

"Okay, you got my attention."

Kettner holds his pen poised over the notepad, ready to write this down.

"Well, see, there were sections of his thigh and calf muscles missing."

"What's in the river that could do that? You were joking about the beavers, right?"

"Yeah. We don't have anything that could take away big hunks of flesh like this up in the Alegash. We got trout, some crayfish, the usual small fish species, a few turtles and catfish in the slow parts. Makes for shitty fishing to tell you the truth. Nothing you wouldn't throw back."

"So you think those parts might have been missing before he went in the water?"

Kettner hasn't written anything because he doesn't know what to think or where this is going.

"That we can try to figure, but it'll be hard. No, the bigger thing is how the wounds present themselves. They're clean cuts, detective. Not, like, scalpel clean, but not an animal or getting pounded on the rocks either.

These wounds were made with a knife or some other sharp instrument."

Morris give a furrowed brow look. Kettner matches him.

"So you're saying someone cut out pieces of him?"

"It looks that way. Thighs front and back and calves on both legs."

"Huh."

"Yeah."

Neither man says anything for a while, each pondering their own theories.

"When can I expect your full report?"

"By end of day today. I wanted to get you the info quick, though. Shit, I just wanted to tell someone. I've never seen anything like it."

"No, that's a new one on me, too. And that's saying something."

"Okay, I'll get back to it. I'll send you something as soon as I've got it."

"Thanks for the call."

He hangs up, so does Morris. They watch each other, seeing if either one has the answer.

"Curiouser and curiouser," Kettner says.

"Two more to go, huh?"

"Yeah. No telling what tomorrow may bring."

Kettner taps his chin with a finger, trying to imagine what could have really gone on out there.

OUT THERE

DAY 17

THEY SET OUT EARLY, but not until after a fight.

Grady slung his backpack over his shoulders and took up his walking stick.

"Okay, let's head out."

He pointed his body downriver.

"Wait, aren't we going to walk back up to the camp-site?" Maia said.

"No. We're going this way."

"Why wouldn't we go where we know they're looking for us?"

Grady turned and stepped closer to Maia. "Because they've already been there and seen we're not there. Because following a river downhill is the way to reach the mouth of that river which is the best place to find people."

Sean and Wes stood ready to lift Ken's stretcher. Nobody else argued about the direction of the hike. Maia searched their faces for some support.

"I still don't think we should be going anywhere," Lara said.

"Oh, for fuck's sake." Grady opened his arms wide, asking the entire forest. "Anybody else got a problem with what we're doing?"

"Let's get going," Ken said. Everyone turned to him. Flat on his back on top of the home made stretcher he pointed downriver. "Let's get the hell out of here."

Sean and Wes bent their legs and lifted the stretcher. Grady started walking, Nathan close behind. They left behind the shelter and warm coals of the dying fire.

The hike was slow going. Grady walked ahead about a hundred yards in search of a good way down. He veered farther from the riverbank to try to find flat terrain and a break in the trees. The ground sloped evenly down with occasional sharp dips in the earth. The landscape remained dense with trees, ferns, other bushes and grasses.

Moving efficiently while holding a stretcher was difficult. Sean and Wes picked their way slowly through the forest, Sean in front with his back to Ken and Wes in back trying to see what came next underfoot with Ken's body blocking all view.

Ken remained quiet unless he was encouraging the others.

"We're gonna make it out of here. Don't you worry about me."

His fever seemed to have broken, or at least the idea of moving had energized him.

Maia walked between Grady and Nathan in the lead and the boys in back. Lara hung close by. She spoke to Maia, to the air, to nobody. She began telling stories of her life. Confessions. Like she was shedding skin. Every bad thing in her life she wanted to leave in the forest. Maia tried to tune her out, but with only the sound of the birds and the plants brushing past their legs, Lara's voice played like a song you were tired of hearing.

"I cheated on my college boyfriend. It was one summer so we weren't even together. I didn't tell him when we got back to school. I should have, but I knew he'd break up with me. The guy over the summer, he kept calling me at school. He was hot and the sex was great, but he went to a school, like, six hours away. It wasn't practical. Plus, I really did like Paul. But then by the end of sophomore year, we'd broken up. I barely ever saw him after that. It was a big campus.

"One day near the end of senior year I ran into Paul. I had dated, like, three guys since then but wasn't dating anyone then. I never hooked up with the summer guy again, either. But when I saw Paul I figured I'd do the right thing and tell him, so I did. I told him that I'd cheated on him that summer. I figured he'd thank me or say no big deal it was a long time ago. But he totally freaked out."

Maia kicked a fern out of her way. "Well, no wonder."

"He was all like, 'You didn't have to tell me that. I was better off not knowing. Now I feel like crap'. Well, excuse me, y'know?"

Sean and Wes called for a break. They set Ken down.

"You guys are doing great," Ken said.

Sean and Wes panted for breath. They could still

hear the river flowing but it was a long way off, and they needed water.

Maia called ahead to Nathan who stayed midway between where Grady was up ahead and the group. He called to Grady and told him they were stopping.

Sean bent down to get Ken's water bottle and fill it for him when he went to the river. He noticed Ken was sweating.

Ken smiled, but it was weak. "It's hot in here inside this sleeping bag. When you guys walk it closes up nearly all the way over me. But it's a smooth ride, I have to say. You guys are killing it."

"Thanks, Ken," Sean said. He went away with concern in his eye.

Grady stomped back to the group.

"What's the holdup?"

"We need a break," Sean said. "And some water."

He started to walk in the direction of the river. Wes followed.

"We've only gone a half a mile."

"We've done more than that," Sean said.

"Barely. We have a long way to go, potentially."

"If you want to come carry half of this, be my guest."

Grady pointed to the stretcher with his walking stick. "That's all your idea. Don't try to shove that off on me."

"All I'm saying, Grady, is that you have a tiny little backpack and we're carrying a whole person."

Grady spun around, pointing back downriver. "Well, not a *whole* person."

Maia tried to keep her voice low. "Grady, don't be an ass."

Grady dropped his voice to a whisper but put

venom in it. "I'm saying you all wanted to bring him and now he's slowing us down exactly like I said he would."

"What if it was you in that stretcher? What if it was you who lost half a leg?"

"I'd say leave me behind."

"Bullshit, you would."

"I would."

Sean stepped closer, trying to keep Ken from having to hear a debate about his life.

"Knock it off. That debate is over. Now if you shut up and quit fighting we can get to it and back on the trail before we waste too much time."

Sean turned toward the river and Wes ran to catch up.

———

After they'd filled their bellies from the river, they each straightened up on their knees. Their pants were soaked in mud from the side of the river where they'd bent through a break in the weeds to find a good place to drink. Sean dipped the plastic water bottle into the flow and watched it fill.

Wes examined his palms, the start of a blister on each hand.

"We would go faster," he said as if talking to his fingers.

"I know that, but we can't leave him at some random place in the woods."

"Maybe we could mark the spot somehow."

"Are you serious, Wes? Are you on Grady's side?"

"Look, I know Ken. He's tough. He wouldn't have

made it this far with all he's been through if he wasn't. Maybe we need to ask him again."

"No. Screw that. He's doing better now. We can do this."

Sean thought about the sweat on Ken's face. About what happened last time they moved him.

Wes shook his head, clearing his thoughts.

"You're right. I'm sorry. You're totally right. I'm just tired. My energy...it flags after so little. I mean, look at us."

Wes raised his shirt. Ribs showed prominently, his hips bones jutted out above his pant line. Sean knew he looked the same.

"We'll keep going slow and steady. We can do this."

Wes nodded.

When they returned Grady didn't say a word. He wore his furrowed brow look back into the woods. The others followed.

———

"There was a guy at my first big job," Lara said. She sounded to Maia like she was speaking from a dream. Her words were slow and a little slurred like she'd had one too many drinks. She spoke, prompted by nothing, answering no questions other than what was in her own head. Maia listened patiently, her energy failing her.

"I knew he sucked at the job and I knew I could do it better, so he used to piss me off. We used to get together for drinks after work, all of us. He'd be there and I wouldn't talk to him or anything. So one night I'm in the ladies room and this girl comes in all giggles and smiles and she's pulling this guy in after her. I ducked back into a stall so he wouldn't see me, but I couldn't believe it. This girl starts, like, eating his face she was so wasted. Well, he gets out a little vial and lays out two lines on the sink there and hands her a straw. They both do the lines and then go into the stall next to me and start doing it. I ran out of there so fast."

Lara stumbled, putting a hand on Maia's shoulder to steady herself.

"The next day, I phoned in an anonymous report to HR. I told them to pull a random drug test or at least search his bag. He used one of those, like, messenger bags that was leather. Well, they did and he got fired. I always felt really guilty about that."

Lara started weeping as she walked. Maia didn't bother to console her or comfort her. She didn't have anything to spare, emotionally or otherwise.

Sean felt his ankle turn. He dropped to one knee before it twisted and tore something. Ken went down hard on one side. He cried out.

"Sorry, man."

"It's okay," Ken said, though his voice sounded weak.

Wes set down his two sticks. He looked at his palms. His blisters had grown now into two pus-filled sacks rimmed by angry red skin. It hurt him to bend his fingers.

"I need a break," he said.

Maia called, "Grady."

Nathan relayed the call. Soon Grady was clomping back through the path he'd cut.

"Again? Are you serious?"

Wes held up his palms. Maia sucked air through her teeth. The blisters were painful to look at.

"Fine. Water break, then."

Grady threw down his backpack, leaned back and stretched. The rush of water was more distant, but Grady walked that way. Nathan followed on his heels.

"Where does he get all this energy?" Maia asked.

"He's not carrying anything but that," Sean said pointing to his backpack which looked empty.

"Still, he's had more energy than the rest of us for days. I'm fucking exhausted."

"I know."

Lara stood next to a tall tree and wept, leaning into it like it was a long lost relative.

"I bet that fucker is hoarding food," Maia said.

"I wouldn't put it past him." Sean sat down on the damp ground. He called over to Wes. "How you doing, Wes?"

Wes continued to stare at his palms as if they might heal from his vision.

"Are you getting these blisters?"

"Not yet. I will, though." Sean watched Ken try to adjust himself on the stretcher. "How about you, Ken?"

"I'm hanging on. The ride seemed smoother at the start."

"Sorry."

"Not your fault, man. This is just..."

He tried to swallow but his throat wouldn't cooper-ate. Finally he got it down.

"This is how it is."

"You sure you're all right?"

Ken pushed up on one elbow, tried on a smile that fooled no one.

"I tell you what, I'll be all right when get the hell out of all this nature. Get me back in front of a nice computer monitor, let me at some design tools and let me lead a team to build a platform for optimized web-based interactive performance and I'll be all good."

Sean smiled back at him, wanting to believe they'd all be there soon.

"That mother fucker."

Maia had Grady's backpack held in her hand.

"I knew it."

"What?"

"He's got meat in here. Dried meat he must have cooked into jerky." She pulled out several strips of dark brown meat clenched in her hand. "That son of a bitch killed the younger possums and didn't tell us. No wonder he's got all that energy. He's been eating all our protein."

Wes put his hands down and studied Maia's evidence. "Are you kidding me?"

"Can you believe the balls on this guy?"

Lara cried louder. Everyone ignored her.

"When did he do that?" Sean said.

"I have no idea, but it's shitty. He's eating the shares for six of us all himself."

Wes came over for a closer look. "He probably thought since he killed it he was entitled to all of it."

"Some of us could use that meat," Ken said.

"Hey!" Nathan came running back, twigs snapping under his feet. "Put that down."

"Look what we found in Grady's pack," Maia said, holding out the dried meat for Nathan to see. He ran right up and snatched the pack from her hand, the strips of meat falling to the ground.

"That's not your pack. You have no right."

"Holy shit, he knew about it," Sean said.

Nathan took two steps backward. He held the backpack to his chest. Suspicious eyes scanned the group.

Sean picked up a strip of meat from the ground and held it out.

"Did you know? Was he sharing it with you?"

Nathan said nothing. They heard Grady's heavy footfalls coming from the direction of the river.

Sean turned the meat over in his hand. He thought about how satisfying it would be to eat it right in front of Grady. To let him know he hadn't gotten away with it. To pass out his spoils to the whole group and leave him with none. Then maybe take the lead, steal his walking stick and—

"Maia," he said.

"Let's see what the lying son of a bitch has to say for himself."

"Maia," Sean said again.

Grady arrived back to the group. He saw Nathan clutching his bag, saw Maia and Wes's angry eyes on him. He saw Sean holding out a strip of meat to Maia.

"Look."

Maia finally turned her attention to Sean. Wes leaned in closer for a look, too. Sean held the strip out to her but she didn't know what she was supposed to see.

"It's not the possum."

She followed his finger. The tip pointed to a shape. A circle, half black and half white looping into each other. A Yin Yang. And words. Peace on Ea—before it got cut off. Maia didn't know what she was seeing.

"It's a tattoo," Sean explained. "It's Rick."

Lara's sobs turned into a scream.

Grady stood as still as the trees around him. His hard eyes dared anyone to challenge him.

Maia spoke, "Oh, my God," as softly as the beat of a bird's wing through the air.

Sean looked at Grady, at a face defiant but tortured. He saw the doubt and maybe guilt moving under his skin like insects below the soil they stood on.

"Did you do this?"

"You wouldn't listen to reason."

"Reason? This is reason to you?" Sean held out the strip of flesh, then seemed to realize what it was he held in his fist. He flung it down to the ground and wiped his hand down the side of his pants.

"We need to survive out here."

The group stood in silent judgement.

"You came to me at the new camp. You needed someone strong."

"How did you...?"

Nathan stepped forward. "He cut the pieces off then let the body go. He kept the pieces tied up in the river to keep them cold, then cooked them and dried them."

"And you knew about this?" Maia said.

Nathan nodded. "We needed food. We were gonna die."

"The rest of us didn't die!" Maia couldn't face them and turned away. "Fucking animals."

"Don't you dare judge me," Grady said. "He was dead. We were surviving."

Wes was near tears. "You didn't have to—"

Lara screamed again and ran into the trees.

"Lara!" Maia called.

Lara kept moving. She crashed through the low

plants and was soon gone in the thicket of trees, her cries trailing off.

Maia called to her again but got no response. "I should go after her."

"Let her alone," Grady said. "She needs to cry it out, if that's even possible. Is that what you want out here? Weak people like that? You want *them* leading you out of here? Or do you want someone strong? Someone willing to do whatever it takes to keep on living?"

"But there has to be another way," Sean said.

"That was my way."

"What's done is done," Nathan said. "We need to keep moving."

Maia turned away from the woods where Lara had run off. She faced Nathan.

"You can say that because you did this, too."

"I didn't know until after."

"Don't sell me out, you little shit," Grady said.

"It's true."

"It's also true that you ate your fair share."

Nathan hung his head in shame.

"I can't believe this," Maia said. "You need to get out of here. I can't look at you."

Grady stepped over to Nathan and grabbed his backpack, jerking it out of his hands.

"Oh, I'll gladly leave you all behind. Good fucking luck on your own."

Nathan kept a hand on the pack. "No. We shouldn't split up."

Grady pulled a hand back and punched Nathan in the jaw. He went down. Grady slid the backpack over his shoulders.

"Stop it," Sean said. "He's right. If we split up we won't make it."

"Oh, I'll make it," Grady said.

"We need to stick together." Sean faced Maia. "We need to get out of this forest and get back home. We can deal with all of this then."

"Oh, my God, you're with them."

"No, I'm not. But we can't fall apart now. Not if we want to live."

"Yeah, Maia," Grady said. "Sometimes you do whatever is necessary."

"Don't you fucking talk to me."

Ken coughed and then spit. "We need to make it out of here or I'm gonna die." All eyes turned to him. "And I'm only gonna be the first. So quit fighting and get moving."

Bird sounds filled the air. Nobody spoke for a long time. The anger slowly dissipated.

"We can't go anywhere without Lara," Maia said.

"She'll be back," Sean said. "Let's get some rest in the meantime."

They sat in factions. Sean and Wes by Ken, Grady and Nathan near each other, Maia alone. Nathan rubbed his jaw. Grady offered no apology.

They were done for the day. By the time they thought to gather kindling to start a fire, the sun was too far down to catch enough light in the compass glass to make a flame.

Lara had not returned.

"Someone should go out and look for her," Maia said.

"And get lost? That will make two," Wes said.

"I bet she's not lost, she's curled up somewhere afraid."

"Maybe."

Nathan approached the others. "She's not coming back, is she?"

"What if she made her way out?" Wes said. "What if she found a road or a cabin or something?"

"She's lost," Sean said.

They tried calling her name some more. They walked twenty, then fifty, then a hundred yards into the woods calling for her. They walked until they couldn't see each other, then scurried back like frightened children in the dark.

The sun fell and they were six.

BACK HOME

SEAN SCOOPS green beans onto a tray. The smell is getting to him. First it was the industrial cleaner that burned his nostrils, now it's the soft, semi-congealed food in metal bins in front of him.

His hairnet is itching his scalp.

Grace, the volunteer coordinator, passes down the line with a smile and an encouraging pat on the shoulder for all six volunteers.

"Nice work, Erin," she says to the plus-sized woman next to Sean. When she reaches him he can't quite muster a smile back to her.

"Good work, Sean. So glad you decided to join us today. I hope it does your heart some good to help others."

She moves down the line without waiting for a response.

His heart is empty, and it bothers him. He thought coming down here and donating his time, his energy, would fill him in some way, but it's left him more empty than before.

He can't look at the line of men and women holding trays and not feel drained. He can't watch them salivate over the slop he's dishing out and not feel disgusted. He can't help people he doesn't know and not feel like it's pointless.

This was supposed to help. He turned over this new leaf but only found a writhing bunch of maggots. It's how he sees these people. There is no empathy here, only disgust.

He knows it's wrong. He knows he should feel more. Maybe with time. But there won't be time enough. This is his first and last shift at the shelter. He won't be back, not even on Thanksgiving.

A woman steps up in line with a small child behind her. She pulls her daughter along by the wrist. The kid is limp and grey. Sean's empty heart cracks. He can't do it, can't live in their misery. He gives each an extra heavy scoop of beans, then with his left hand gives them extra rice.

He is angry this didn't work. That the scales haven't tipped any further toward the middle. His search for balance will need to continue. His anger is with himself. With each weathered face he wills himself to feel more, but he can't. He's seen things. He carries a burden, too.

A man comes through the line smelling worse than the food. Sean faces him and scoops, glances at the clock to see when his shift is over.

It's weird, with the sun down the streets are more colorful than in the daytime. Grady notices the lights, the neon, the bright beacons luring people and their wallets to the flames. He's hunting, prowling. He knows he won't find Nathan walking the streets, but he needs to do something. He needs to be hunting.

He parks his car and gets out. Being sealed inside a box isn't the hunter's way. He walks the sidewalks and feels the glow of the lights on his skin. He can see the reds and blues tint his hands as he passes by the storefronts.

He spots orange dots glowing from the tips of cigarettes outside on the sidewalk like sparks rising from a campfire.

Overhead he knows there are stars, but the lights down here are like a million stars fallen to earth. He doesn't need to see what's in the sky. This is enough. It ought to be enough for anybody.

He spots other hunters. A trio of men moving away from one bar, one feeding spot, to another. You go where the prey is. They laugh and show teeth. They own the territory. Grady follows them.

One peels away, the one who is smoking. He steps into an alley.

"I gotta piss," he says.

The others don't stop. They keep laughing and walking.

Grady follows the smoker into the alley. He can hear the piss hitting the brick wall. By the smell, he is not he first one to go here tonight. His back is to Grady, a cloud of smoke over his head picks up the red of a neon sign at the mouth of the alley.

Grady can't find Nathan, but he can still hunt.

He shoves the smoker in the back. His hands otherwise occupied, he doesn't have time to protect his face. He hits the brick wall and the cigarette curls, the cherry stinging his cheek where it hits. The man staggers back. Grady grabs the back of his jacket, pushes forward. He slams the man's face into the brick again. The smoker's pants fall all the way to his ankles. He has barely made a sound other than a grunt of shock.

Grady lets the man fall to the concrete. He lays on his back, his nose a bloody mess. He stares up, unfocused. His urination had been interrupted but now he finishes, the piss arcing up and then landing on him.

Grady walks out of the alley and back toward his car.

———

"I've told him, like, ten times he can't stay here all night."

The girl in the short kimono is talking to her boss. The older woman scowls.

"Perez!" She calls the bouncer.

A thick, shaved-headed man in a tight T-shirt rounds the corner.

"We got a clinger in room six."

The girl in the kimono puts a soft hand on Perez's arm.

"He's nice. He didn't...nothing happened. He wants to stay all night. I told him he couldn't but—"

Perez is already walking away, he knows his job.

"He wants to stay, he has to pay for his time," the boss lady says. "This ain't a hotel."

"That's what I said. But he's nice. Just don't let Perez—"

"This ain't a hotel," she repeats.

Perez doesn't knock. Nathan is in the small room,

fully clothed. He didn't even get the massage. He wanted to talk and to sleep. The girl, Kimmie, remembered him and he remembered her. She is always on the lookout for signs of the weirdoes. Not wanting anything is a big red flag. But he was good to her. Didn't seem like he was gonna freak out. Too late now, though.

Perez doesn't speak. He grabs Nathan by the collar of his shirt and lifts him like a kitten in his mother's mouth. Nathan moves with the big man. He knows the drill. He doesn't want trouble. That's why he came here. He wants no more trouble, ever.

"It's fine," he says. "I'll go, I'll go."

But Perez is on the job. He doesn't take the john's word for it. He's seen that ruse before. He lets go, the guy starts kicking or punching. Then it gets ugly.

He drags Nathan past Kimmie and the boss lady. One is defiant and enjoying the parade, the other is sad.

Nathan is out on the street. He feels eyes on him. He slinks to his car, wary of predators.

"Four down, one to go."

Detective Kettner strides past Morris' desk.

"They got another one?" Morris asks.

"Yep. The girl."

Kettner sits hard into his seat. The weight of unanswered questions seems to push him down like a bag of rocks on his shoulders.

"Let me guess," Morris says. "Another weird one."

"Not weird as much as all fucked up. I guess it makes sense. She's the only one not found in the water. Something got at her, though. Doc says real bite marks this time. Lots of trauma and blood loss leading to cause of death. Not as simple as the others."

"So either the gang went full Manson family on her, or she really did get gotten by wolves or something."

"Doc says bites are consistent with wolves, yeah."

"Still..."

"Yeah, still."

Kettner taps the file on his knee. He chews the inside of his lip. He tries to remember the faces of the survivors when he interviewed them. Tries to remember any cracks.

"I'm thinking," he says. "I was gonna go get the transcripts and go over the parts about the girl again. What if we go get it from the horse's mouth one more time?"

"They've had a few days to recover."

"And to develop inconsistencies in their stories."

Kettner raises his eyebrows to Morris. Morris slaps his hands down on the desk.

"Which one do we start with?"

"First one that's home."

They stand. Put badges, guns, wallets in pockets.

"I think we play this one close to the vest," Kettner says. "We don't mention that we found them. Not yet."

"Yeah. I'll go with that. More chance to let them make up something dumb."

On the way to the door, "Are we looking for something that isn't here? Are we trying too hard on this one?"

"Something isn't adding up. We, at least, have enough to warrant asking more questions. I think this is a give-em-enough-rope situation here."

Sean answers the door. He's given up guessing what to expect. The reporter? Kerri again? Maia on the prowl?

It's two cops.

"Mr. Boyle," the shorter one says. "I'm Detective Kettner. This is Morris. We spoke to you right after you got back."

Sean remembers. Through his racing heart and his body eating itself after so long in the woods, he can't recall what he said except to know that he stuck to the script. He's mostly sure he did. It was all that was on his mind when he sat down with them.

"May we come in?"

"Of course."

Sean steps aside and let them pass. The kitchen counter is littered with takeout containers and dirty dishes. He feels embarrassed to be such a stereotype. Wife leaves and his housecleaning goes to shit. Truth is he did most of the dishes when Kerri was around. But he hasn't felt like it lately, and now he's ashamed.

"Can I get you guys anything? I got beer or a Coke, maybe."

"No, thank you. We wanted to check in and see how you were doing."

"Oh, y'know. Hanging in there."

"You look better," Morris says. He sounds sincere.

"That's not hard. A shave and a few good meals can do that for you."

"Yeah." Morris pats his belly. "That's a hell of a diet plan you went on."

They all politely chuckle.

"Do you want a seat?" Sean asks. He realizes he is in a T-shirt and old jeans with paint stains on them. No socks on his feet. He must look a mess.

"No, no that's okay," Kettner says. "Just a few quick follow up questions if we could. The guide, Rick, when was the last time you saw him?"

Sean thinks back, fakes that it is harder to remember than it is.

"On that first day. When it all...when the accident happened. He went in the river and, him and Ron, they fell in and just were...whoosh. Swept away."

"And you never saw him again?"

"No. Neither of them. The river just, the river took them." Sean crosses his arms and tries to think if that is some sign of lying. He knows these guys are studying his every move.

"Did anyone else see him again?" Morris asks. "That you know of?"

"I doubt it. We were all together, so if someone found his body, we would have known it."

"So you knew he was dead when he floated away?"

"Well, it's...I guess he could have been alive but the river was moving so fast and—I mean, there was no way he could have survived." Sean uncrosses his arms. He wonders if *that* is a sign. "And he hit his head. I remember that. He hit his head when he fell in with Ron."

"Right. I remember that from the report. Everyone corroborated that account."

"What about Lara?" Kettner asks. "When was the last time you saw her?"

"Well, like I said, she ran off. Ran away into the woods."

"And what do you think made her run away like that? Seems dangerous."

"It was very dangerous, obviously. She was freaking

out. She didn't deal with it well from the start. She was always crying. Always, like, every day. And it all got to be too much, I guess. I don't know. She just took off. And she was crying. Again. But yeah, just ran away and we tried to find her and we called her name for, like, all day and all night. But once she was gone, she was gone."

"And you never came across her again, either."

"No. Never."

Sean feels their eyes scanning him like a cat scan. Like they can read his thoughts. He tries to think of nothing, make his mind a blank so there is nothing to see.

"Thank you for your time, Mr. Boyle."

"Yeah, sure. Anytime."

Sean walks them to the door. When they leave he goes to the kitchen, turns on the water as hot as it goes, and does the dishes.

Kettner and Morris stand at the car before getting in.

"Bullshit?" Morris says.

"It's not *not* bullshit. That's about all I can say with certainty"

"I can't say a goddamn thing about this case with certainty. Other than we got four people dead and one still missing."

"And five people hiding something."

OUT THERE
DAY 18

THEY WOKE early after a fitful sleep of only a few hours. Sean, Wes and Maia huddled together. Nathan and Grady slept nearby but separate, not utilizing any body heat. Ken was wrapped in his sleeping bag stretcher and had the warmest night of the group.

Lara hadn't made it back.

Sean lay awake and thought about what it was like to be lost, like he was, and what it meant to be lost in the world, like he was becoming. When they first went down the river, they became lost. Now people at home must think they were dead. They must be moving on. He was lost to the world. To Kerri. To his job.

They were all lost in the world.

Ken noticed Sean awake and spoke low so the others might not hear.

"My leg feels funny, man."

"How do you mean?"

"I don't know. Not pain, though that's still there. But just...funny. Different."

Sean checked the others. Wes was stirring and Maia had risen to go pee.

"I can check it out, I guess."

"Thanks."

Ken got himself up on his elbows. Sean leaned over and spread the sleeping bag apart. The leg had started to smell again. Not a good sign. Sean lifted the long scrap of fabric that used to cover his lower leg. His hand jerked away and he dropped it.

"What is it?"

Sean could see the concern on Ken's face the same as he was sure Ken could see the revulsion on his. Wes looked up from his patch of ground.

"Everything okay?"

Sean tried reaching for the flap of pant leg again. "It's...I don't know. Maybe."

Wes crawled over to them and peered over Sean's shoulder. He lifted the fabric and Wes had the same reaction. Sean held on to the scrap.

On Ken's stump where his leg ended abruptly at the knee, the wound writhed with tiny white maggots. There must have been two dozen, their bodies twisting and rubbing against each other.

"Holy shit," Wes said.

"What the fuck is it?" Ken said.

"You have some..." Sean started. "There are a few bugs on there."

"Bugs? Shit. Get them off."

Ken reached down to swat at the maggots. Sean stopped his hand.

"Hold on, wait. Wait. I think I read that maggots are good for wounds, especially burns."

"Maggots? What the fuck."

Ken swatted again and Sean gripped his wrist.

"He's right," Wes said.

"What they eat is the dead stuff. They actually help it heal."

"You're telling me maggots are eating my skin?"

"But it's a good thing."

Ken struggled a bit more against Sean, but gave up and fell back.

Maia came over to them.

"No sign of Lara. I'm worried." She looked at the men huddled over Ken's leg. "Is he okay?"

"Yeah," Sean said. "It's good actually."

Ken laid an arm across his eyes. "Get me off this goddamn mountain. Get me out of these fucking woods."

"He's right," Grady said. He stood behind them, backpack on, walking stick in hand, ready to move.

"What about Lara?" Maia said.

"What about her?"

"She's missing."

"She ran away. That's her fault. We can't wait around for her temper tantrum to end. That puts all of us in danger."

Maia threw her hands in the air and brought them down with a slap against her thighs.

Sean and Wes stood. Wes checked his blisters. Shrunken a little from yesterday, but still red and irritated.

"We can't wait, Maia," Sean said. "If we want to save ourselves, we have to keep moving."

"Are we still following this monster?"

"We're all together. We're headed the right way.

We'll see something soon. We have to. The river will lead us there."

"I can't even see the goddamn river anymore."

"We can hear it." He paused to let them all train an ear toward the distant sound of running water. "We'll turn back closer. Right, Grady?"

Grady sharply exhaled, then gave in. "Sure."

Sean moved in close to Maia, put a hand on her arm. She shrugged it off.

"Ken really needs a doctor. He needs to get help."

Maia studied his face. Awake for five minutes and already exhausted for the day. She nodded and reached for her backpack.

Grady watched Sean and Wes flex their fingers trying to get motivated to lift the stretcher.

"How you guys doing with him?"

"It'll be fine," Sean said. Wes stayed silent.

"We could walk him right to the edge of the river, make him easy to spot from the air after we get rescued."

"I said no, Grady."

"How fast did we move yesterday?"

Sean bent down to adjust the poles. "Just stop it. We're fine."

Grady shrugged. "Let's move out."

Sean and Wes assumed their positions with the stretcher. They hoisted Ken and both grunted. It was going to be a long day.

They found Lara after three hours of walking. They'd only traveled a mile.

Maia was the one who heard her. Soft mewling like a wounded animal, which wasn't far off.

Before she said anything to the group, Maia stepped off the path carved out by Grady and Nathan ahead of her. They had turned closer to the river and the ground sloped away steeper than the day before. About twenty feet from where Grady had passed only a minute before, Maia spotted her.

"Guys! It's her."

Sean, close behind, perked up. "It's Lara?"

"Come quick."

Sean and Wes set Ken down on the path. Ken waved them on. "Go. Don't worry about me."

They came up behind Maia and stopped with a jerk. Wes saw Maia's eyes and followed her gaze. Sean was already holding in a breath.

Lara lay in patch of greenery tamped down by her body. It reminded Sean of a crop circle on a farm. She was on her side, one arm reaching out for her friends. Blood streaked her arm from wrist to elbow. Her hair was dark and matted to her scalp with blood. Her nose leaked blood, her lips ran red with it. Her shirt was torn away from her shoulder exposing a bite mark and a ragged tear of exposed muscle.

Lara wheezed out a sound, not a word. A plea for help in any language.

"Oh, my God," Maia said with tears in her voice.

"What happened?" Wes said.

Nobody got close to her. Sean looked around the surrounding trees for whatever animal had done this to her, anxious it might still be around. Grady and Nathan came crashing through the trees retracing their steps on the path.

"You found her?" Nathan said. The others did not answer.

Now four of them stood and watched her slowly twist from one side to the other. As she squirmed her left leg became exposed. Her ankle and foot and most of her calf were a meat grinder of torn flesh. Her pant legs were stained red and the deep green grasses and leaves around her were tinted a deep burgundy with the blood.

She moved slowly, her eyes unfocused but pleading.

"Jesus fucking Christ," Grady said. "Wolf must have gotten to her."

"Or a bear, maybe?" Nathan said.

"Something," Sean said.

"What do we do?" Maia asked. "How can we help her?"

Nobody had an answer. Sean stepped slowly forward, inching toward her. She reached out for him, the blood stains dry on her arm and over them moved a flow of new, fresh blood. He crouched down and took her hand.

"Lara, what happened?"

"Help me," she whispered. A single bubble of red formed on her lip then popped, spreading tiny dots of blood across her chin. Closer now he could see a dark stain in her abdomen and through the tears in her shirt he saw open wounds, exposed muscle.

"We're gonna try." He squeezed her hand but she was too weak to squeeze back.

"Don't make promises," Grady said.

"We have to do something," Maia said.

"Like what?"

She opened and closed her mouth, but no answers came.

Sean could see the dark stains on the earth around her. "She's lost a lot of blood."

"Did it get her in her sleep, you think?" Nathan said.

"Maybe she stumbled over it when it was sleeping, whatever *it* was," Wes said.

"I think bear."

"More wolves in this area," Grady said. "That's what the website for the tour company said. It was all in the waiver we had to sign."

"Does it fucking matter?" Maia said.

The men went quiet. Lara lay flat, out of energy. Sean watched her eyes shut and her chest rise and fall in slow, struggling breaths.

"So what do we do?"

"What can we do?" Grady said. "She's dying."

"But she's not dead."

"If we came by a half hour later she would be."

"We're here now."

"Are you really gonna make me say it?"

Nobody would look at Grady. They knew because they were thinking it, too.

"Don't leave me," Lara wheezed. Her eyes never opened.

Grady swiveled his head between all the averted eyes.

"Fucking weak." He planted his walking stick firmly in the ground. "We can't take her with us."

Nobody argued right away.

"She's not going to make it. She would only slow us down more."

"We can't leave her here to die," Maia said.

"If it happens in an hour or if it had happened an hour before we got here, what's the difference? She ran off. This is just like Rick and Ron falling in the river. It's not our fault. It sucks, but it shouldn't put us in more danger of not getting out of here."

"It's cruel." Maia's tears fell down her cheeks but she did not sob.

"Nature is cruel," Nathan said.

Wes moved closer to Lara. He checked out her wounds and had to look away.

"It's bad."

"How are we gonna move her, anyway?" Grady asked. "We don't have material to make another stretcher. And that's slowing us down enough."

"This whole thing is so fucked." Maia cursed into the canopy of trees. She screamed out the obscenity until her throat hurt.

Lara lay there on a bed of fallen leaves and pine needles. Dead things being absorbed back into the earth. Her blood had already fed the ground. The iron would feed the soil, insects had already feasted on her blood. More were lined up to devour her corpse until nothing remained. The way of the forest, the way of the world.

Sean thought of Ken's leg. The piece of him they left behind after the amputation. Was it already gone? Absorbed by a world built for recycling its own?

Grady was right. He knew it. He suspected they all knew it. Lara was dying. A countdown had begun.

"I think we should vote," he said. "We all need to agree."

"You're still gonna make me the bad guy in this," Grady said.

"No. You're right. She ran off. That was her choice. And we're not prepared to help her now. So let's vote. Leave her here?"

Sean raised his hand.

"Look," Grady said, "as long as we're voting and as long as I'm the asshole here, maybe we should be voting on whether to put her out of her misery."

Maia turned away and stomped a few feet into the trees. "This is goddamn absurd. I won't be a part of it. I won't. It's fucking barbaric."

"Is it, Maia? Is it?" Grady followed her. "You'd rather her sit there and suffer? She's already gone. All we'd be doing is ending her pain."

"I won't say yes to that because of how much you'd probably enjoy it. What's your plan, Grady? Huh? Cut her throat with your precious knife? Cut out pieces and eat her? You saw what that animal did to her? That's what animals do. That's what *you* did. Because you're a fucking animal."

"This shit again."

"Yes, this shit. It's all this shit. We can't get out of it. It's all around us. It's killing Lara and it's killing all of us."

"That's why we need to get a move on and get out of here."

"Guys!" Sean cut in. "Can we vote?"

Wes waved his hand dismissively. "I don't think we should...I won't vote for Grady's thing."

"No way," Ken spoke up from his spot on the ground. Sean wasn't even sure he'd been listening.

"Okay. We're not unanimous on that one."

Nathan pulled in tight to himself, glad he did not have to vote. His hand had been ready to rise, to agree with Grady. His stomach roiled. Empty and eating itself, the stress boring a hole through him and into his gut. He could feel it grow. He wanted out. Time to keep moving.

"I vote we keep going," Nathan said and raised his hand. "We don't need anything else to slow us down."

Grady lifted his hand. "I vote we go."

Sean looked at Wes. Wes lifted his hand. "We go."

Ken raised his arm. It poked up beyond his stretcher cocoon like a sapling tree. He said nothing.

Sean raised his hand. He looked to Maia, who had her back turned to the group again. After a moment, her arm lifted and her shoulder shook as she sobbed.

"Okay. We go and leave her here. If we can send help, we will."

Everyone knew it would be futile.

Grady followed his footsteps from before and continued down the slope, Nathan at his heels. Wes and Sean lifted Ken and followed. Maia fell in behind Wes, never looking back at Lara.

Lara moved again, pushing up on one hand, lifting her face to the backs of her coworkers. She summoned every remaining bit of strength and cried out.

"Don't leave me."

After that she screamed. Her cries were weak, but loud enough to make birds flitter away from the trees above her. Lara's screams followed the group into the woods as they trudged away. Each cry for help pierced them like a thorn. No one spoke. They walked on until the screaming faded away.

BACK HOME

GRADY PRESSES the button on his steering wheel. The phone connects through the speakers.

"Hello?"

"Mr. Beyers, this is Detective Kettner."

Grady checks his rearview, scans the street outside. Can they see him? Do they know?

"How are you, detective?"

"We're wanting to speak with you if we could. We went by your place and you weren't home."

"No, I'm out. Won't be back for a while."

I'm out hunting a man seems like the wrong thing to say.

"We could stop in later."

Don't say anything to make them suspicious. Be agreeable.

"If you'd like. I wouldn't want to keep you out too late." He tries to put a smile in his voice. "Unless you want the overtime."

"We're on our way to talk to Wes Brock right now. How about after?"

"What about first thing in the morning? I'm not sure how late I'll be."

"That would work. Can you come to the station?"

"Sure. Of course."

"We'd appreciate it Mr. Beyers."

"No problem."

A man lightly jogs across the street, jaywalking in front of Grady. He knows if he accelerates he could hit the man, take him down. Maybe not kill him. Maybe send him to a wheelchair. Maybe roll over him, drag his body under the car for a block. If he accelerated.

"Have you spoken to Nathan yet?"

"No, sir. He wasn't home, either."

"No. He's not, huh? He was supposed to meet us out and I haven't heard from him. I thought maybe you knew where he was."

"No, sir. So, see you in the morning. Say nine a.m.?"

"Works for me."

They hang up. Grady knows where they are headed next. He doesn't know what Wes will say. He pulls to a stop at a traffic light. The red reflects down into puddles like pools of blood.

———

Maia knocks on her new agent's office door. Amy comes to the glass door, already smiling. Her hands are clenched into little fists that she shakes in victory up by her shoulders. She's excited.

Amy opens the door, the receptionist gone. The office empty after hours.

"Sorry to keep you until late," Maia says.

"Girl, for this, I'll stay until midnight. Sit, sit."

Amy guides her to the reception couch, too excited to make it to her office.

"I've been on the phone all day. You wanna know why?"

"Why?" Maia has picked up Amy's infectious smile. She knows good news is coming.

"Fielding offers. I swear on a stack of Bibles, Maia, I have never had this kind of response to a book. *Everyone* wants it. And you know what that means."

When Maia clearly doesn't, Amy waves jazz hands at her and sing-songs, "Bidding war."

"Oh. That's great."

"Better than great. It's amazing. Played one off the other off the other all day until about a half hour ago." Amy is bouncing on the couch. "You know you wanted a six figure payday?"

"Yes. Oh my God, you got it?"

Amy lays her hands on Maia's and sets a look of smugness behind the smile.

"Try seven."

"Seven figures?" Maia takes a second to focus on what that means.

"A million two."

Amy waits for the news to sink in. She helps it along. "One point two, Maia. They gave you one point two million for the book."

"Holy..."

"That's right. Okay, now look," Amy tries to push past the excitement and get down to business, "they want it fast. Strike while the iron is hot, y'know? I have a writer lined up to help you. One of the best. She'll do it for a flat fee. All you have to do is dictate. Tell your story, she'll write it up and then we're on the best seller list by fall. Fast track, baby."

"What did they think of the title?"

"Loved it. Didn't even suggest another. They're getting a cover artist on it this weekend. Maia, this is amazing. It never happens this fast outside of political memoirs or prisoners of war. But we've got to deliver. It's got to be raw. It's got to have details. And it's got to be exclusive. We can't have anyone else beating us to market. That's key."

"Okay, yeah. I'll make sure of it. One point...holy shit."

"I should have paperwork by tomorrow. But you need to start getting shit together tonight."

"Okay, yeah, I will."

Amy stops and looks Maia deep in her eyes.

"Congratulations, girl. At least some good will come out of what you went through."

"Yeah."

Maia feels the high hit her brain like a jolt of cocaine, if she remembers back to college that well. She'll have to figure out how to keep Grady from being pissed. Maybe with this much money she can pay him off. Or maybe her book has a great villain. Maybe she can tell the story without any of it. What they went through is compelling enough. People will still want to read it.

But if she came clean about some of the things Grady did...

Wes answers the door to his hotel room. He expects the manager. Someone to tell him to keep it down. But he realizes he wasn't making any noise. He'd come in from the bar, taken off his shoes... He looks down. His shoe. He kicks the other off.

He sat in the chair, must have dozed off, then the knocking.

"Okay, okay."

Three more knocks like firecrackers. He flinches at each sharp noise. Wes opens the door. Two men in dull suits.

"Mr. Brock? Detective Kettner. We spoke directly after the incident."

"If you say so."

Kettner trades a look with his partner. Wes jumps slightly. He hadn't seen Morris there at all.

"The fuck are you?"

"Detective Morris. Is this a bad time?"

"Depends what for."

They can see he's drunk. Anyone could. His eyes are lidded. His cat nap on the chair still hangs over him like a fog. He holds on to the door tightly like it is keeping him up.

This many days in and Wes is up to his old speed. Falling back in went much faster than the initial descent those years ago. Habits came back easy. Three drinks per bar, then move. Nobody can toss you out. Only interact with the bartender to order your drink. No chit chat. That'll get you in trouble. Order your three at once and make like you're getting them for you and two friends. Call out the first two, pretend to forget the third and then go with, "Oh, screw it. Just three of the same. Jack and Coke. They can deal with it."

Take your three drinks and retreat to a dark corner. Drink them and then leave.

"Mr. Brock," Kettner says. "We wanted to ask you some more questions about what went on out when you were lost."

"Ask me? Go ahead. I can tell you some shit."

A raised eyebrow and piqued interest push Kettner over the threshold. "You mind?"

He's in before Wes can answer, Morris behind him.

"What exactly can you tell us?" Morris say. "Anything you might have left out in our first interview?"

"A shit ton. Shit load. A shit lot, a lot."

Kettner and Morris are excited and skeptical at the same time. He's drunk as anyone still standing can be, yet it might have loosened his tongue. Kettner gets his cell phone out, clicks open his voice recorder app.

"What do you want to tell us, Mr. Brock? It's Wesley Brock, right? And we're here at..." He checks the digital alarm clock by the bed. "Nine fifty three on Tuesday..."

As Kettner lays down the court-required setup, Morris looks around the rented room. The bed is untouched. Couch cushions at odd angles. The hotel stationary is in a pile on the floor.

"Were you trying to write something down, Mr. Brock? A confession of some sort maybe?"

"Me, confess? What do I need to confess? Ask them. They're the ones."

"Ask who?"

"Them. All of them. Spilling bullshit. Ron and Ken. I worked with them, y'know. And friends. They were friends. Work friends."

"What about them?"

"They're fucking dead, that's what."

"Yes, we know that. Is there something about their deaths you want to tell us?"

"Yeah. That it's bullshit. All of it."

Wes looks like he might tip over. He reaches a hand back behind him and sinks into the chair. Kettner steps closer to him with his recorder held out. Morris taps his partner on the shoulder, gives him a slight head shake. Kettner waves him off.

"What about it is bullshit, Wes?"

"They're dead. That's what's bullshit. Dead and dead."

Wes's eyes begin to shut.

Kettner shuts off the recorder.

"Even if we get something it's not admissible."

"Sounds like he's got a lot to say."

"How much of it is the liquor talking?"

"Hard to tell."

Kettner taps Wes's socked foot with the toe of his shoe.

"Mr. Brock. Would you come down to the station in the morning after you've had a good rest? Would you come in a talk to us, tell us what's bullshit?"

"Who?"

"Us. Would you come and tell us what you know?"

"I go home tomorrow. They let me go home."

"Yes, well, maybe we can still stick to that if you come see us early. We can be all done in time for you to head home no problem."

"Ask them. You should be asking them."

"We are, sir. We're talking to everyone. We want you to come down to the station tomorrow morning at ten. Can you do that for us, Mr. Brock?"

Wes was still, his eyes closed.

"Fuck."

Morris goes to the room desk, picks up a sheet of paper from the floor and writes out their information. He underlines ten a.m. twice. He pulls a business card from his shirt pocket and leaves it on top of the note.

"You willing to bet he knows something the others aren't saying?"

"I'm not gonna bet the house on it," Kettner says. "But I'm willing to lay out a few chips on the table and spin the wheel, see what he knows."

"Tell you one thing he doesn't know is when to say no to a drink."

In the lobby they set a wakeup call for Wes. Nine fifteen. They leave cards from each of them with the front desk. Ask them to make sure Wes calls in as soon as he gets up, and to remind him of his appointment at the station.

The front desk clerk nods and writes it all down. He puts the notes in a slot for the morning crew, then promptly forgets about it.

Grady watches the cops leave the hotel. They climb into their car and drive off. Wes isn't with them so he's not in custody. Maybe he worked a deal. Maybe he sold out the others. Maybe he sold out just Grady.

He doesn't want to talk to the front desk. He's done his asking already, over the phone. He knows Wes's room number. Grady crosses the lobby on the far end, away from the desk, which is unmanned at the moment, anyhow. A light murmur of voices comes from the lobby bar riding a wave of smooth jazz. Grady gets on an elevator. Presses fifteen.

He double checks. This is one of those buildings that doesn't have a thirteenth floor. Most hotels do that. Nobody wants to stay there. They get tired of relocating people so they trick them and their stupid superstitions. Send them to fourteen and no one complains. Same goddamn floor.

He gets off at fifteen (fourteen) and finds the room. He knocks. Quiet at first. Louder when there is no answer. The door swings open. Wes looks like a sleep-walker. Half unconscious.

"Wes. How are you, buddy?"

"The fuck you want?"

Grady enters the room, pulls the door closed behind him. Wes is pliable, moves anywhere Grady touches him to go. One finger on his chest and he's moving backward into the room. If only everyone were like this.

"What did those cops want?"

"What cops?"

"The ones who were just here."

"Questions. More questions. It's all bullshit."

"Right. And what did you say?"

Not that anything he said could be trusted. Or used in court.

"Bullshit. Talk to them, I said. I told them. Told them all."

Grady can see the room is a mess. He spots the note on the desk, the cop's card with it. The time, the inter-view request. They got nothing. He's too drunk.

Wes can't make that meeting.

"Hey, Wes." Grady holds up the note. "Wes."

Wes looks at him, unfocused eyes.

"See this? Those cops need to talk to you. They need you come down to the station."

Grady brings the note over to Wes, holds it in his hand so his fingers are covering the ten a.m. underlined at the bottom. Wes stares at it and rereads words, but little sinks in.

"You gotta go, buddy. Can't keep the cops waiting."

Grady puts a hand under Wes's armpit. Guides him toward the chair. He sits him down, moves his shoes closer so he can reach them.

"Get set, bud. You gotta go. Don't want to be late." He stands and moves to the night stand. "Where are your keys?"

"What keys?"

"To your rental car."

Wes toes the shoes with his sock feet. "I just took these off."

Grady finds his keys and his wallet. He helps Wes into his shoes then stands him up. Easily moveable. Like leading a dog on a leash. He gets Wes to the elevator. He's excited when he sees a button for P1. He doesn't have to parade Wes through the lobby.

They get to the garage and Grady keeps one hand under Wes's armpit and he guides him. With his other hand he holds the key fob for the rental and presses the button over and over. Finally a beep.

He puts Wes in the passenger seat and drives the car out of the garage. He parks on the street in front of his own car. Grady gets out and helps Wes slide behind the wheel. He does not attach his seatbelt.

"Can't keep cops waiting, buddy."

"Fuckin' bullshit."

Grady gets into his own car. Honks the horn lightly

once. He sees the brake lights dim and Wes pulls into traffic. Grady follows. At first Wes is slow. When they get clear of most traffic Grady honks the horn at him again. Wes speeds up a tiny bit. They travel straight. Wes doesn't turn off or change lanes. He passes through a stop sign with no incident. Traffic is lightening up.

Grady moves his car closer to Wes. There is a break in the traffic. Grady sets his bumper on Wes's rear bumper. Grady slowly picks up speed. Wes is pushed along. They pass forty miles an hour. Wes starts to veer. Grady guns the engine.

As Wes turns slightly the full force of Grady's engine shoves him off the road. He doesn't hit him, only a gentle push. Nothing to show up in any investigation as a rear-ending accident.

Wes drives off the road, the car speeding up as it skids sideways. Grady hits his own brakes and Wes flings off ahead of him. The car tilts until it is sideways, then the road ends and the tires catch on the curb. Wes's rental car, a sensible compact, flips sideways and rolls. One complete rollover.

Airbags deploy, glass shatters. The car comes to a stop. Grady pulls over. The rental steams from under the hood. The engine ticks as it idles, the tires bent and keeping it from rolling.

Grady gets out and runs to the car, peers in the driver's side window which has shattered. Wes is breathing, but battered. He slumps over, his legs in the driver's side and his torso in the passenger side. Blood seeps from cuts on his forehead. He is passed out, either from the impact or the alcohol.

But he is breathing.

Grady checks the street. Still no one coming. He

leans in and presses Wes's face into the passenger seat, nose and mouth down into the fabric. He pushes hard on the back of his head, cutting off any airway.

He checks behind him, up and down the non-residential street. A closed bakery, a closed print shop, a vacant storefront with a FOR LEASE sign. No people. No life. Even in the forest there was life everywhere. When you couldn't see it you could hear it. When you couldn't hear anything you knew there were insects underfoot.

Here there was nothing. Concrete and brick, lifeless. No trees. No water. Rivers of pavement. Buildings where the trees would grow. But they're as tall as they're going to get.

Grady presses and presses, hoping any bruising from his hand on the back of Wes's head will be accounted for by the accident. He can see no more rise and fall of Wes's chest.

He leans out of the window, gasping for air. With Wes gone, Grady is the only living thing. His territory. His kingdom.

OUT THERE
DAY 19

THEY HAD TRAVELED MORE than five miles. Nobody knew this; to them it seemed like twenty. The terrain became more unpredictable. Gentle slopes gave way to larger dips, which backtracked in sharp inclines for several hundred yards. Through it all the river cut its path but the rocky shore made it impossible for the group to follow directly.

They passed several short waterfalls and sections of protruding rocks which made them all thankful nobody had pursued the raft idea.

They slept in fits, napping in the afternoon when energy reserves ran low and catching short stretches at night in between shivering from cold and waking at every snap of a twig or skittering sound in the trees above.

They fed on earthworms pulled from the ground, fat grubs and larvae from under the bark of rotting wood, hard green berries that were so acidic they made everyone fight cramps for the next hour as they walked.

And there was Ken.

Blisters leaked fluid as they burst on Wes's palms. The sleeping bag showed signs of tearing at the seams. If that failed they were done. Sean could barely open his fingers once they were clawed around the poles for an hour at a time as they walked in slow trudges through the maze of trees.

Ken tried to encourage them. He called out his support. He urged them on. He also grew weaker and his fever had returned.

The maggots feasting on his leg grew in numbers. There was a short discussion about eating them, but there were some things the group could not get past.

The night before Sean lay on his back looking up through a break in the trees. Thin clouds moved over the scattering of stars, dimming them and then revealing them again like a magician's cape. Far off he heard the howl of a wolf.

He wondered, was it the same wolf who found Lara? Was this a cry of victory?

He thought about her back in her circle of trampled greenery. How long had she lived after they left? He wondered if the animals returned. She would be food for any number of creatures who lived in the woods. Birds of prey overhead could spot her and dip down under the canopy for a meal. Insects would scarcely wait for her pulse to stop before starting their rituals. The rodents and scavengers of the forest would move in, lured by the scent. Would they know she'd been left like a gift by the group who voted for her death?

We can't tell anyone, he thought. We can't speak of

any of this. So much had gone on that nobody should know. Nobody would understand. Not unless they were here, fighting for life.

He felt like they were losing the fight.

They hadn't taken in enough calories. They'd had virtually no protein. Each walk to the river for water added twenty minutes to their journey. And they might be walking in circles, for all they knew. They only way they had to judge their progress was the constant slow fall of the land and the path of the river.

From a world measured in city blocks, they had no way of knowing how far they had come or how far they had to go.

He thought of the difference between a bad person and a bad deed. Good people could still do bad deeds, right? It didn't fundamentally change the person, did it? And you had to factor in circumstances. You had to.

He had to. If not, he'd go insane. Perhaps that's what happened to Lara.

He thought about it and tried to justify. He tried to explain it to himself, to rationalize all they had been through with all they had done. They were good people who had done bad things. They weren't bad people. But he saw there was a line that could be crossed.

He wondered if Grady had crossed it. He wondered what it would take for him to step over that line.

Morning came before he had a chance to fall back asleep.

They trekked to the river to drink. Maia brought Ken's water bottle to fill. They'd drink their limit before they started out and resist stopping for as long as they could.

They followed the sound, Grady in the lead and the others tracing his footsteps. Maia brought up the rear. She told herself she was strong. She repeated it like a mantra. She felt like she was lying to herself.

She'd kept up, done her part, not asked for help from anyone. She hadn't panicked like Lara or lied like Grady. She hadn't given up. But now each footstep was a journey. The endless rows of trees blurred her vision. They never stopped. They'd changed as they descended. The pine trees were almost all gone now, replaced by a thick leafy tree she didn't know the name of. Low bushes were more common and more apt to give up berries, although they were sour and unripened and burned her stomach.

She stopped thinking about the things she was eating. She had to. Put it out of her mind and she could overcome. But the woods were relentless. At night she felt eyes on her. She longed for direct sunlight to hit her face. The constant shade overhead was worse than spending all day under fluorescent lights in the office.

She wanted her view back from the sixth floor. To see the world from anywhere but ground level. To see a world with variety, with some difference. The architect's mark on a building. Not the cloned sameness of trees.

They reached the water and found a small pool. They stepped upriver a few feet to where the water tumbled over a small rise and made a three foot fall like a drinking fountain. The men had long ago given up on deferring to her first because she was a woman. Grady dunked his head in and drank.

When it was her turn she tilted her head and sipped. In the pool below she saw movement. She lifted her head. Silver scales glinted in the dappled sunlight.

"There's fish."

She pointed to the small pool. It was like a stocked pond on someone's property. The still water had made a refuge for weary fish and they gathered there in a dense school. Maybe a hatchery, she thought. She didn't know and didn't care. There were fish.

The others crowded the shore and counted in their heads. A dozen or more. The pool had one narrow entrance back to the free flowing water of the river. An easy escape route.

"Get a log or something," she said. "Block that gap."

"Hold on," Grady said. "If I tie my knife to my stick I can make a spear."

"You waste your time doing that. I'm getting us some fish." She pointed at Sean. "Get a log or a big rock."

Sean moved into the trees, Wes followed. Maia searched the shore for a suitable spot to enter the pool without scaring the fish.

Grady enlisted Nathan to run back to where they'd left their packs and get the rest of the rope. Nathan obeyed the order.

Sean and Wes came back each holding an end to a four foot section of dead tree. It dripped dead bark and looked worm-eaten and rotten, but it would do the trick. It was plenty wide enough.

"Drop it there," she pointed. "Don't scare the fish, though."

With gentle steps, the two men waded through the water on the edge of the pool. Two fish darted from the still water back into the river. The rest huddled together.

They came to the opening and set the log down. It closed the gap in the rocks and left only a thin layer of water on top of the log for the fish to swim through to escape the pool.

Maia stood ready with her hands outstretched. She tried to follow any single fish but they moved quickly and the flashes of silver made it hard to track. Hunger took over. She dove. Plunging her hands into the water in the midst of a school of at least six fish clustered together, she clamped her fingers shut like a claw. Soft, slick skin slid across her palms. She curled her fingers and her uncut nails dug in. She lifted out of the water with a fish in her grip.

Sean and Wes reached in after the others who swirled around like dancers at a punk rock nightclub, slamming into each other, thrashing and slapping tails.

Sean had one, then it slipped away. Wes brushed against two. Maia had thrown hers to the shore where Grady stood waiting for Nathan to return.

"Don't let it flop back in," she called.

Grady pounced, his knife already out and open. He stuck the fish through the head.

Maia hurled a second fish to shore. Wes had one in his hands and Sean came up with a small one.

The others had escaped in a panic, sliding over the rocks in the inch of water that led them back to the river, their backs touching the air in a glint of scales.

They had four fish, all at least ten inches long, Maia's first one being the biggest.

Nathan returned with the rope. He saw Grady already lopping off heads with the knife.

They ate the meat raw, careful to pick out bones and not get scales stuck in their teeth. Nobody knew what kind of fish they were eating. Nobody enjoyed the flavor, but everyone ate all they were given.

They moved on, a new energy in their step.

They made decent time for the first hour. They came to a steep drop. The ground fell away, exposing rock for a six-foot groove in the earth. Grady, ahead, scouted the area for an easier passage. Sean and Wes put Ken down and peered over the edge.

Grady returned. "This is the best it's gonna get unless we keep walking, who knows how far away from the river."

"I don't see how we're gonna get him down that," Sean said.

"Better think of something," Grady said, defiant.

Sean and Wes walked the ridge looking for a way down, a set of footholds, a gentler slope. They found none.

"I'll walk it," Ken said.

They turned and saw he was up on his elbows, pained expression on his face.

"I can get up on one leg and use you as crutches. I can do it. You've been carrying my ass long enough."

"Are you sure?"

"More sure than you guys seem that you can get this stretcher down there."

"Worth a shot," Grady said.

Grady stood on the lip of the drop-off. He held out a hand to Nathan, who took it and helped lower Grady down. He found slender footholds in the rock and let go of Nathan's hand with only about three feet left to climb. Using an exposed root as a hand hold Grady scaled the rest of the rock and landed on the ground below and stood like it was nothing.

He got set to help Nathan down from below. He pointed out footholds and the root to hold on to. Nathan made it easily. Not too hard when you had two legs.

Maia refused any help and climbed down on her own, scraping her palm on a rock in the process, but she kept the cut to herself, pressing her shirt into her palm to stop the flow of blood.

Sean passed the stretcher down to the others, and then he and Wes stood Ken up, bracing him like a pair of crutches.

Ken's head swam with the sudden shift in his body. He had been prone so long he felt like he might faint. He leaned hard on Wes.

"Whoa."

"You okay?"

"Little lightheaded is all. Standing up feels weird."

Sean noticed a few of the maggots fell from the stump of his leg to the ground.

"So I think we should turn and face the rock wall like they did," Sean said.

"Maybe one of us goes first and we sort of hand him down?" Wes said.

"I don't know. I think we need to give him as much support as we can."

Ken put pressure on his leg. It hadn't held any weight in a long time.

"I think I can support myself. I just need you to help guide me."

"Can we make it three across, though?" Sean asked.

"Guess we'll find out."

They backed to the drop-off and started down.

Grady and Nathan stood below, pointing out areas of footing.

"Sean, to your left. Yeah, there."

Sean could feel the heat of Ken's body next to him, the fever making him sweat, the effort of standing after so many days pushing his temperature even higher. They bent at the waist and began to move down the rock face.

Only the height of an average man, the six-foot drop felt like a mountain crevasse. Sean and Wes both felt the full weight of Ken when they moved over the edge, fully supporting themselves on thin rock footholds and a one-handed grip on the lip of the drop. One arm each was wrapped around Ken's waist, holding him up as much as guiding him down.

"Wait, wait, wait," Ken said. Sean could see his eyes roll back in their sockets. He was lightheaded again, about to pass out.

"Get that root," Grady said below.

Wes let go and tried to reach for it, but missed.

The three of them began to pull away from the rock wall. Sean grabbed tighter onto the lip of the drop, but he felt the pull of Ken's body on his shoulder. Ken was out, his one leg slipped from the foothold. They were going down.

Grady and Nathan made a reach for them, but the three tangled bodies sailed past and landed hard on the ground.

Ken fell on top of Wes, mostly, and Sean fell free from both of them, landing on his side. A fallen branch poked into Wes's arm, digging a cut along his bicep and his hand was wedged under Ken as he fell. Ken lay still on the ground for a moment before coming to and jerking his body.

He turned his head and vomited the fish and water he'd eaten for breakfast.

"God dammit," Grady yelled.

Maia ran forward, crouching next to Sean. "You okay?"

"I think so," he squeaked out, fighting for his breath.

Ken moaned and rolled his body in a way that reminded everyone of when they first pulled him to shore on day one.

"Could've killed us all," Grady said. "He's a fucking liability."

"Just relax," Maia said. She moved next to Ken and tried to see if anything was broken.

"My arm," Wes said. He slid his arm out from under Ken and grimaced in pain. He held out his left hand, his wrist in the clutch of his right hand. The pinky finger on his left hand angled sharply and unnatural.

Maia gasped.

"Oh, perfect," Grady said.

Nathan stepped in next to Wes. "It looks like a dislocation. We need to get it back in place."

"How?" Wes asked through gritted teeth.

"I'd have to pull it. You pull it straight out and then let it sit back in the socket. At least, I saw them do it in a movie once."

"Yeah, I've seen that, too," Maia said.

"But you've never done it?" Wes said.

Nathan shook his head no.

"Fuck," Wes yelled. He held out his damaged hand to Nathan. "Go. Do it. Make it quick."

Ken's moans made a morbid soundtrack. Sean got

his breathing back to normal and pushed up on one arm to watch Nathan take gentle hold of Wes's arm.

"Maybe someone should hold him."

"I'll do it," Grady said. He moved behind Wes and bear hugged him. He pulled tight, unleashing some of his frustration. Wes wheezed for air.

"Do it," Grady said.

Nathan pulled. The pinky finger came forward. Wes screamed and Grady turned his head away to protect his ears. Nathan got it as close to lined up as he thought he could and then let the finger go. There was a light pop and his finger was straight again.

"Holy crap, it worked," Nathan said.

Maia patted his shoulder. "Good job."

Grady let Wes go with a shove. He stood and walked away from the group and picked up his walking stick again.

Nathan examined Wes's arm cut. "Just a cut. We should tie it off." He tore a section of Wes's sleeve and used it to wrap around the cut and cinch it tight.

"Great. How's he gonna carry all that weight with a bad arm and a busted finger?"

"We'll deal with it," Maia said.

"Yeah," Sean said. "It's over now."

"That's what I'm fucking afraid of," Grady said. "It's over for all of us."

He grabbed his walking stick and stomped away. They were done for the day. The rest of the afternoon was spent recovering and making a small camp.

BACK HOME

GRADY LEAVES THE POLICE STATION. He's answered their questions. The same answers. The truth of things left so far behind in the woods that he's starting to think they really didn't happen. Repeat it enough and maybe it will really be true.

They thank him, but the frustration is clear on their faces. They haven't revealed anything. Typical cops. Playing it close.

On his way out Grady asks, "So did you hear from Nathan at all yet? I never got word from his last night."

"Not yet," Kettner says. "We're meeting with Mr. Brock next."

"Oh. Well, good luck with that."

"Mr. Beyers," Morris says, stabbing in the dark. "Is there any reason you can think why the guide, Rick, would have had pieces missing from his leg?"

Grady stops in the hall. He faces the cops, face a blank, trying to decide how to react.

"Animal, I guess. We heard a lot of wolves out there. I heard there were bears."

"Wolves don't swim."

"Maybe you have it wrong. It was Ken who ended up missing a leg. But we explained, we had to amputate to—"

"Not a whole leg missing. Just pieces."

"I have no idea."

Morris nods his head, eyes a hard line at Grady.

"Thanks for your help," Kettner says.

Grady turns and leaves.

"Worth a try, right?" Morris says.

"Hard to gauge that one. Feels like his eyes are stalking you."

"Like a wolf?"

"Maybe."

———

Kerri doesn't call first, just shows up. She has a man with her, a friend Sean recognizes from her work. He avoids eye contact, clearly uncomfortable. On the street behind them while they stand on the porch is a rental truck. A big U-Haul waiting to gather the rest of Kerri's things.

"I wasn't sure if you'd be home," she says. "You remember David."

"Yeah." Sean gives a weak wave, which David returns.

"I figured you might be at work. Y'know, earning a paycheck."

"I'm still on leave. Paid leave."

She throws a look over her shoulder to the truck.

"I'm here for the rest of my stuff."

Sean nods. He can see that.

"And to give you this."

She holds out a file-size envelope. It has the return address of a law firm on it, a name he recognizes from late night TV ads. He knows what's inside.

"Divorce papers?"

Kerri nods.

He's thought of it, briefly. It would have felt good to beat her to it, he thinks. But either way he won't contest it. Get it over with. Move on.

"There will be stuff to settle like selling the house."

"Selling the house?"

"It's an asset."

"So you're forcing me out?"

"You don't need a place this big."

"We never did."

David shuffles his feet on the concrete pad of the porch. "Maybe I should give you guys a minute to talk in private."

"No," she says. "This is all better handled through the lawyers, anyway. I'll get my things and leave." Sean hasn't moved from the doorway. Kerri juts out a hip. "This might be easier if you aren't here."

"Yeah. It might."

Sean thinks he can see David breathe a sigh of relief.

"Just let me get changed," Sean says. He turns into the house, leaving the door open. An invitation without having to invite her in.

"I'm going to talk to that reporter," he says over his shoulder. "Sell her my story."

"Good for you." There is bitterness in her voice.

Before seeing the divorce papers he may have taken the offer for the money as a way to get her back. Now he wants her to know he's going to do it to piss her off. To let her know she missed out. But he doesn't even know if he really will do it. He wants to hurt her. To prove some point.

But everything seems pointless these days.

Grady sits in his borrowed office staring out the window. He's claimed his territory, but isn't sure it's what he wants. Nothing feels right. His skin feels too tight, then too loose.

Nathan is out there. Beyond the glass, down below. Telling someone? Who knows? Grady grips a pen in his fist. *None of us are innocent.*

There is a slight knock at the glass door. Maia is there.

"You enjoying this? Your little power grab?"

Grady swivels the chair, Allison's chair, to face her.

"Someone needs to lead around here."

"Where have I heard that before?"

"What do you want, Maia?"

"To make sure you know you can't just take things. It's not that easy. This isn't like out there. There are rules and ways of doing things."

Grady sets down the pen, laces his fingers together.

"Word on the promotions should be coming down soon. Seeing as you and I are the only ones coming back to work, it seems, it looks like we have them. We don't need to compete with each other anymore. Why can't you let it go?"

Maia laughs. "That sounds good coming from you."

Her cell phone rings. She steps out of the office to answer. It is Detective Kettner.

"We were wondering if you could come down and answer a few more questions we have about your time out there. Just some follow ups. Around lunchtime?"

"Sure, of course," she says. Take notes, she reminds herself. Keep details. It all goes in the book.

"And have you seen or heard from Wes Brock or Nathan Heyes? We haven't been able to reach them."

"No. They haven't come back to work. Didn't Wes go back home?"

"He was scheduled to today but he had an appointment with us that he missed. His hotel says he hasn't checked out yet."

"Well, no, I haven't seen them. Either one."

"Okay. Thanks. Can we expect you at noon?"

"Yes."

She hangs up. Two missing. She can see Grady through the glass—watching her.

A tap on the shoulder makes her jump. It's Sean.

"What are you doing here?"

"I needed to get out of the house. Figured I'd stop by and see how things were going around here."

He's dressed casually, not for work. Maia wonders where he's been and what he's been doing. Getting rid of Wes and Nathan? Does he have that much to hide?

Don't they all?

"What's Grady doing in Allison's office?"

"Doing what he usually does. Pushing his way in." Maia watches him through the glass with a look of disgust. They walk back into Allison's office.

"Sean," Grady says. "Good to see you."

Sean nods. "You, too." The lies come so easily now.

"Look, I won't be back for a while. I'm taking a leave of absence," Maia says.

"Too much too soon, huh?" Grady says.

She hates the smug satisfaction on his face. "The company set it up for us to take time off. I think it's a good idea not to rush things."

"I guess. If you need it." Grady leans back in the plush chair.

Allison's assistant pokes her head in the door.

"Oh, congratulations, Maia, on the book deal. That's awesome."

Maia's face goes pale. "What?"

"I read about it online. The article said 'Hollywood ready'. Do you think it'll be a movie?"

Grady sits up straight. He dismisses the assistant with a curt command to shut the door behind her. Alone now, but still on view behind the glass walls, Grady speaks low and slow. "You're writing a book?"

The news is out. Maia knows she can't backpedal now. She straightens her jacket. "Yes. About our experiences."

A thick fog of tension fills the room. Grady leans forward in the plush leather chair and it creaks. "What about our experiences?"

"That's up to you, really."

Maia grins, knowing she has the upper hand. Liking the feeling. It's been too long coming with Grady. She wants to see him squirm.

"Spit it out, already."

"Sean already knows," she says and nods toward Sean. This gets a sharp look from Grady. "But if there are...events you don't want discussed in the book, then that can be arranged. But it's a tradeoff."

"And what if I don't want any events discussed at all?"

"I'm writing the damn book, Grady. What it needs to be is exclusive. I can protect you. All you need to do is keep quiet. No other deals. No other stories out there to compete with mine."

"It's not your story, Maia. And it's not one I want out there at all."

"That ship has sailed."

Grady stands quickly, shoving the chair back against the wall of windows. Sean flinches but Maia does a good job of standing firm.

"It's not happening. We've discussed this. Nobody says a goddamn thing."

"Not without your approval, you mean?"

"Not at all."

Grady aims an angry finger at Sean. "You might be able to get a pissant like him to submit to you, but I won't. No book. No way. Everyone needs to keep their damn mouths shut."

"It's not up to you, Grady. I'm giving you a chance to keep what you want hidden. I know I can get Wes and Nathan to agree, too."

"Wes isn't a problem anymore." He says it like a threat. Maia thinks back to her phone call with the police.

"Why not?"

"Maybe you'd like to find out."

"What did you do, Grady?"

Sean leans in. "Wait, what's up with Wes?"

"What did you do?" she says again.

"He wanted to talk. I didn't let that happen. You could learn a lesson here, Maia. Before it's too late."

"You're fuckin' nuts. I was crazy to think I could reason with you."

She turns and heads out of the office.

"Maia." Grady comes out from behind the desk, passes Sean, ignoring him. He's not the threat.

Maia is walking away, fast. Grady follows after her. Sean trails behind.

OUT THERE
DAY 20

THEY HADN'T MOVED since the tumble down the ridge. Ken's leg began seeping a yellow-tinged pus. Many of the maggots had grown big enough that they transformed into flies. Deep bruises on Ken's back and a heavy rash of abrasions from the fall were swelling and growing infected.

Wes's finger had swollen where the dislocation was. They used a bit of the remaining rope and tied a stick to his finger to act as a splint. He didn't think he could hold the stretcher. Nathan offered but Grady didn't like the idea. The others thought Ken shouldn't be moved.

"I don't really give a fuck what you think," Grady said. "I'm about to leave your sorry asses here and go on my own."

He'd caught two more fish that morning with his knife-spear, gutted them and passed out the rations.

"I still think we should stick together," Sean said.

"Do we need to hold another vote on this? I know Nathan is with me. Leave Ken behind. We can be out of this shit in another day and send help. They can follow the path we lay down."

Sean watched Nathan's face for any faltering. "Is that true?"

"We would go so much faster," Nathan said.

"We would, Sean," Wes said from behind him. Sean jerked his head around.

"You, too?"

"We gotta face facts. We almost broke our necks."

"There's no way they'd find him."

"All we do is tell them to follow the river," Grady said.

"I'm not leaving another person behind."

Sean looked to Maia for support. She didn't throw in with the others, but she said nothing. Everyone had a moment of reliving Lara's screams in their ears. Nobody could agree to go through that again.

"Fine," Grady said. "Nathan can carry the stretcher. We've already lost half the goddamn day. Let's get going."

After a failed attempt to catch more fish before they left the small pool, they set out.

Sean and Nathan's rhythm was off from the start. After three hours they had made it only a half mile. The terrain took more sharp drops and jagged rocks stuck out from the soil.

Sean saw a hawk on a high branch watching them while pulling apart a rabbit with his beak, his bloody talons clenched hard to the animal. The hawk turned his head as they passed underneath, pulling and chewing bits of flesh and innards. Tufts of rabbit fur floated down like fat snowflakes.

The trees were becoming less dense. At one break

they could see a flat plain of grasses below in a small valley between hillsides covered in trees. The break in monotony made them all feel like progress was being made.

They walked past the dried pelt of a small fox, long dead and sinking into the ground. The meat was all gone but the red-orange fur remained for the moment. It shocked each of them to feel pangs of hunger as they passed it. Meat was nearby, they could feel it in their caveman brains.

Night came swiftly with a low cover of steel gray clouds that blocked the sun well before sundown. Without speaking about it, by habit now, they formed a crude camp with gathered leaves for bedding, tall trees to shelter them.

Exhausted and raw, they took turns drinking from the river. They moved slow and lacked the energy to speak unless they needed to. The only advantage to being so tired was they fell asleep early and soundly.

Sean awoke to a rustle of leaves. Afraid of animals he stayed still. He felt movement and smelled something that could be animal, but he wasn't sure. He opened one eye.

Nathan was there, crawling slowly past him toward where Ken lay. In his hand he held the scrap of shirt that had been tied around Wes's arm. They'd removed it earlier now that the cut was starting to heal. It was stained with blood and balled in Nathan's hand.

Sean watched in silence, unsure what Nathan was up to, but not sure he wanted to get involved. He tried to see if Grady was nearby but couldn't see much from his one open eye.

Nathan reached Ken who breathed hard, a raspy clog of something in his throat.

He hovered over him for a while. He seemed to be muttering something quietly.

Sean opened both eyes. Nathan's back was to him and he seemed obsessively focused on Ken's sleeping face. Nathan lifted the rag in his hand and held it above Ken's slightly open mouth.

Ken's eyes opened. Nathan hovered over him like an angel of death. He knew immediately what that look in Nathan's eyes meant.

Too weak to shove him off, Ken tried to stare a hole through him.

"Don't do it, man."

Nathan held the rag over Ken's mouth, inches from shoving the balled up fabric into him. Tears came to his eyes as Ken spoke, while inside a screaming war raged.

"I got a kid, man. I have a family."

Ken reached up and put a hand over Nathan's wrist. It would have been simple for Nathan to twist away, to force the rag down over Ken's mouth, to pinch his nose shut and lean over him until he stopped breathing. They could cover twice as much ground tomorrow.

Grady would be pleased.

"Nathan, please," Ken said. Heavy tears rolled off the side of Ken's face.

Sean shot out a hand and slid across the bed of leaves and grabbed Nathan's arm. He pulled his hand away from Ken's grip and Nathan relaxed. His muscles went soft and tears tracked down his cheeks.

Staying quiet to keep the others from hearing, Sean

pulled himself close to Nathan. He saw him sob silently, agonizing over what he'd done. Sean didn't need him to explain. He was trying to take Ken out of the equation. Sean doubted it was Nathan's own idea.

Sean pushed Nathan away and they crawled off into the tree line. Once far enough away from the others, Sean whispered.

"What were you thinking?"

"We need to get out. If we don't we'll die. And we won't with him around."

He broke down crying again.

"Did Grady put you up to this?"

Nathan didn't answer, but kept on crying. As good as a yes for Sean.

"That's not who we are," Sean said. "We're not going to kill anyone."

"We left Lara to die."

"That was different."

"Was it?"

"Yes."

It bothered Sean that he felt like he couldn't call out to the others and get them to rally against Grady. Wes wanted Ken out now, as well. Grady might lose it. And if he was setting people up to kill for him, Sean could put a target on his own back.

"I didn't want to do it," Nathan said. "I don't think I could have gone through with it."

"I don't, either. You're not a killer."

"But he's in bad shape. What if we're just speeding up the inevitable and making our chances better at the same time?"

"Just the fact that it's a question and not a fact is

enough to know it's wrong. We haven't sunk that low. We haven't lost our humanity."

But Sean knew what Grady's counterargument would be. That there is nothing more human than doing anything and everything to survive. There were no limits to what the human animal can do if faced with death. And all of it justified in the name of staying alive.

"I'm going crazy, Sean. I can't take it."

"We're almost there. We have to hold on a few more hours. One more day. We can't come this far and then succumb to this. We'll make it out and then you'll have to live with it."

"I can't go back to Grady."

"Yes, you can. Tell him you couldn't do it. Tell him you won't be his executioner."

"I'm already out of my mind."

"No. You didn't want to do it. That proves you're still sane. And guess what? Grady didn't want to do it, either. That's why he sent you. Even he's still got some humanity left inside."

"The human inside...he scares me."

Sean knew exactly what Nathan meant. He nodded. "Me, too."

Sean kept his gaze steady, not letting Nathan know how close he had been to cracking these last few days. How close he'd come to flinging his own body into the river. To rushing Grady and stealing his knife only to plunge it into his own throat. Or maybe attack Grady and know that he'd be killed in the fight.

Sean had fought back those thoughts, and more. Each time telling himself that as long as he knew it was wrong, there was still hope inside. When he stopped seeing the difference was when he knew he would give up.

That day hadn't arrived yet.

Nathan sat and cried for another fifteen minutes. Exhausted and spent, Sean lay him down where he was and took the balled up cloth from his hand. He sat next to him as Nathan collapsed into sleep. Sean sat up the rest of the night keeping watch over Ken and Nathan both.

BACK HOME

NATHAN AWAKES STARING up at a tree. For a moment he thinks getting rescued was a dream. But it sounds different. The river sound is not quite right. It's traffic. The trees are too far apart, the grass too short. He's in a park. He remembers. He came here, the edge of a cluster of homeless tarps and tents, and slept out last night.

He walked for hours, afraid to go home, feeling Grady's predator eyes on him wherever he went. He thought hard about the police. He almost went. But what would he say? I tried to kill a man. A man who is now dead. I know how he died and it wasn't me. But why would they believe him?

He could explain that Grady was trying to kill him. But why? To keep secrets. And what secrets, they will ask. He'll have to tell. He knew once he started, like the river that swept them away, he wouldn't be able to stop.

So he lay down against the bark of a tree and slept. He is amazed how easily sleep came outside, exposed.

Was this something in him now? A permanent part of him?

He saw the makeshift homes. The garbage scavenged lean-tos and tents. He used to pity them, these urban nomads. Now he thought how weak they were. Resources at every turn. Discarded food you didn't have to hunt for or fight for. Building supplies thrown out in every alley in the city.

He wonders if these people formed a group to keep each other alive. He wonders if they will fail like he and his group did.

Sunlight brings little comfort or safety. Grady is out there, hunting. Nathan must decide what to do. He doesn't know how much longer he can defy Grady. He only knows he must.

The police. The reporter. Keep running. Every option is open to him. He walks, moves on from the tent village. In his pocket is a wallet. An ATM card. He can eat what he wants. He doesn't have to merely survive.

So why does he feel so close to dying?

Detective Kettner gets a visit at his desk. An Officer Seely, someone he's seen around the precinct but doesn't know well.

"What's up?"

"Got a name that sparked something and it took me a minute but I realized it was one of your survivalists. Wes Brock."

Kettner perks up. "Yeah, he's one of mine. We've been looking for him. Had an appointment this morning that he missed."

"Yeah, well, he would. Turned up in a vehicular DOA, solo crash, blood alcohol off the charts."

Kettner is shocked, but mostly because of the flashing red light of coincidence. Too many people are dead or dying around this thing. And in all the wrong ways.

"Vehicular? He was out driving? Shit. Coming here for his interview."

Kettner hung his head, thinking he added to the death of this man.

"No. Happened last night. Around nine fifty-five p.m. according to the report from the guy who called it in."

"Solo crash, though. Nobody with him. No other cars on the scene."

"None reported. Just thought I'd pass it on since it was a name I recognized."

"Yeah, thanks, Seely."

Seely gives him a two fingered salute and walks away. Kettner stares into the blank near distance and thinks. This is too much. He's thinking he needs to get all these people in a room together before there's no one left to interview. First things first, check other divisions for word on Nathan. He might be somewhere else in the system waiting for the same discovery.

Maia drives her heels into the ground, walking hard through the parking garage toward her car. Grady speed-walks to keep up.

Upstairs the workers watched them go, three in a line, wondering about the strange behavior of the

survivors since their return. Maia aimed for the elevators, but then veered away when it was clear she
wouldn't be alone for her ride down. Sean brought up
the rear, wondering if he had it in him to stop Grady if
he got violent. He's seen what Grady was capable of.
Then again, after his time out there he's seen what he
was capable of, too.

"Come back here, you bitch." Grady reaches for
Maia's arm. She jerks it away.

"You think about it, Grady. You'll come around.
Believe me, I want to use your story. It'll be a fucking
bestseller if I do. But believe it or not, I respect the
agreement we all came to."

"You write one goddamn word about me and you'll
regret it."

Maia spins on him. "How about you, Grady? Do you
regret anything you did?"

Grady slaps her. Sean steps in, grabs his arm. "Hey."

Grady pivots on his heel and drives a fist into Sean's
chin. Sean falls back and goes to the ground.

Grady turns back to Maia, fist clenched at his side. "I
should have left you in the woods with Lara. You'd make
a great fucking team."

Maia has a hand in her purse, car keys gripped
between her knuckles like claws. Her eyes dare Grady to
come forward.

"Not a bad idea," he says. He takes a step.

Maia yanks her hand from her purse, the fistful of
keys raking the air. Grady slaps her arm away, gets
behind her and wrenches her arm between her
shoulder blades.

Sean is up again and rushing them. A fierce stare in
his eye he hopes Grady recognizes. The unleashed

Sean. *Temper, temper.* Grady swings Maia in front of him as a shield.

"Let her go," Sean says.

Maia grimaces, but refuses to cry out.

"I'm gonna take her to the woods and dump her body with the rest of them," Grady says.

"It's over," Sean says. "That's behind us. We're home now. This has to end."

"She's going to tell. Nathan's probably already told. It's not over."

Grady reaches down and pulls his knife from his belt. He thumbs open the blade, still tarnished from his time in the wilderness. He holds the blade to Maia's neck. She gasps in short bursts.

"It doesn't have to go like this," Sean says.

"This is exactly how it has to go, Sean," Grady says. "You know that. They can only push you so far, right?"

Grady drives his knee into the back of Maia's knees and it puts her on the ground. She lets out a grunt of pain as her kneecaps hit the concrete. Grady brandishes the knife at Sean.

"Maybe we should finally have this out. Like we should have done a while ago."

"I don't want to fight you, Grady."

"You don't want to die is what you mean."

Grady smiles, folds the knife away and picks up Maia by one arm. He shoves her toward his car. She struggles and he punches her hard in the gut. He finds his key fob and presses the trunk release. He lifts her and dumps her in.

While his back is turned, Sean charges. He hits Grady in the back and makes him pitch forward into the trunk on top of Maia. Grady straightens and turns. Sean hits him on the side of the head. A slight stun, but not enough to knock him cold. Grady winds up and pounds Sean first in the chest and then across the jaw. Sean goes down.

While he's on the ground trying to focus his eyes again, Sean hears the car start and squeal out of the lot. He pushes himself up and gets to his own car. Grady said he's taking her to the woods. He knows exactly where they're headed.

OUT THERE
DAY 21

IF GRADY WAS SURPRISED to see Ken still alive come morning he did a good job of hiding it. He couldn't exactly chastise Nathan in front of everyone for failing his mission the night before. Nathan stayed far from Grady as they packed up and got set to move again.

Nathan stood over Ken, getting set to lift the stretcher again. He didn't meet Ken's eye.

"Nathan," Ken said. Nathan pretended not to hear Ken's weak voice. "Nathan," he said louder. Nathan peered down.

"I know you weren't gonna do it. Not really. I don't blame you. I really don't. We're all a little crazy out here. I want to thank you."

"Thank me? Ken, I—"

"Thank you for giving me a chance to see my son again. Even if Sean hadn't...I know you wouldn't have done it."

Nathan stared in to the thick trees ahead. He wasn't as sure as Ken.

Sean walked over to Grady and put a hand firmly on his arm, staring him squarely in the eye. He was keenly aware of how much taller Grady was than him, but he could also feel the bone in Grady's arm. They were all thinner, bones protruding, blood closer to the surface.

"I know that little stunt you tried last night with Nathan."

"What are you gonna do about it?"

"I'm telling you not to try it again. Nathan won't do it."

"He'll do what I say. He respects a leader."

"If you want Ken dead that bad you'll have to come for him yourself."

"What makes you think I won't?"

Grady jerked his arm away. Sean felt ashamed how easily his grip released.

He'd thought about mutiny. Turn everyone against Grady. It wouldn't be hard. They could all see how Grady had seized power, how unstable he'd become. But what then?

Leave him behind? Veer off and take a different path down?

Sean couldn't make a point of not leaving a man behind and then abandon another because he disagreed with him. And if he made an enemy of Grady any more than he already had, his colleague would become as dangerous as the wolves in the night.

Perhaps it was already past that point.

Maia gave Ken his water bottle. Ken was sweating, eyes shut, not talking. He got half the bottle down then turned and vomited.

Maia stood with concern in her eyes. She went to the others to confer.

"His leg looks really bad today. It's still oozing something and now it's red."

She lifted Ken's pant leg to show. Ken didn't seem to notice anyone touching him, he was too much in the throes of his fever and the pain. Where there used to be a thin red line rimming the stump of his leg, now there was a deep red color rising two inches up his thigh from the wound, like a creeping death devouring him. The burns leaked open sores and with the maggots gone to hatch, the wound was untreated and festering.

"Today's the day, right?" Sean said. "We'll make it out today and get him help."

The others shared a look.

"If we really are that close, we can get there and send someone much faster on our own."

"We can just as easily keep him with us and get him immediate help."

Maia gave him sympathetic eyes. "You know that's not true. We'll be faster without him."

"If you leave him, you leave me, too."

Grady turned to face down the hill. "Fine by me. Let's roll."

"No," Maia said. "We can't leave them both."

"Yeah," Wes said. "That seems wrong."

"Make up your fuckin' minds," Grady said.

Ken's moans when they lifted the stretcher again brought Lara's cries to mind. They aimed down the slope and marched in shuffling steps toward either salvation or death. One would come soon, but nobody could be sure which.

BACK HOME

MAIA WORKS her cell phone out of her pocket. Dazed, she doesn't know where she is at first. Doesn't know why all the darkness. Her head clears. In a trunk. Grady driving. Said something about dumping her in the woods.

She dials the phone. Nine-one-one. Asks for Detective Kettner. They patch her through.

"It's Grady. He has me in his car. I think he's taking me back to where we were lost."

"He hurt you?"

"Yes. And Sean. I think he did something to Wes, too. And I haven't seen Nathan."

"Okay. Hang in there. We're on our way. Is there anything you can tell about where you are?"

"No. It's been a while. Feels like we're driving at highway speed."

"Okay. And he said or did something to indicate he might be bringing you back to the woods?"

"He said he should have left me there, like Lara. She was...she's out there."

"We know," Kettner says. "We found her."

"You need to know," she says. Panic is pushed aside for a moment of cold calculation. "There are things we didn't tell you. He made us. Said if we didn't..."

"Who said? Grady?"

"Yes. He did things. Out there. He...to Lara. To Rick. He was...he went insane. He threatened us, said if we told anyone he would come after us. It was him. All him."

"The initial accident? Everything?"

"No. That was true, an accident. But everything after. Everyone who died after. He went wild and now he's gonna..."

"Keep your phone on, Maia. Do you have enough battery?"

"I think so."

"Then stay on the line, I'll see if I can get a trace or get you tracked by the cell signal. Send a text if you get any information that shows where you might be. I'm alerting the rangers and we're headed out right now because I think I know where he's heading. Probably the only place he knows up there."

"The drop-off."

"Right. That's what I was thinking."

"I think he wants to kill me."

"We're on our way."

But Maia knows they're too far.

"Don't worry," she tells the detective. "I'm not going to let that happen."

Sean has one guess to get it right. It's been a long time. In many ways, a different life when they were driving up into the mountains. He remembers signs. Some landmarks. But he has to watch each mile marker and road sign closely. The trees start to rise around him. The buildings vanish. Like stepping back in time.

If he gets there, if he makes it in time, he knows he will face a choice. Saving Maia and getting her away from Grady might mean killing Grady. Sean tightens his grip on the wheel. He knows he can do it. He calls on the animal inside—the human inside.

———

The car slows. She hears the tires leave pavement and roll over the soft shoulder. Maia quickly punches in a text.

WE STOPPED. CAN'T TELL WHERE YET.

She can hear footsteps crunch in the gravel so she hides her phone, stuffs it in her front pocket. The trunk opens. Grady reaches in and grabs her by the wrists. Maia is hauled out of the trunk, hips banging the edges, legs knocking together. Her knees still sore.

Bright sunlight blinds her at first. She squints against it, catching glimpses of Grady through slitted eyelids. His face is stoic. Eyes hard.

"Couldn't keep your big mouth shut, could you?" he mutters.

Her phone chimes. A return text. With fire in his eyes Grady jams a hand down her front pocket and retrieves the phone. A quick glance at the screen and he throws the phone down to crush it underfoot. She never sees what it said.

She is tugged forward. They are on a path. She remembers. The bus, the drop off, Rick and Karina. The path into the woods slopes down in front of them. Her feet struggle to keep up, ankles scraping along the rough ground.

She looks for an opening, a chance to get away. She knows she may only have one chance.

Being dragged back into the trees is like being pulled down a long hallway towards a dungeon. The sky darkens around them as the sun is blocked. Shade feels like an executioner's hood dropping over her head.

"I can share the money," she says. Grady does not stop. "It's a lot. I'll split it with you and leave you out of it. I won't say a thing about any of it."

"You didn't want me as the leader. You never did. You didn't want me to get that promotion, either. I saw you and Allison whispering."

"Seriously, it's a lot of money."

"You'll see," he says. "Out here, I'm in charge."

He twists her arm up behind her back. She cries out a low whimper of pain, biting down the rest of it, not wanting to give him the pleasure of hearing her suffer.

Above them the birds screech out a welcome home.

Sean crosses over the yellow lines, then veers back. He thinks he's gone too far. He knows it. None of it looks familiar and yet all of it does. A dark green shroud over the landscape. Trees like knives on end.

Then he spots Grady's car, trunk still open. He's not

hiding. He's not lying anymore. He's living his true self out in the open. That's dangerous, Sean knows.

Sean parks and gets out, faces the woods and the path. He can see deep scars in the ground from Maia's feet. Signs of struggle. He looks out over the thick trees ahead, like a curtain he must pass through. A test.

He is frozen in place. Beyond the tree line he is not the same man. He is who he became. Stripped raw and exposed. He feels the weight of his backpack from the first day. He feels the tightness of his shoes. Now he's wearing running shoes. Jeans. A plaid shirt.

Before, when he was outfitted for the journey, he barely made it. What now?

But Maia is in there. He can't let another one die. Maybe he can fix it a little bit. Maybe he can bring one back, undo the evil. Reverse the clock.

He steps onto the path. One step, then another. Then he is running toward the tree line like it is a wall he needs to break through. But he knows what's on the other side. Grady will be waiting for him. And the other Sean will be there, too. The one he thought he left behind in the woods.

Kettner hangs up with the rangers. He turns to Morris who is driving.

"I told them where and they knew the spot. Said it's where all the tour groups get dropped off."

"I hope we're right."

"Even if we're right about where, he has a hell of a lead on us."

"You think he had something to do with Wes?"

"I think it makes a lot more sense with what she said. I wish she'd said it earlier when we could have helped."

"He threatened them, right?"

"Sounds like he's backing up those threats."

Morris urges the car up the tilting incline as they rise higher into the hills.

———

Maia can hear the river. At once she knows his plan. She's going in, whether dead or alive she doesn't know.

He is right. She never wanted him as leader. He does not control her. Not then, not now. The river grows louder like the crowd at a Roman coliseum cheering for blood.

Not today.

Maia lets her legs go loose. She slips in his grip and she turns. As she slumps to the ground she flails her legs and tangles them in his. They are falling together. They land in a twisted mass of limbs.

She is moving. Every part of her—arms and legs and shoulders and head. She scrambles like she is trying to burrow into the ground.

Grady is grabbing for her, trying to get a grip again. His chin takes an elbow, his knee takes a heel. She is slipping out, clawing at dirt and flinging it in his eyes. He grunts, growls at her.

Maia is out, on her belly, crawling. The sweet smell of decaying leaves, freshly overturned soil from her clawing, fills her nose. Birds overhead complain loudly about the intrusion.

Grady reaches out and gets a hand around her ankle.

She pulls and frees herself, his nails like claws on her flesh. She know she must stand so she gets her knees on the ground and pushes up. He is behind her, leaping forward from a crouch and landing on her back. She knows she is strong and pushes herself to a stand with him clinging to her. She spins and flings him off. He lands hard.

As he spins off she rakes her hand along his waist and when she stands straight she is holding his knife.

Grady turns to her, hair falling in his face, on his hands and knees in a canine stance. He sees the knife, gets a sly grin on his face, fangs exposed. He rushes her.

Maia plants her feet, rooted as deep as the trees around her. No backing down. She slashes. The knife digs into Grady's forearm, tears through the shirt and bites flesh. He flails to the side with a yelp. She expects the wolves to howl back in answer.

He rolls in the dirt and dead leaves. She could pounce, could stab and stab and stab until the threat is gone. But she's seen too much killing. So she runs.

Sean can see her coming. She has a knife in her hand. He steps off the path and ducks behind some trees. She rushes past, chest straining with heavy breaths. She looks uninjured, but there is blood on the knife. Has she killed Grady?

From out of the dark line of trees comes a bellow like a lion's roar.

"Maia!"

Sean takes a step deeper into the trees. Soon heavy footfalls ricochet off the trees around him filling his ears. The river close by fills in the gaps between heavy steps. Grady is coming. Sean waits, watches the path. He feels rising mercury inside him. The threat all along has been Grady. Sean knows he can fight back. He knows he can stop him. He knows he can kill if he needs to. He knows he can kill.

Grady appears in a blur of movement. Sean dives out from behind the tree and tackles him.

Kettner answers his cell. "Anything?"

"We got word from the rangers, but not on the woman."

"What is it?"

Morris steals glances away from the road to see what the news is. Kettner is poised to pass on any info.

"The rangers found the last body."

"They found Ken?"

"Yeah. He was half buried in some brush like someone was trying to keep him hidden."

"Keep him hidden?" Kettner repeats for Morris's benefit.

"Yeah. His cause of death...it wasn't the leg."

OUT THERE
DAY 22

THE MAKESHIFT POLE slipped from Nathan's hand. Ken tipped and started to fall. Sean dipped to one knee to balance the stretcher, banging his knee on the hard ground.

"Dammit."

Nathan leaned his head back, face to the sky, and sucked air. His hands were red with blisters. Sean set the poles down and rubbed at his own blister and welt-covered hands.

Up ahead Grady stopped his progress and huffed loudly in frustration.

The trees were more sparse, the ground more slick and harder with protruding rock. Moss and short weeds covered the ground and made small, slick patches that could send feet sliding forward without notice.

A pair of hawks circled overhead, watching them.

Maia took the pause in walking to sit down, her muscles extended beyond their limits.

Grady hurled insults at the sky.

"How fucking long is this gonna take?" He took his

walking stick like a baseball bat and swung it at a nearby tree. It splintered in two around the thick trunk. He turned to the group.

"I mean, how goddamn lost are we? Are we walking in circles? Did we go the wrong direction? Someone tell me."

The only answer came from Ken's pained moaning.

"It's him," Grady said. "We can't go more than a mile an hour, sometimes less. He's killing us."

He got no argument from the group.

Sean bent over Ken to look at him. His face had gone ash grey. Sweat seeped from him, leeching out every last drop of moisture from his body. He could see Ken's tongue through the open gape of his mouth as he moaned and it was a dull, lifeless color. Ken's eyes opened briefly and they looked yellow.

Grady continued to rant.

"I can't take this shit. I'm walking ahead. Whoever wants to come with me, come on. We can't wait another day. We can't."

For the first time, Maia cried.

Sean peeled back the flap of fabric covering Ken's half leg. The redness had grown, creeping up his thigh like a marker pointing toward the inevitable. The charred and infected end had gone putrid again, the smell of death hung in the air around them.

"I'll go with you," Wes said. He walked the few feet farther down the path to where Grady stood. Loose rocks slid under his feet.

Nathan held his hands out with open palms toward Sean. They shook with the pain of the raw skin as if he'd just pulled them from a fire.

"I can't carry anymore, Sean. I just can't." His

apology was on his face as he stepped away and joined Grady and Wes.

Maia cried, her arms clutching her thin ribcage. She stepped slowly toward the others leaving Sean with Ken.

Sean looked at the four of them. Clothes were torn and sweat stained. Greasy hair hung lifelessly, red welts adorned skin where insects had fed. They stood crooked, tilted and slumped as if holding themselves up was an act of will.

"So what now?" he asked. "You leave us both?"

"You can come with us," Maia said.

"So it's like Lara? Her screams weren't enough? That doesn't keep you up at night? Because it sure does for me."

"We can still get five of us out of here," Nathan said. "We have to think of the team."

"Are you still on a corporate retreat, is that it? Still bucking for that promotion? I hate to break it to you, Nathan, this isn't a part of the exercise anymore. This is a man's life."

"He's already half dead," Grady said. He stepped away from the others and moved closer to Sean who sat on the ground next to Ken. "Look at him. If we get him back he'll lose the rest of that leg. He's got an infection in his blood. He's half crazed, dehydrated, who knows what else. He's already dead. All you're doing by carrying him is being a pall bearer."

"Anything to get your way, huh Grady?"

Grady fixed him with a stare as hard and craggy as the rocks all around them, "Anything to stay alive."

Sean felt the fight slipping away. Four against one. He also felt the fight inside him slip. His fight to maintain his humanity. His decency. His empathy. Grady was right. Stay alive—that was the only directive. Stay alive. The only purely human instinct. Stay alive at all costs. Self before all others. Grady had known it all along.

"So what now, we put him out of his misery? That's what you want, isn't it Grady? You wanted that for Lara. She was as good as dead. So is he, right? So why not?"

Sean reached beside him and picked up a rock a little larger than his fist. One edge was sharp and ridged like the mountain above them. It was dark, with lichen growing in spaces. It looked like the earth had only recently coughed it up from below.

Sean held it tight in his hand, the pain from his blisters driving his rage deeper. Everything he'd fought against came rushing forth like the unstoppable river that tore them away from their old lives.

"Is this what you want?"

Sean brought the rock down. Ken's eyes were closed. He didn't see the blow coming. A split ran along his forehead, blood flowing immediately. He grunted, but didn't open his eyes.

"Is this it?"

Sean brought the rock down again. Bone splintered as the jagged edge of the stone cut into Ken's skull. As he tore the rock away, blood came with it and dappled Sean's cheeks. He raised the rock again.

Maia turned away and buried her face in her hands. Wes thought to move forward and try to stop him, but he stayed put. His body drained of any energy and he knew it would be futile.

Grady watched as Sean brought the stone down again. Ken's head cleaved open, splitting through his hair line. With one sharp spasm, Ken went still.

Sean brought the rock back and paused. He looked down at Ken, the horror crawling over his face. He stared into the gap he'd made in the bone. He dropped the rock. It slid from his hand, turned over twice and spun blood off as it went. It landed on the ground, bounced once and stopped, a line of blood tracing the contours as it dripped down the side of the dark stone.

All was still. Maia's muted sobs mixed with bird calls. The river near them had flattened out and gave a gentle sound as it flowed over rounded stones.

Sean got to his feet. He kept his eyes on the rock, then turned to face the others.

He met no blame and no judgement. He saw people welcome someone as broken as they were.

"Let's get him buried some," Grady said. "Then we can move out."

BACK HOME

SEAN AND GRADY roll through the blanket of pine needles. Sean on top, then Grady, then Sean. Blood from Grady's arm smears over Sean as they grapple.

They come to a stop, Sean's back to a tree. Grady pushes off. He stands in a crouch, his arm hanging limp in front of him. His shirt buttons are torn in front and his chest hair peers out like an animal pelt. He watches Sean with murderous eyes.

Sean turns and runs toward the sound of water.

Grady chases. Each man knows the other is capable of killing. Each man knows their chance of leaving these woods may depend on them doing it again.

Grady leaps and tackles Sean around the ankles. He climbs his legs and gets his pelvis over Sean. Grady reaches for his belt but finds his knife gone, a small detail forgotten in the brawl.

Sean struggles under him, bucking and clawing like any cornered animal would.

"Did she make you promises?" Grady asks. "And you believed them? Just like you believed Ken could be saved. Like you believed we could all make it out and leave it behind. And not pay for what we'd done?"

Sean gets a thigh up into Grady's crotch. He takes pressure off for a second and Sean wriggles free. He is up and running again.

Did he think they could leave it behind? Yes. He needed to believe. He couldn't live with what he'd done unless he separated it in his mind. That was out there, where things were different. That wasn't Sean. It wasn't the real him.

He could see now that Grady had instead found the real him out in those woods. And he could never go back.

———

Maia makes it back to the head of the trail just as Kettner and Morris arrive. Their car kicks up gravel as they stop behind the open trunk of Grady's car.

She has folded the knife away. She falls into Kettner's arms as he gets out.

"Down there." She points down the trail toward the river. "Grady. He's going to kill Sean."

"Okay, stay here."

A dark brown pickup truck with the RANGER SERVICE logo painted on the side pulls to a stop from the other direction.

"They'll take care of you." Kettner taps Morris on the shoulder and they move off down the path, two Rangers from the truck close behind them.

Maia reads the name tag on the chest of the ranger who steps over to help her. She'll need these details.

This is the final act in her book. She wants to remember it all.

———

The broken rigging of the river crossing rope is still there. A long tail of rope snakes through the water, attached to the shore on one end. Beyond the fast flowing water are the remnants of the campsite. Only one tent is still standing.

Sean had made it there once. Been to the other side. To safety.

At the end of the path Sean can either try to cross the river without ropes, or turn and face Grady. He remembers the river flowing much faster then. He remembers Rick telling them it was an unusually high flow year. He remembers the river sounding like a hungry animal.

The crossing looks impossible. He stops at the edge and turns.

Grady emerges from the tree line.

"You know we were being tested out here, right?" Grady says as he stalks slowly forward. He has to speak loudly to be heard over the water. "But it wasn't about the job. It was bigger than that."

"I think we all failed."

"No. We didn't." Grady holds his arms up, ready to grab. Blood flows from the slash down his forearm. "We survived."

"No. We failed. I did. You did. The difference is, I know it. I regret it."

"I'm alive. I got the job."

"You failed worst of all."

From behind his back Sean brings out the rock. He hurls it at Grady and is running before it has cleared the distance between them. The throw is off. It bounces off Grady's shoulder, but it's enough. Sean is on him, shoving him down.

Grady rolls like he's seen alligators do on TV. Spin and spin with your prey in your grip. They roll as one to the edge of the water, hitting rocks and feeling the spray. Sean's gambit hasn't worked. Grady is too strong.

Behind him, Grady sees the snaking rope in the water. It's been there a month, dancing and swaying in the current. It slithers, ready to strike. Grady throws an elbow across Sean's nose, he is stunned and still for a moment. Grady lunges forward, reaching into the frigid water and gathering up the loose rope. He brings it out and lashes it around Sean's neck.

Sean tries to jam his hands in between the rope and his neck and gets three fingers from one hand in. Still the rope pulls tight. Grady gets up to his knees, higher than Sean now, and pulls.

Sean sees stars behind his eyelids. The rope is cold from the river, like a coil of ice around his neck. Grady grunts with the strain. Sean struggles but his legs are out in front of him. He can't get any leverage. The river rushes in his ears, or maybe it's his own blood.

———

Kettner and Morris are panting as they run. Their tan suit jackets and slacks aren't good outdoor wear, and their flat soled shoes offer no traction. The path is well worn and easy to follow from tour groups in years past.

They can hear the river, and above it, sounds of a struggle.

Guns drawn, they keep the pace toward the river.

Grady's arm is weakening from the cut. He's lost blood and his arm muscle is ripped along a ten inch gash. The rope is wound tight, but Sean is still getting air. Grady moves his arm to make a second loop around Sean's neck.

At the movement, Sean shoves back with what little grip his feet have in the soil next to the rocky riverbank. He gets one leg bent under him and shoves up. He gets his second leg under him, but his knees are bent and he is sitting on his shins.

Grady grunts in his ear, his hot breath pulsing against the back of his neck as Grady tugs tighter.

Sean shoves up with both legs, pushing with all he has left before the air stops coming to his lungs. He lifts Grady a few inches and shoves them both back. Grady falls backward toward the water and rocks. His head strikes a large rock and his arms go slack.

Sean sees motion. Two men coming from the trees. He continues to push back.

Grady's body goes limp. Stunned for a second by a strong blow to the head. Sean pulls away and Grady is now fully in the water. Warm blood seeps down the back of his neck from where his head stuck the rock. It warms his skin while the river shocks him with cold.

He can see Sean tilt forward and land on the bank, the rope still around his neck in a loose loop.

Grady pulls his legs under him and tries to reach for

the shore. He spots the two detectives running out of the trees, looking ridiculous in their sport coats and ties. Grady lunges for the riverbank but his feet slip on the rocky bottom. He hits the water face down and feels the pull of the river.

Arm over arm he tries to swim what is only a few feet to shore, but the river has ahold of him. First his legs, then his hips turn. He reaches for rocks along the bottom, but each one he grabs comes away in his hand. It is a jumble of loose stones along the riverbed. He has no grip, no strength against the current. He bounces off a rock, tilts to the left and enters the fast center of the river's flow. He can see the remnants of the camp as he drifts quickly by. He never made it to the other side.

Sean leans forward, gasping for air.

Kettner bends beside him, holstering his gun, and uncoils the rope from around his neck. He stands by Sean as he spits and coughs, but his eyes are on Grady as he disappears around the bend, the river taking him quickly away and dunking his head under before he disappears.

OUT THERE

DAY 23

THEY WALKED IN SILENCE.

Sean shivered like the world around him was suddenly colder. He couldn't stop seeing Ken's skull. But it wasn't what he saw there—the blood, the bone, the blank eyes. It was what he saw about himself. What he was capable of. The fog through his brain when his instinct took over. *Temper, temper.*

They walked faster, running away as much as running towards something. The ground settled and flattened out. When the sun started to descend behind the line of trees, nobody stopped. If they stopped walking, legs would cramp up, muscles would revolt. If they kept moving they would go until they collapsed.

The sky dimmed, the trek became harder. Grady slowed but kept on, the others at his heels.

By seven thirty they found a road. When they stepped onto the flat, man-made surface Wes, Nathan and Maia all wept. Sean collapsed to his knees and slumped forward like he was praying to the asphalt, but he was merely exhausted.

After a break to process the emotions of it and to regain some strength, they moved on along the side of the road. This deep in the woods traffic would be rare, more so at night, but the road would lead somewhere even more reliably than a river.

Hi-beams shone from around a bend in the road. They all raised their arms and waved, too weak to cry out for help. A truck appeared and slowed, coming to a stop with a hiss of brakes.

Each one of them fell to the ground and sat in the gravel of the soft shoulder.

The trucker called the rangers, and in twenty minutes a full crew of medics, rangers and state police were there.

In that twenty minutes the group talked, huddled in a mass while the trucker ignored them and made calls on his cell phone and radio to share the news that he'd been the one to find the missing hikers. They agreed to leave what happened out there in the past. They discussed particulars. What to leave out, what to say about the ones who had died. Everyone felt a degree of guilt. They each held a fear of Grady, but didn't say so out loud. They all understood how far down they had broken and knew how each of them could have been the next to crack like Lara, or to lose it like Sean.

They talked over their retelling of the initial accident. They all agreed on how it happened. Grady kept Karina's accident with the rope to himself.

They put hands in the middle of a circle like a sports team and all shook on it. They carried a secret now. None of them knew keeping it would be harder than surviving in the wild.

Interviews were conducted. Examinations held. Wes

had his finger splinted. They were treated for bruises and cuts. They were given water, protein bars like military rations.

They wept for joy, they wept in pain, they wept for what they'd seen. Some wept for what they'd done.

The next morning they were taken off the mountain and back into their lives.

BACK HOME

MAIA AND SEAN are wrapped in thin blankets as the rangers secure the scene. Kettner and Morris are answering questions for them.

Maia and Sean can talk quietly to each other and not be heard.

"I put it all on Grady," she says.

"Everything?"

She fixes him with a gaze. "Everything."

Sean can't help seeing Ken's skull crack open, the rock splashed with blood. He nods to her.

"We can keep ourselves clean. It works out perfect."

"Perfect," Sean says. He stares off into the woods.

Kettner and Morris return to the car.

"Okay, these guys are all set. They don't need us anymore. Ready to go home?"

"Yes," Maia says.

When Sean doesn't answer Kettner speaks directly to him.

"Listen, Sean, we saw what he was doing to you. We saw how you defended yourself. Don't be worried about this. It's self-defense and with two cops as witnesses, I've never seen an easier call on that. You're gonna be fine. It's behind you now."

"That's what we thought the first time we got taken off this mountain."

"This time it's for real."

On the way down Sean leans his head against the cool glass of the window and falls dead asleep.

———

It's five o'clock by the time Kettner drops Sean off at his empty house. Kerri has taken maybe more than her fair share of things, but Sean doesn't care. The house is quiet and feels safe.

At eight Maia calls him. She wants to meet.

"A few last things," she says.

"I'm really tired, Maia."

"Nathan," she says.

"What about him?"

"He knows the truth. They still haven't found him."

"Maybe Grady..."

"Maybe. But if not, he's the only loose end."

Sean studies his house. The gaps in the furniture, blank spots on the walls, missing items on the shelves.

"What do you want to do about it?"

"That's what I want to talk about."

She gives him an address. He agrees to meet. He checks the fridge. He'll get beer on the way home.

———

He arrives at the address, realizes he's never been to Maia's place. Never been to anyone's house or apartment or condo who he works with. He still barely knows these people.

She is waiting outside in her car. She steps out when he pulls up. She is wearing a short navy blue trench coat and it makes Sean feel like a spy.

"How are you doing?" he asks her.

"I'm okay. I thought that was it, y'know? I thought I was gonna die."

"Me too. I thought I'd almost gotten used to the thought. Y'know, after being out there for so long and thinking it every second of every day. But it still hits you just as hard."

"It's wired into us. The survival instinct."

"Yeah, I guess so."

He is glad they are outside. On the drive over he thought she might be luring him to her apartment for another night together. He isn't sure what that would do to Kerri's divorce proceedings. Probably gouge him for more money and more assets.

"Look, Maia, if this is about us getting together, I don't think—"

"It's about Nathan."

Sean has a brief moment of being hurt. She doesn't want this anymore? What was it then, a power play? Of course it was.

"Okay. So what do we do?"

"I asked the detectives specifically if they'd heard from him. They said no. They'd been trying to reach him but he wasn't answering his phone or hadn't been home."

"If they can't find him, we can't find him."

"But if we could…he's the only one who can screw up our story. And you said he was really close to telling the cops."

"A few days ago, yeah. I don't know what he's thinking now. And with Grady gone, it might all be different."

"And when my book comes out? What then?"

"I don't know, that's up to him."

"It doesn't just affect me."

"You mean he'll talk about Ken?"

It's the first time he's said anything about it since they got back. The silence about what went on seems silly now that nearly everyone is gone.

"Yes. And you'll be on the hook for that. And so will I for lying about it." She tries to feel out Sean's feelings on this. "Don't you want your life back? Finally? You get a chance to move on now that Kerri's gone. You can't do that from prison."

"What are you suggesting?"

From her pocket she pulls Grady's knife. It is dirty and the blade dull. It does not shine in the street lights. It sits in her open palm like a volcanic stone.

"This is Grady's knife."

"Yeah." Sean doesn't know where this is going yet, but his hands are trembling.

"If he hasn't already, what if Grady killed Nathan?"

"But Grady is—" He starts to see it now.

"If they haven't seen Nathan then they don't know if he's done it yet or not."

"You want us to kill him with Grady's knife?"

"You've done it before."

And just like that he knows what he is. He is a killer. One time and now he is marked for life. Three minutes of his life carved out into a hollow that bores straight through his soul. It marks him, defines him. If it were only in Maia's eyes that would be bad enough, but it marks him in the mirror. Killer.

One is out of the way, what's one more?

"Maia..."

"It's the last step. No more loose ends after that."

"But..."

"We never talked money. I have enough now that I can share some. It's your story, too, after all. Fifty thousand. All yours. I'll work it into the contract so nothing is fishy. You'll be a paid consultant. Like there to help me remember things."

"This is crazy."

"Free and clear, Sean. Only one more thing to do. Remember when we were out there, walking. It was always that one more step that we needed to bring us home and make us safe again. One more step and we kept on doing it. And eventually we hit that last step and were saved."

Sean can see her eyes, clear and serious. They remind him of the woman he's seen in presentation meetings and sales pitches. The confident, career woman he knew would go far. The one he knew would do anything to get ahead.

"One more step, Sean."

"We don't even know where he is."

"Wrong." She casts a glance to her right at the modern box structure of the condo complex they are in front of. "I called him. He wouldn't answer for the police, but he answered for me."

"Where are we, Maia?"

"This is Grady's condo."

He can see her plan. If Nathan is found here stabbed with Grady's knife, open and shut case. But they can tell time of death. They'll be able to see he died after Grady. But Sean can see it in her sales pitch. She has it figured. Any question he could ask, she has an answer. In the time he was at home cataloging the missing pieces of his life, she was planning. She attacked it like a business problem. Allison would be so proud.

"Maia, what happened...with Ken...that was—"

"Are you guys okay?"

Sean sees Nathan over Maia's shoulder walking toward them. She hides the knife and turns to him.

"I saw something on the news. Grady kidnapped you?"

"We're fine," Maia says. "It's over now."

She takes a half step in front of Sean. Nathan approaches them, unafraid. Behind her back she presses the knife into Sean's hand and closes his fingers around it. She has opened the blade.

"Right, Sean?" she says. "It's all over."

The last loose end, Sean. You've done it once, Sean. What's one more?

"We should go upstairs," Maia says.

Nathan looks around the street, worried about who might see them and why it matters. Maia leads, Nathan follows and Sean brings up the rear with the cool blade pressing against the inside of his wrist.

When they reach the door to his ground floor condo Maia pushes inside, the door already unlocked. An uneasy feeling sinks Sean's stomach. She's been inside already. It seems like a bad sign.

Inside Grady's apartment Maia closes and locks the door. Sean catches the movement of a curtain waving gently in the breeze coming from the back patio. He sees broken glass, the sliding door open the width of a person turned sideways. Maia's way inside. The stone in his gut sinks lower.

"I'll make us drinks," she says. "You two should talk."

With a look to Sean, she leaves. Nathan is watching him expectantly.

Sean knows what he has to do. This last risk to their freedom, their safety. But the knife is tight in his grip, reluctant to come out.

"What's up, Sean? What happened with Grady?"

"He's dead."

Nathan deflates, seems to shrink. "He is?"

"Yeah."

You will be, too, in a second, Sean thinks. The thought doesn't settle with him, though. Facing Grady he knew what he had to do. Looming over Ken was a momentary loss of reason, a lapse he's been trying to recover from and put right ever since.

Here it is in front of him. The way forward. But not the way Maia wants it. His muscles stiffen, lock him out of any commands.

He knows he can't kill Nathan. He does know the thought sprouting in his head is how he puts it right. Will it balance the scales for Ken? Maybe not. But one more killing might tip things to an irreversible end.

"She wants me to kill you," he says. He lets the words tumble out before thinking it too far through.

"What?"

"Maia," Sean says. He turns his hand and like a magician he shows how he has the knife blade hidden against his wrist, ready for a big reveal. Nathan takes a step back, feral instincts of the woods come back to him.

"But I'm not going to," Sean says. He sets the knife down on the coffee table between them. "I'm going to the police. I'm going to tell them everything."

That part comes to him in a flash of clarity. It's the only way to get things back in order. It will ruin his life, their lives. But they're ruined already. It's the right thing to do.

"We have to do it," Sean says.

The world turns lighter. Maybe it's fear, maybe the deep knowing that he is finally doing what's right.

Sean sees Nathan as the same man he left in the woods. The same defeat, the same weakness and blood-drained weariness has come back over him like a fever sweat.

"Why does she want to kill me?" Nathan steals glances at the knife.

"She's writing a book. We could stand in her way. I don't know. Maybe she's more messed up from being out there than we know."

Nathan rubs a hand through his hair. Every inch of progress since they returned has been wiped away. His eyes hold the same look from when they were lost—like he's staring into his own grave.

"This is so fucked up. Everything since we got back. It's like we came home to a different world."

"Telling the police is the only way to make things right."

Nathan looks at him with tears in his eyes.

"Things will never be right."

Sean knows this is true. Movement startles him. Maia is behind Nathan, looking impatient.

"Nobody is telling the police."

Nathan spins in place, his body going stiff like he's confronting a vision from a nightmare while he is awake.

"Where does it end, Maia?"

"What do you mean?" She is playing it calm. Sean can see the anger in her eyes that he didn't complete the task.

"I'm not going to do it, Maia," Sean says.

"Do what?"

"Come off it," Nathan says. "He told me."

"He told me a lot of stuff, too. I think maybe Sean is as unstable as Grady was."

"Cut the shit."

Nathan picks up the knife from the coffee table. He holds it out at Maia, the tip low and facing her gut.

"Nathan, think about this."

"I've thought about it. The whole time out there I never did anything to stop Grady. I helped him when I knew I shouldn't. But I wanted to live and I knew he was my best chance. But I should have stopped him. But now I can stop you because I still want to live."

"Nathan, you didn't do anything wrong," Maia says. "Grady manipulated you and he—"

The knife sticks in her gut. Sean gasps out air, but can't scream. The room is like a vacuum. Maia's face goes slack, her eyes wide and watery. Sean can see Nathan's shoulders tremble as he starts to cry.

"Nathan..." Sean tries a soft voice to see if it will calm him, but the room is the picture of calm. Three people, all standing nearly still, quiet and waiting for the next second to pass.

Maia has her hands wrapped around Nathan's wrist,

the knife still deeply embedded in her. No words are said. Air passes from her lungs into his, they are so close.

Nathan jerks back, pulling the knife to the side as it leaves her. A long, jagged cut opens from her center to her side. He drops the knife on the floor. He stands and becomes a flow of tears.

Sean hovers behind him, a hand out to maybe calm or maybe grab him and tackle him to the floor. The damage has been done. Maia sinks to her knees. She lets out a slow leak of air, still no scream. No crying. Shock over pain.

Nathan turns to Sean, face wet, eyes pleading.

"Things will never be right," he says again.

Sean nods his head slowly. It's the truth. Nothing has ever been more true.

Nathan cries out in pain. He pitches forward, lands on one knee. In his calf muscle on his right leg is the knife, Maia's hand wrapped tight around the hilt. Nathan falls face forward onto the carpet.

Sean backs up toward the door.

Maia holds one hand against her belly, blood coating her up the elbow. Her right hand holds the knife. She pulls and it comes free of Nathan's leg. He grunts animal sounds and squirms as he grabs his bloodied calf in both hands.

Maia leaks blood from her mouth as she leans forward and brings the knife down again, this time on the back of Nathan's neck. The knife sinks in. He stops moving. She lets go. The hilt protrudes from the base of his skull. The blade is long enough that the tip has poked out the side of his neck where her stab was off center.

She falls forward and lays tangled over the top of his legs. Both lay still.

Sean is unmoving by the door.

They're in Grady's apartment. They've used Grady's knife. Nobody knows they were here.

Loose ends. The last one.

What's to confess? What's to explain? Who can he help anymore?

He wipes the hilt of the knife. He uses his shirt to cover the doorknob as he turns it. Sean walks out into the night.

THREE MONTHS LATER

HE GOT the chair from his old office. He liked it better than Allison's.

She's taking time off. A year at least, the doctor's said, until she regains full motor function. Maybe longer for her brain to get back to the way it was. Maybe never. She'll be able to hold a job. Just not this one.

Sean's job.

He gave his interview to the persistent reporter, got a little money. So much of it was half stories, versions of the truth, they got what they paid for.

They came after him with Maia's book deal. They still wanted the story. He didn't want to write it. He put down a three page summary of his story and gave them permission to sell that to whoever wanted to write it and he'd allow himself to be interviewed. They could bring it to Hollywood and they could bastardize it all they wanted. The story was already so skewed, anyway.

He saw Kerri twice more at meetings with lawyers. Already he rarely thought of her.

They found Grady's body tangled in reeds along the

river six days before they found Maia and Nathan. Sean had stayed inside his house the entire time so when Kettner showed up at his door to tell him, the hollow-eyed shock was real.

He returned to work the following Monday. The promotion was his. Three weeks later it was clear Allison wasn't coming back so they offered him this job. He thought about sending Kerri a note or a text saying TOLD YOU I'D GET THE JOB, but he didn't.

Kelsey, his assistant, brings him a tall Starbucks cup with the name SHAHN written on the side.

"The guys are here a little early for the two thirty," she says.

"Okay. Show them in to the conference room, but they'll have to wait."

"Will do. Anything else?"

He looks at his view through the wide window behind him. Over the city streets, the traffic, the glass and steel, he can see hills rise in the distance. Hills covered in trees. Wild land, undeveloped. Maybe not for long, but for now. He wonders what's out there.

But he knows. The trees hold secrets. The river holds confessions never spoken.

A LOOK AT: MCGRAW
THE COMPLETE SERIES

Meet the McGraws. They're not criminals. They're outlaws. They make a living by driving anything and everything for the Stanleys —a criminal family who has employed them for decades.

In *Rumrunners*, Tucker McGraw wants to go straight, much to the disappointment of his father, Webb. But when Webb goes missing after a job—with a truck load of drugs—and the Stanleys want their due, Tucker is forced to enlist the help of his grandfather, Calvin, the original lead-foot McGraw. In a dash to save his father, Tucker learns a whole lot about the family business in a crash course that might just get him killed.

Going back in time, *Leadfoot* centers on Calvin as he grooms his 19-year-old son, Webb, to uphold the family name. When a delivery goes wrong, Calvin steps knee-deep in a turf war between the Stanley's and a rival Midwestern crime syndicate.

In *Sideswipe*—the never-before-published third book in the McGraw trilogy—Calvin is on the sidelines with a broken leg. But when he finds out he was a pawn in someone else's set-up to fix a race, he makes it known that he doesn't play that game. Webb, on the other hand, is sent on a simple job: pick up a car and drive it back. Unfortunately, the pickup goes sour, and he finds himself at risk of missing the birth of his son and losing his life.

Strap in and hold on tight. These outlaw drivers are about to take you on the ride of your life.

AVAILABLE OCTOBER 2022

ABOUT THE AUTHOR

Called the "New Maestro of Noir" by Ken Bruen, Eric Beetner is the author of over 25 novels of crime, mystery and suspense–described by Paul Bishop as "the standard by which all current hardboiled and noir writers should be judged." Beetner has been nominated for an ITW award, a Shamus, a Derringer and three Anthony Awards. He hosted the podcast *Writer Types* for more than one hundred episodes and has been host of *Noir at the Bar L.A.* for more than a decade.

Made in the USA
Las Vegas, NV
02 November 2022

58631003R10208